USURPER OF THE SUN

HOUSUKE NOJIRI

USURPER OF THE SUN

HOUSUKE NOJIRI

TRANSLATED BY JOHN WUNDERLEY

HAIKA SORU

SAN FRANCISCO

Usurper of the Sun
© 2002 Housuke Nojiri
Originally published in Japan by Hayakawa Publishing, Inc.

English translation by John Wunderley
Cover illustration by Katsuya Terada
English translation © VIZ Media, LLC

HAIKASORU
Published by
VIZ Media, LLC
295 Bay Street
San Francisco, CA 94133

www.haikasoru.com

Nojiri, Hosuke, 1961-
  [Taiyo no sandatsusha. English]
  Usurper of the sun / Housuke Nojiri ; Translated by John Wunderley.
     p. cm.
  "Originally published in Japan by Hayakawa Publishing, Inc., c2002."
  ISBN 978-1-4215-2771-0
  I. Title.
  PL873.5.O52T3513 2009
  895.6'36--dc22

                                                                 2009015309

The rights of the author of the work in this publication to be identified have been assert-
ed in accordance with the Copyright Designs and Patents Act of 1988. A CIP catalogue
record for this book is available from the British Library.

Printed in the U.S.A.
First printing, September 2009

CONTENTS

—◆◆◆◆◆◆—

Chapter 2: United Nations Space Defense Force

Chapter 3: Contact

Chapter 4: Mind to Mind

Afterword
About the Author

PROLOGUE

AT DUSK, THE third day of the third month, in the fifty-seventh year of the Empire of the Great Ming, a farmer entered a teahouse. Every year, on this auspicious day, villagers harvested shepherd's purse, a weed of the cruciferous order. Setting down his woven bamboo basket, the farmer offered a bundle of the white flowers to Zōngyuán, the teahouse's proprietor. Drying the grass in the shade and placing the shepherd's purse next to a lantern distracted moths because the moths would feed on the grass instead of entering the flame. In traditional medicine, the weed was added to formulas to treat blurry vision and spots that floated before the eyes.

The farmer described a new star to Zōngyuán. He stated that the star had appeared next to Shēn Xiù, the asterism of three stars that eventually became known to the West as Orion's belt. Surprised, Zōngyuán followed the farmer out into the street. The stars shined dimly through the sand-filled air, with the last vestiges of sunset glowing crimson along the western horizon. Despite the dusty air, Shēn Xiù was clearly visible in the southern sky.

Where the farmer pointed, next to the three stars, Zōngyuán saw a faint light. The farmer said that he knew the night sky as well as shepherds knew their sheep and insisted that the barely visible star had not been there the previous night. Zōngyuán returned to his house. With his record book and inkstone, he wrote, "1424: Guest star appeared next to Shēn Xiù." Below his note, he drew a rough map to indicate the location of the celestial body.

Later that season, standing in his garden, Zōngyuán located Shēn Xiù, slightly west of where it had been. The guest star was still next to Orion's belt. The star remained visible whenever Zōngyuán checked. Eventually, he grew old and his eyes no longer worked.

Fourteen years after the original sighting, the farmer returned to the teahouse and told Zōngyuán that the star had disappeared. Wetting the inkstone, wondering how legible his entry would be, Zōngyuán wrote, "1438: Guest star no longer next to Shēn Xiù."

PART I

USURPER OF THE SUN

ACT I: NOVEMBER 9, 2006

THE SUN IS often studied by high school astronomy clubs, partially because it is usually the only celestial body easily observable during the day. In terms of astronomical distance, the sun is nearby. Every once in a while, other celestial visitors appear and make the day's light show more interesting.

Aki Shiraishi was getting ready to stare at the sun. She was excited this particular morning because Mercury did not normally get much attention. Mercury was considered uninspiring by some astronomers because its craters are less attention-grabbing than atmospheres or volcanoes. The swift planet once posed the question of how its center of gravity wobbled gyroscopically as it orbited the sun. Mercury travels elliptically as it passes through the sky, but Albert Einstein solved that mystery by explaining general relativity and the Mercurial perihelion shift about a hundred years ago.

On this particular day, the only people bothering to watch the Mercurial eclipse were amateur astronomers. Tons of them, from high school kids to citizens in their backyards with binoculars, were ready to record their observations and upload them to the Internet. There were contests and prizes to be awarded for the most accurate measurements, and Aki Shiraishi, even though she was only a high school junior, wanted to win very badly. Her school's astronomy club could not afford a digital camera to record the eclipse. Her club needed money for something better. Aki wanted to rectify the situation. A good camera could have them all watching the eclipse instead of sharing one eyepiece.

Hoping she could get accurate results with their inferior telescope, she pushed on the doors that opened the slit in the building's domed roof. Waiting for the planet to come into view, Aki felt the warm air of the clear summer sky.

"Can you give me a hand?" she asked a junior club member she was training.

"Sure."

Just her luck, the doors were not opening all the way. With help from a classmate, Aki managed to shove hard enough to get the roof's slit open. Sunlight glared off the reflector telescope that rested in its ancient equatorial mount. Peering into the eyepiece, Aki said, "The optical axis is still wrong. Weren't you supposed to fix it?"

"Sorry, I didn't get a chance," apologized the junior club member.

There was just enough time. Aki grabbed a screwdriver and changed the angle of the main mirror. She made the adjustments and got the line of sight to work just as her target came into view. Closing the aperture, she saw the edge of the sun shimmering through the telescope's light-reduction filter. After a minute, a speck of darkness appeared on the sun's outer rim.

"There it is!" she called out. "First contact! Record it as 19:12:04 Universal Time." Her friend recorded the time into the club's PDA.

Aki knew that first contact, when the outer edges of celestial objects first touch, is hard to measure accurately by eye through a telescope. With Mercury about to appear on the face of the sun, Aki strained her eyes in anticipation of second contact.

Tiny, like a poppy seed, Mercury's silhouette was gradually eaten by the edge of the sun's brightness. Mercury fully entered the solar sphere, making second contact. The shadow of Mercury morphed into the shape of an elongated bead of liquid, the teardrop effect.

The planets do not actually change shape. Astronomers realized a long time ago that the teardrop effect was an optical illusion. Even though Aki had known the illusion was coming and prepared her mind, the teardrop effect still looked strange.

"Second con—" Aki stopped suddenly, forgetting to finish her word.

"What's wrong?" asked the club member.

"I must be hallucinating. I see this gigantic tower..."

As crazy as the idea of a gigantic tower on Mercury was, it looked real. Through the telescope, she clearly saw a tower rising from the surface of Mercury. It was unlike anything discussed in astronomy club. Second contact passed. Mercury was swimming inside the boundary of the sun's outer rim. There was a long, thin object stretching out from the silhouette of the planet, trailing behind it, looking like a piece of yarn being spun, flailing up from the surface, connecting to the edge of the sun.

Aki rubbed her eyes one at a time so she could keep watching before her turn was over. The object stuck up from near Mercury's equator, extending outward an unfathomable distance three times the diameter of the planet, where the tower gradually faded from view. Aki asked her partner to look to make sure it was not just in her mind.

"What in the world?" he said, voice cracking.

That was all she needed. It was not illusory. Something bizarre, bigger than anyone could ever build, was protruding from the surface of Mercury. She was not sure whom to tell. She was not even sure she should tell anybody at all.

ACT II: DECEMBER 2006

MERCURY GROWS AN IMPOSSIBLE ANTENNA

INCONCEIVABLE STRUCTURE DISCOVERED ON MERCURY

———◆•✦•◆———

AT FIRST, MOST scoffed at the reports. Sensational headlines made their way around the globe and phones at observatories rang off the hook, but the landmark discovery was dismissed as conspiracy theories and hype for the first few days. Then, the general public's apathy toward space vanished. Astronomy turned into the latest craze. So many people visited observatories and planetariums that there were waiting lists and lines around the block.

Aki had been elected president of her astronomy club in a special midterm election. Before her discovery, she had been called a bright underachiever, still seeking internal drive and motivation for learning. Now, she had found it in astronomy. As the first witness of the Mercurial event—and a media-friendly one as a poised and well-spoken female student—she was bombarded with questions from reporters, classmates, and teachers. Aki had to stay on top of the issues because people asked her opinions day and night. She even carried a laminated sketch drawn from memory, diagrams, and graphs in order to describe what she had witnessed and what the strange phenomenon meant to the world.

"It was built by aliens?" a podcaster had asked.

"No one knows for sure yet," Aki answered. She felt it was her job to present the facts and not get swayed by the media speculation.

"Do you think aliens are taking over Earth sometime within the next few weeks?" she was asked in an online chat.

"We are not even sure that the object was built by intelligent life. We need to make more detailed observations and not go willy-nilly with spacey ideas," she had responded. She regretted the phrasing when a small-town paper ran the headline EXPERT SAYS DO NOT GO WILLY-NILLY WITH SPACEY IDEAS! but she got over it. The experience was a lesson to be more careful in choosing how she expressed the concepts she was studying.

"If you could see it with just the little telescope on the roof, wouldn't it be awesome to look at it again with an even bigger telescope?" an interviewer who giggled behind her hand after each question had asked on an hour-long talk show special devoted exclusively to Aki.

Aki explained that it was not possible, saying that, "Transits of Mercury, when we can watch Mercury pass between the earth and the sun, are somewhat rare, though more common than those of Venus. Otherwise, Mercury is always too near the sun to be seen well with even the best telescopes in the world—except for just before sunrise or just after sunset. Even viewed along the horizon, the angle distorts observations because of fluctuations in the atmosphere. State-of-the-art equipment, like active optics, cancels out some of the distortion, but my astronomy club would only get what, at best, could be called a rough approximation of the appendage's shape. With slightly better equipment, we would also get peeks at Mercury during the day when it was high in the sky, but the sun is bright enough that it is hard to see with enough detail because of the severity of the contrast."

It got to where classmates who had never listened to a word Aki Shiraishi said would revere her as a newly famous authority on astronomy. Before her discovery, Aki was shy and unpopular. Now, she had to turn kids down when they invited her to go shopping or attend concerts because she was too busy giving interviews and reading scientific journals.

She spoke at a science convention and mentioned that her astronomy club wanted better digital video cameras; donations poured in and the new equipment was delivered by the end of the week. Becoming a voice in the astronomy revolution and the theories people were calling "cultural exobiology" made her even more committed to her studies. Students and teachers from all over the world asked every kind of question, putting her on the spot. She had to become a reliable expert. Her knowledge started with Mercury's physical properties but quickly moved to more obscure topics like Mercury's orbital resonance and tidal force. Eventually, she gave lectures on the history of humankind's belief in life on other planets and related how people got half their ideas about aliens from books and TV—but that even U.S. president Jimmy Carter had claimed to have seen a UFO. While some of her public appearances were less formal than others, she was committed to understanding the cutting-edge quantitative research and presenting it objectively.

Aki wished there were more pictures of Mercury, but there was only one good set. The outer planets always got more attention, with tons of photos and other data collected by the Voyager probes, but Mercury only had the ones from *Mariner 10*'s three flybys in the mid-1970s. There were over four thousand photos, but Aki came to the gradual conclusion that *Mariner 10* might have overlooked something extremely important.

The diameter of Mercury is about a third of Earth's. At first glance it looks like the moon but has fewer dark spots. *Mariner 10* had taken pictures of almost half the surface, but there was no hint of the tower. Nor had anything unusual been observed in 2003 during the previous transit of Mercury. Thinking about it one night falling asleep and again the next morning while brushing her teeth, it worried Aki that some unknown entity could build such an enormous structure in less than four years.

One month after the phenomenon was discovered, NASA decided to resort to using one of its space telescopes to take a closer look. Although under normal circumstances NASA would never dream of pointing such a costly piece of equipment anywhere near the sun, this case merited an exception. NASA took over the telescope's time slots, which were normally booked solid months in advance, and after careful preparations, began to collect images of Mercury.

When the photos were released to the public, the world lapsed into speculation again. Aki stuck to peer-reviewed sources and used the best-resolution images available. The strange and gigantic tower looked like Old Faithful, even though the tower dwarfed the famous geyser by six orders of magnitude. Near the surface, a thick rod jutted up before fading into a cloud of countless, blurry particles that got fainter and fainter, eventually dissolving into space.

Since Mercury's magnetic field is 1 percent as strong as Earth's, Aki was certain that all seismic activity on the planet had long ago ended. Some experts were clinging to the idea that dirt or dust was being shaken up into space because a similar phenomenon occurs on Io, but most admitted that the tower could not possibly be a naturally occurring phenomenon.

A few days later, newer pictures showed that the surface of Mercury was being covered with ridges and furrows. The flowing material at the root of the tower had lifted and formed a solid line along Mercury's equator, with branches and veins stemming from the equator like tributaries. A giant red seaweed covered the planet, surging in every direction, obscuring the craters and the mountains. Under the highest magnification, Mercury looked like a monstrous bloodshot eye with pulsing capillary vessels, with areas of land that glowed with grayish red mud, reminiscent of the swampy agar fields of Japan.

Aki kept talking about the facts, but inside her head she knew that the fountain, or tower, or antenna was only the beginning. The equatorial structure, which had kept growing until its line was seventy-five kilometers thick, was somehow feeding and powering the tower construction. With no atmosphere on Mercury, payloads were easy to launch into space. Aki presumed that the constantly flowing material was launched by a series of mass drivers—electromagnetic catapults that launch payloads. As much as it was an impressive engineering feat, a different question remained for her: *why is any of this happening?*

The material being ejected from Mercury trailed along its elliptical orbit. The laws of orbital dynamics said that the material would flow away from Mercury toward the sun and eventually come to rest between the two.

SURFACE MINING TAKING PLACE ON MERCURY!

HEADLINES ABOUT MERCURY were in the most recent daily newspapers. No one could keep track of all the blogs. The images produced by the space telescope resolved to the square kilometer—not enough detail to show any vehicles, machinery, or even the residences of hypothetical alien engineers. Psychics and abductees made claims of mind-melding or being probed by the supposed Mercurians, but their stories were inconsistent, even lunatic. Aki had no choice but to hear the rumors. That side of the discussion meant little to her investigations.

Most of the experts came to the conclusion that the work was not being done by native inhabitants of Mercury. Even for the most respected scientists, it was considered unlikely that intelligent life from beyond the solar system was behind the mysterious activity, but to Aki Shiraishi, the conclusion that aliens were involved was the only rational explanation.

Was Mercury a good choice for aliens? It had a wealth of metallic minerals and, naturally, a plethora of solar energy for the harnessing. Because it was also close to the sun's gravity, Mercury had a high concentration of heavier elements, including an iron core just beneath its crust. With solar radiation on Mercury seven times the level on Earth, there was a more-than-sufficient power source for excavation and building.

With the possibility of an extrasolar life-form only a hundred million kilometers away, humanity's great institutions had to make a show of doing something proactive. The United Nations created rules for interstellar diplomacy based on the Post-Detection Protocol that had been adopted by the International Academy of Astronautics in 1989. PDP was devised by researchers in the Search for Extraterrestrial Intelligence (SETI) project and gave important instructions about what to do when extraterrestrial contact appeared imminent:

1. *Duly confirm the existence of the extraterrestrial civilization.*
2. *Inform the relevant organizations and agencies, starting with the U.N., followed by the mass media.*
3. *Share observational results.*
4. *Protect the communication frequencies being used to make contact.*
5. *Do not respond to any incoming messages without the proper authorization.*

Replies were to be sent only after thorough discussion among the U.N. Peaceful Use of Space Committee, national governments, and certain non-governmental organizations. Based on the consensus reached, the U.N. would adopt a resolution finalizing the response to the communication. There was doubt that the PDP could pass a vote because the planet had so many political, religious, and personal differences about how to handle communication with other people on Earth that it seemed unlikely they could agree on how to talk to an alien species.

Finally, the U.N. hammered out an addendum to the PDP that said, simply, "Communication will be restricted until there is confirmation that the other party is an intelligent form of life." In other words, the sanctioned dialogue with the extrasolars was limited to, "Greetings. We are intelligent beings. Are you?"

Nevertheless, scientists began devising means of communication, since there was no point in deciding what to say otherwise. The first message composed at the SETI Institute at the University of California at Berkeley was a pulse that transmitted a series of prime numbers, followed by symbols indicating that the message was coming from the third planet from the sun. Inspired by the message that was included with the Pioneer plaques, the first human-made objects that ever left the solar system, the communiqué also included a schematic of the spin-flip transition of hydrogen. Prime numbers do not occur randomly in nature. A communication composed of them would be *prima facie* evidence of intelligence. The transmission used the Arecibo radio-telescope observatory and NASA's global deep-space network. The transmission points were synchronized with the earth's rotation. The message was always sent from the side of Earth facing Mercury. To avoid interference, global restrictions were placed on using radio waves and the signal was broadcast on every possible frequency. Given the size of the construction project the extrasolars were conducting on Mercury, it seemed logical that the extrasolars would have at least one communications receiver in place. Still, Mercury remained silent.

━━•◦••◦•━━

MATERIAL CONTINUED TO seep from the planet's surface. Before long it was visible even with consumer telescopes. Scientists observed particles entering a circular orbit around the sun with a radius of forty million kilometers. The behavior of the mass could not be explained by gravity or orbital dynamics. Scientists speculated that the floating particles were acting as planar mirrors, using light pressure to correct their orbit. That would require the production of eighty thousand tons of miniature space machines per second, a preposterous amount to Aki, but she knew that such a level of production was the only possible answer.

Eighty-eight days of head-scratching passed on Earth—and a year passed on Mercury—before the shape became clear: a ring eighty million kilometers in diameter encircled the sun.

News outlets scrambled to explain:

"This light bulb, with a diameter of 16.5 inches, is the sun," explained one newscaster, the camera following as he walked. Then, panning out, there was a circle twenty-six feet wide with the light bulb at its center, slightly tilted and not quite parallel to the floor.

"This circle represents the enigmatic Ring that extrasolars on Mercury seem to have built, though perhaps this could *still* simply be a natural phenomenon never before seen by humanity. Our artists have made it thicker so you can see it, but if it were drawn to scale it would be as thin as a piece of dental floss. Magnified observations show that it's about three kilometers tall and shaped like a ribbon standing on its side and wrapped around the sun like a wall. There are also reports of some kind of gas cloud, or particulate cloud, surrounding the Ring."

The anchorman jogged past the ring. A table placed near the edge of the large room had a small blue pellet resting on a white china plate.

"I'm fifteen meters from the light bulb; the relative position of Earth. This little ball is our home planet."

Over time, the Ring became more and more pronounced until it was visible to the naked eye. When the sun set each evening, people gathered on rooftops, hillsides—any spot with a clear view of the horizon—and stared at the western sky, chanting, weeping, and sometimes just sitting in lawn chairs drinking beer or barbecuing. For an hour after sunset and an hour before sunrise, the Ring could be seen in the dim sky, looming diagonally above the horizon like a glowing silk thread.

At first glance, it looked like the fibrous rings of Saturn or Uranus. Closer observation revealed that it had no orbital movement and was stationary relative to the sun. People wondered what kept it from getting sucked into the sun's gravity well, and the best theory was that the Ring was composed of solar sails, giving it the power to stay in orbit. The inner side of the Ring was black. By absorbing sunlight across the inner vertical face, one square meter of surface could hold 0.7 grams of material in position. By Aki's calculation, the Ring was as thin as a sheet of aluminum foil.

Then, a newly discovered fact shook the world. The height of the wall formed by the Ring was growing at the rate of fifty kilometers per day.

There was no visible form of construction observed. At the current rate of expansion, most experts calculated that it would take fifty years for the height of the Ring to cause total solar eclipses twice a year in May and November, when the plane of the earth's orbit intersected the plane of the Ring. Meteorologists and planetologists predicted a crisis; though the total eclipses would only last a day, the eclipses would be preceded and followed by partial eclipses that would last more than two months, thereby blocking 10 percent of the earth's annual sunlight.

"We don't need to wait the fifty years," a famous astrophysicist, Harrison Godwin, explained. "Reducing the amount of sunlight will increase the ice and snow enough to raise the earth's total reflectance ratio, and we will be robbed of even more sunlight. This will start a chain reaction of cold spells around the world. In three to five years, we will have entered a new ice age."

ACT III: SEPTEMBER 2007

"WOW, AKI. NOTHING is stopping you these days," said Hiromi with some bitterness, looking at the results of their exams.

"Yeah, I guess. The grades are not why I do it."

"You have been a different person since 5/9."

"I found my heart's deepest desire, something that drives me…"

"Really? My parents said it was fine to skip college and stay with them since the world is coming to an end."

"You do not want to end up one of those girls that live with their parents well into their thirties, Hiromi," Aki said.

"Maybe I do. Thirty sounds far enough away that it will never happen."

"I cannot believe you would waste your life at a time like this."

"Nobody cares anymore," Hiromi said. She clenched her teeth. "It's easier." Aki shook her head as Hiromi stalked out of the room.

The astronomy club observed the Ring through the school's new telescopes as often as they could. Aki had trained some juniors to watch for her and call her if there were new developments. She left school and walked to the subway. A man standing on top of a van parked near the entrance to the station shouted doomsday rants into a megaphone. Aki tried to tune him out. There was always someone talking about the destruction the Ring was bringing; if you tuned one rant out, another arrived within fifteen minutes:

"Glaciers are coming back! Glaciers are going to crush us all!"

"Do not let the government put you on a starvation diet! Rationing is coming! Horde food now!"

"Extraterrestrials are going to enslave the strong and use the weak for food!"

"Everyone is wrong and will regret their negativity when humanity is invited to join the Intergalactic Age. Bliss will be delivered upon us all!"

As hard as Aki tried, the level of concern among everyone she knew was as frightening as the wall around the sun. The ignorance and fear were inescapable. She could not help but notice. People stockpiled food and fuel. New nuclear power plants were built rapidly. New Age cults and doomsday religions flourished. People who could afford it moved to warmer climates or built underground bomb shelters. For a while, the stock markets fluctuated violently, then the markets flatlined. Nobody knew how to prepare for a tomorrow of unknowns that might never even come. Aki, on the other hand, never considered resigning from life. She was frustrated by how most people gave up easily. Through it all, her focus remained on astronomy.

In astronomical time, human society consists of a ten thousand–year blip on a 4.5 billion-year history. Aki knew that human civilization was not special in the grand scheme of astronomical time. From her perspective, the blooming of the human race and all its grand civilizations, from the perspective of the universe as a whole, was the light from a beat-up flashlight with a cracked bulb and dead batteries that only work for a few seconds if you shake the flashlight really hard before pressing the button, even at the bottom of the Grand Canyon on a moonless night. To Aki Shiraishi, the insignificance of humans in the eyes of the universe meant that she, as a human, was responsible for her species' fate no matter how bad the situation became.

If Mercury and the Ring were the work of intelligent life, it was startling to ponder a civilization advanced enough to cross the nearly infinite gap between their sun and Earth's and then change the surface of an entire planet. Aki could not get over it and thought of the extrasolars all the time. What other people saw as terrifying only tantalized her. She wanted to solve the mysteries of the Ring, of its builders. The Builders—that was what media outlets had started calling them. It became the popular descriptor, replacing extrasolars. The Builders might soon be the only ones left alive in the solar system. The fact that everyone she knew might die did not bother Aki. They would all be dead in a hundred years, and even that was merely a sunspot or a solar flare in terms of astronomical time. Her only fear was dying before her questions got answered. Responsibility and answering questions were the fire that drove her.

Graduation came and went, and Aki was offered full scholarships to colleges and universities that she had never even heard of, let alone applied to. She was more interested in the space probe—*Ikaros*—that had been launched toward the Ring and the astronomical developments of the past year and a half. To many, her discovery seemed like the end of everything, but to Aki, it still looked like just the beginning.

Sending a space probe close to the sun was a historical first and an amazing feat of engineering in its own right. The distance from Earth to the Ring was farther than the distance from Earth to Mars. The solar radiation around Mercury was hot enough to melt lead. There was no atmosphere on Mercury that could be used to decelerate the probe upon arrival. The stakes were too high to fail though, and the combined scientific and economic might of the world came together to build *Ikaros*. *Compared to the Ring though, it is nothing,* Aki thought on more than one occasion.

The mission of the first probe was a high-speed flyby past the Ring's outer surface, which appeared smooth and metallic. The only surefire method to get detailed observations was to launch a probe that could maneuver itself into a static position relative to the Ring. The spacecraft would need the ability to accelerate and decelerate quickly. Engines fueled with chemical propellants would lack the fine control necessary for such maneuverability. An ultra-lightweight probe with solar sails, like the collectors on the Ring, was designed and deployed.

The first images, taken from less than two meters from the earthside face of the Ring, were finally obtained the year Aki entered graduate school. All she had done during the interim was study. She could have graduated early, but there was too much to do in the lab, and precious little that interested her outside of it. Other than the Ring there was little else. People frayed and developed haunted looks, jails grew overcrowded, and people would just leave their life one day without a moment's notice, but she followed her love of astronomy, knowing that it would lead her where she wanted to go.

The images from *Ikaros 1* were compared to mold growing on carbon paper. Although the surface appeared shiny and silver from a distance, a closer look revealed a black substrate covered with countless cilia. The cilia caught particles being flung up from the surface of Mercury and then added them to the Ring to expand its height, like a daisy chain of minuscule centipedes handing grains of sand to each other.

Although the Ring appeared durable, a blast from *Ikaros 1*'s positioning jet accidentally burned a hole in it. The hole was repaired immediately—like cells replicating to fix broken skin, growing back without even a scab or scar. Because of that discovery, *Ikaros 2* was sent to collect samples of the Ring's surface to discover how the regenerative process worked. This mission failed miserably. After collecting its sample, the container corroded, then the probe itself was eaten away until nothing was left.

But the death of *Ikaros 2* was not in vain. It reminded scientists of K. Eric Drexler's conceptions of molecular nanotechnology, a disputed idea that suddenly burst back into vogue. The destructive energy must have come from the sun, which meant that there had to be a dense array of solar energy storage inside the material, because the corrosion had continued after the ring material was separated from the Ring and sealed in a container that prevented the material from receiving any additional air or light.

A third probe with more advanced collection technology that could withstand the corrosion was planned immediately. The decision-makers soon realized, however, that bringing such a deleterious substance back to Earth could be disastrous. The plans were canceled. If it had a taste for the probe, it was likely to find many other substances on Earth just as palatable.

While no progress was made in understanding what the Ring was composed of, it became clear what kind of mechanism was at work behind maintaining its fixed position relative to the sun. Observations had revealed that the structure of the Ring's surface could alter itself on a microscopic level to control the albedo and angle of reflection of sunlight.

RCT IV: MAY 2014

AKI CHOSE THE Comparative Planetary Research Department at the Sagamihara Astrophysical Science Center to continue her studies. The choice was arbitrary since her work was only nominally related to planetology. In fact, no department yet existed for her field of specialty: the Ring and the transformation of Mercury by an extrasolar intelligence. Her research mainly involved analyzing data received from the probes, though she also worked on developing the center's own sensing devices to be used on future *Ikaros* missions.

The center's research budget increased each year, inversely proportionate to the declining global economy. There were also rumors that the center was going to become an independent organization. It was the perfect location for Aki to pursue elite studies in the field of *ringology*, as she and others began to call it.

Young students, most too scared to get their hopes up but some dreaming of seeing something that would change their lives the way the Mercurial eclipse had for Aki, looked to the heavens. Every television showed real-time images of *Ikaros 5*. When *Ikaros 5* passed the three million kilometer mark, it had to pass through an invisible barrier recently generated, it was presumed, by the Ring as a defense mechanism. Asano, one of the assistant instructors, was at the helm of a wall of monitors, arms folded and reading the countdown.

"The distance to the Ring line of defense is fifteen thousand kilometers."

The line of defense hypothesis was in vogue as an explanation of why communication with previous probes had cut out at three million kilometers from Mercury. The instant before contact with *Ikaros 3* and *4* were lost, the readings from the radiation counter jumped off the scale. Also, every observation point on Earth that was facing Mercury at that time detected an unprecedented burst of radio-wave activity. Even the largest nuclear explosion ever recorded was dwarfed by the energy released by the event.

The probe was functioning normally and the telescopic camera provided by the Astrophysical Science Center showed a clear image of Mercury. It had the sharpest detail ever, clearly showing four mass drivers planetside. Material spewed from the four locations, arcing away from the surface and disappearing into space. At this resolution, the surface of the planet was unlike anything anyone had imagined, covered by a fantastic "highway network"—a term Professor Asano coined on the spot—that extended in all directions, a web of rails creating circular patterns like the canals on Mars.

"Seven thousand kilometers to the line of defense. We are almost there…"

Abruptly, the image stopped refreshing and updating, and the telemetric data came to a halt. A backup meter flashed red, showing that the signal from the most advanced probe ever had suddenly stopped. Terrestrial data lines continued to function normally.

"It can't be gone. It can't be. What about Hiraiso? Shiraishi, what are your readings?"

Aki checked the data coming from the Hiraiso Space Environment Center.

"A ninety-three decibel flux burst, sir."

"We have been shot down," Aki said. "Again."

———————

TWO HOURS LATER, the president of the United States, surrounded by many world leaders with forlorn faces, gave a solemn speech to announce the findings:

"We are now certain that the creators of the Ring are in possession of a gamma-ray laser, or *graser*. These creators of the Ring appear to have secured Mercury as a fortified outpost. Over the past seven years, we have tried to initiate dialogue, using every method of communication that is known to humanity. We have not been able to obtain any response whatsoever. To protect our lives, our homes, our countries, and the existence of Earth itself, we have no other choice but to fight this unknown enemy."

It was then announced that a body known as the United Nations Space Defense Force, or UNSDF, was to be formed under the auspices of the U.N. Security Council. Since NASA was to oversee many of the working units of this new organization, the Johnson Space Center in Houston was selected as the location of its headquarters. However, the UNSDF differed greatly from the PKF, making it the first true military force created by the U.N. since its inception.

The "Space Force" being formed to confront Builders was all humanity had left to cheer for. Sports and mass culture continued as distractions but had become insignificant for most. Many of the countries of the world had succumbed to crime and violence, but the leaders of the world had, slowly at first, formed new and closer ties with each other because the leaders faced such a terrifying common enemy. Finally, humanity was ready to retaliate. With the shadow of the Ring ever present, with the world as it had always been known blotted out by an intransigent and aloof alien intelligence, war appeared to be the only answer. Aki disliked the idea but understood the fear and urge to fight.

———————

"HOW CAN WE prove, without room for equivocation, that this constitutes intentionally hostile behavior?" Asano asked the crowded lecture hall. "If the Builders knew they were building their large-scale mining on a planet with no atmosphere, wouldn't they need a system to protect their extractions from comets and meteorites? The potential explanation that presents itself is that there's a chance they mean us no harm and do not know that we are here." Asano paused.

"Any Builders should have considered the possibility of life in the solar system before they interceded by beginning construction," a student said.

"I just want to know how the Space Force will penetrate the line of defense. Is overwhelming the Ring with a massive attack likely to prove effective?" another student asked.

"The Space Force cannot launch massive payloads or even platform enough war material in orbit. They could try scattering micro-probes, but that would prevent bringing back samples. I suppose other options would include camouflage or stealth." Asano stopped to think for a moment, as he often did, then continued, "The Space Force will try different tactics, but I think that our force will end up avoiding Mercury altogether. Their prime target must be the Ring. The Ring does not have a defense system. They can get a foot in the door. There is, of course, the concern of being infected by the corrosive agent that destroyed that other probe. If it were me, I would follow the plan of sending a manned mission to the Ring."

———————

AKI HAD BEEN sitting in the back because she had 3-D graphical rendering to work on. She had predicted that today would be another discussion composed of wild conjecture, fear, and little grounding in science. Then she heard the words *a manned mission*.

"How many people would go?" she said, louder than she normally spoke.

Instructor Asano raised an eyebrow, then tried to hide that he had just raised an eyebrow.

"Are you volunteering, Shiraishi?"

"No one else is more qualified," Aki answered.

"You would be saturated with radiation. The acute radiation syndrome would kill you even if the Builders did not."

"Acceptable. Where do I sign up?"

Asano shook his head. "We are in a classroom discussing a hypothetical solution to the worst problem this planet has ever faced. Any real 'Space Force,'" he said, his fingers in the air to make quotation marks, "is still a long way off. I hear that the governments are developing, well, more accurately, restarting work on a nuclear propulsion system in Nevada. If they are using atomic engines, then I bet that they are planning to send people along with the reactors."

ACT V: JUNE 2017

THE ROUNDABOUT IN front of Fuchinobe Station was overflowing with water from the rain and gusting wind. Aki considered taking a taxi but decided to walk after remembering how prohibitively expensive taxis had become. Her umbrella proved useless. She covered her head with the hood of her raincoat as best she could and walked. The overflowing water ran across the sidewalk, carrying pink petals in its wake. The cherry trees had bloomed over two months late because of the darkness and pollution.

The wind blowing on Aki's face was warm and moist, like the vanguard of a typhoon. Swept by the whistling gust, the streets were as empty as the morning of New Year's Day. The shuttered windows of the shops had nothing to do with the weather. The world was in turmoil. Though she was too focused to spend much time worrying, Aki could not help but pause and admit that the last few years looked like the beginning of the end of the world.

Economies that had seemed too big to topple had toppled. Food and basic necessities were either strictly rationed or too expensive for regular use. In less than a decade, global weather patterns had changed irrevocably. Average temperatures had dropped. The resultant "global cooling" created environmental chaos. Indonesia was suffering a devastating drought, and over a million people had drowned or been washed away in floods in northern China. Glaciers had crushed entire populations around the globe, and Japan was trapped in sweltering heat. Locusts swarmed just north of Tokyo, beetles infested Hokkaido, and southern Japan reported cases of malaria. Farmers had to grow crops inside retractable plastic greenhouses so growers could adjust the amount of sunlight and temperature. The farmers were barely producing enough food even though the world's population was dwindling.

Aki's favorite professor was waiting for her when she entered the research lab. She was embarrassed that she looked like a drowned rat.

"Shiraishi, I hear you've applied to join the Vulcan Mission."

"Oh, uh…Yes, I did." Aki had forgotten that the names of those who passed the second round of the selection process were announced to the public.

"I'm sorry that I didn't talk to you about it first."

"Don't worry about it. It's not often that we have the honor of one of our students being chosen as a protector of the solar system."

"They're only in the second round of selections," Aki said. "Besides, I don't think I have what it takes to be a…" she hesitated, the words surreal, "'protector of the solar system,' anyway."

"If you ask me, your nerves of steel would make you a perfect candidate for the job."

"I'm not sure I agree, but thanks for the encouragement," replied Aki.

"There's, uh, just one thing, though," her professor added hesitantly, looking for the right words. "You do know that the Vulcan Mission is going to be unlike any other manned mission ever launched, right?" Asano hesitated and looked away.

Aki knew all about it. The Apollo Missions had sent astronauts to the moon and returned them safely, but the Vulcan Mission was a UNSDF military attack. Destroying the Ring was more important than the lives of the crew. For a ship and group of people to destroy an object with sixty thousand times more surface area than planet Earth's sounded impossible. But sixty thousand was also the number of additional casualties dying every day from the encroaching darkness. It was not about research anymore. It was about survival of the species.

The nuclear-powered warship needed so much power and propellant that safety and human comforts were not going to be priorities. One designer had quit the project because the solar radiation shields were not strong enough and she did not want to be involved in creating a deathtrap for the astronaut soldiers.

Aki knew enough to help the Vulcan Mission, even if it meant that she might never set foot on her home planet again. Someone had to try to save the world. It was her duty.

ACT VI: OCTOBER 2017

THE INTERVIEWERS SAT in high-backed chairs, making the three men and one woman appear farther away and shorter than they really were. The jowly bearded man in the second seat on the left asked Aki to stop looking nervous.

"You make an excellent first impression," he said, then ran his thumb and forefinger along the corners of his mouth. "Judging from your size, you would eat less food and take up less space than the other candidates."

Aki was unsure whether he was joking at her expense or trying to make her comfortable and doing a bad job of it. The other three interviewers laughed. Waiting her turn outside in the sterile lobby, another candidate had told Aki that he aimed to look relaxed but keep his guard up. It had passed silently that they were far from relaxed, no matter how hard they tried to appear otherwise.

After covering a few general topics—how her family and loved ones were enduring the solar crisis, what it had been like to see the tower from her school's telescope—the interviewers moved to more probing questions.

"Your Eastern views. Do you believe in the transmigration of souls and animism? Given your background, I'm curious to hear your opinion on the Life-Form Theory," said the other man, the one with gray hair.

Aki answered carefully, "I think it is a possibility."

None of the probes had found traces of life, nor any clues as to where the Builders were from, what the Builders looked like, or why they were constructing a Ring. The question floated as an amorphous unknown over all humanity. In the absence of knowledge, theories that nearly bordered on superstition reigned supreme, at least from Aki's point of view.

The Life-Form Theory was one of the dominant explanations. It suggested that the Ring itself was a living organism. Seeds fell upon the planet, constructing the mass drivers; mineral resources were launched into space around the star; and the Ring was built. With sufficient detachment from the crisis it spawned, the Ring looked like an artifact of beavers building a dam. When the time came to leave the nest, the Ring would scatter into countless seeds, each with a solar sail, flying off to other solar systems. Consciousness was not necessarily guiding the process. But with no evidence of consciousness or even a definition of "life" that could account for the Ring, the Life-Form Theory was hardly a theory at all.

Aki responded with what she hoped was the safest answer. "Despite the fascinating theory, humanity's number-one priority has to be to dismantle the Ring as quickly as possible."

"I'd like to know what fascinates you about the Life-Form Theory," the woman asked.

"If we find an organism that has adapted to the vacuum of space, our views of the universe would be turned upside down," Aki said, speaking with the same polite tone the woman had used. "Presented with a life-form that possesses the power to alter an entire solar system, we would have no choice but to consider the possibility that everything we have observed in the universe until now, every single star, every nebulae, all the way to dark matter and galaxies, could be alive in ways we have never even imagined. Organic beings such as ourselves could have been created out of molds of these cosmobiological organisms when the organisms came to Earth in the distant past. Suddenly, we would not be who we think we are."

"I agree. But the same could be true for any highly developed civilization. Would anyone we interviewed in confidence describe you as having a special affinity for the Life-Form Theory over, say, the Civilization Theory?"

Aki knew that she had entered the high-risk portion of the discussion. She knew the interviewers had vetted her, but she did not know to whom they had spoken. The main difference between the Civilization Theory that the woman with flowing white hair had just brought up and the Life-Form Theory was the belief in an intelligent presence. Followers of the Life-Form Theory subscribed to the idea that evolution takes place without any underlying intentions. As such, believers were labeled nihilists, mostly because the idea that life was moving in a haphazard and meaningless fashion without purpose seemed hopeless. Confessing to nihilism or even an awareness of existential meaninglessness would most likely rule someone out as a candidate for protecting the solar system. Yet, Aki had doubts about any theory that built its validity on the need for hope instead of empirical evidence.

Looking at evolution on Earth, nonintelligent life-forms—those for whom everything is left to the algorithms of evolution because nonintelligent life-forms cannot purposefully shape their own environment—have adapted better than people have. An intelligent life-form changes its environment to suit its petty needs instead of allowing itself to be selected. Yet the ongoing world death toll was revealing human intelligence, despite its efforts, to be losing out to the chaotic whims of its environment. An advanced intelligent life-form would have been able to do a better job. Otherwise, it would be impossible to distinguish adequately developed intelligence from adequately developed non-intelligence.

For Aki, the questions always got sadder quickly. Would ending human life work out better for the other species of Earth? Would learning how to abandon self-awareness and drift like the less thoughtful creatures lead to less pain or even some form of enlightenment? It could not help but make one wonder what would happen if people stopped changing. Perhaps letting go and letting the world have its way with humanity was the ultimate solution to the puzzle of life. In any case, the further one went with the argument, the less one seemed to care about anything at all. Those were the signs of nihilism that Aki knew they were assessing.

She did not want to answer. Mostly because deep down inside she did not know. She could not tell a soul, but it was the answer she was hoping to find in space. All four panelists were the elite of their fields. They embodied Western civilization, were highly educated and were most likely Christians. Greater numbers of believers had found positions of power in the sciences now that their End Times were looking nigh. Aki had met others like them throughout her time as a researcher. Silently, she was grateful for her previous insights into how this sort thought, even if people like these interviewers had never impressed her very much.

"What fascinates me about the Life-Form Theory is that...every step of the process can be explained without assuming that the Builders intend to invade." She bowed slightly and closed her eyes.

"You are hoping that we are dealing with new neighbors who are doing some friendly landscaping before they move in?" interrupted the overweight man, rubbing at his mouth again.

"I cannot take it for granted that an advanced civilization is acting out of aggression for no reason. The Life-Form Theory tends to fit, even if it only fits my bias. But..." Aki trailed off, unsure what to say.

"You think it is possible that the new neighbors did not notice that life was already here?" asked the man with the gray hair.

"It is the same thing, and it would be a shame to think that such an advanced civilization could be insensitive. Such insensitivity is—" She waved her hand, searching for the word. "Unnatural."

"Don't you think these 'Builders' might operate based on values that are different from our own?" asked the polite woman.

Aki was overstepping where she had meant to go. She could not tell if the interviewers had provoked her or if she had changed her own mind and wanted the panel to know what she really thought before they made their decision. "If the hypothetical Builders are truly advanced, I believe they would be willing to listen…maybe even respect our wishes. I doubt that they simultaneously have intelligence and have also concluded that human beings do not matter at all."

"You support the Life-Form Theory?" asked the woman, sounding less polite now.

Aki heard her front teeth click as she nearly bit her tongue. "It is one possibility. If it is a life-form, a single generation must live a long time indeed. There would also be little chance for interspecific competition, which would slow its evolutionary process even further. Despite the possibility, the process appears to be quite sophisticated. There is enough room for speculation that, without knowing anything about its ecosystems for example, it is hard to say anything with certainty. To be honest, I have an easier time believing that it is an automated device created by an alien civilization." She was well aware that she had just lied but was also pretty sure that the three people who were judging her had not noticed.

"I see. Thank you, Ms. Shiraishi. That will be all," said the man with the jowls.

Walking out, Aki heard him whisper, "Cold fish. She lacks charm and has no sense of humor. I like her looks, but I would not pay for a second date if she did not make the first one memorable."

"Which means we have found what we are looking for," said the woman.

Aki kept walking slowly. She could not help but be glad that these interviewers were not as quiet as they thought they were.

The gray-haired man added, "We are looking for people to save the solar system. I believe we will be better off leaving that job to men."

"We need a woman on the team," she countered.

"I know. Why do you have to make my life so difficult, darling?"

TWO WEEKS AFTER Aki returned home, a representative from the Ministry of Foreign Affairs came to the center to notify her that she had been accepted. She was glad that the news came through diplomatic channels. She had expected a soldier to knock on her door.

"There will be a press briefing next week to announce the results. I recommend tying up loose ends," instructed the official on his way out.

Aki worried that her heart might be beating erratically. She took a deep breath. When she came to her senses she realized what he meant by tying up loose ends. He was suggesting that she say her goodbyes.

That weekend, Aki visited her parents at their home west of Tokyo for the first time in over six months. She arrived at the station to find all the nearby shops closed. On the twenty-minute walk to the residential neighborhood where her parents lived, she thought she saw people that she recognized, but they neither waved nor smiled. More tired than she had expected from the walk, Aki found her mother working in the vegetable greenhouse in the backyard.

"Where is Father?"

"He bought two cases of dried horse mackerel online. He went to Shimizu to pick it up and will be back soon."

Retail had collapsed by degrees. Now food was usually sold in bulk by auction over the Internet. While in the garden, trying to coax life into the vegetables that could subsist in diminished sunlight, Aki's mother brought her up to date on her remaining relatives and the neighbors. Rice, meat, eggs, now even milk, were being rationed across the Pacific Rim. Unlike the black market after World War II, farmers in rural areas were suffering just as much as the rest of the country—food was scarce for everyone now that the days were dimmer. Fish was likely to be rationed next. Shorelines had retreated and ocean currents had become sluggish and irregular, both body blows to the fishing industry. The sudden, drastic changes in weather also caused more accidents at sea. Industrial-grade products that could combat the harsh environmental changes were selling well; maybe survival gear was the only thing keeping the economy afloat. What would her parents do when the limping market collapsed? She worried that she would be too many trillions of kilometers away to be of help when her parents' electricity was cut off.

Her father came home just after dark. His face was ruddier and hollow now; he had been healthy, even handsome, when he had worked as a manager at an electronics company.

"Let's grill these up until no one is hungry," he said as he put a pile of fish on the table. "Let's ask the neighbors over too. They have not seen Aki in years."

"They'll smell the grilling meat and come running whether we tell them or not," Aki said. "Let's get the coals going first."

The three of them sat down at the picnic table. Aki's parents asked everything they could think of about the Ring. None of the questions were tough. The subtext of the conversation was clear, even though Aki had not told them yet. Aki smiled when she considered the idea that this discussion might not be any worse than the nights when they had encouraged her to get married or move back home.

"When are the Americans sending up that spaceship?" her father finally asked.

"It's not American. It's an international collaboration, but being run by NASA," Aki said, remembering that the dinner conversation was atypical after all. If she was going to break the news, now was the best opportunity she was going to get.

"Actually, since you brought it up...I was afraid to say anything. I am going to be on it."

"On it?" her mother asked. It was obvious that she did not comprehend.

"Yes. Aboard the spaceship. When it goes up. I found out on Thursday that I have been selected."

She showed them the letter. It was in English. They did not understand the letter any better than they understood when she told them out loud in Japanese. The reality of the situation eventually began to sink in.

"When will you leave?" asked her mother.

There were no words of protest. Aki was surprised. She had always made her own choices. They had rarely been supportive and had always tried to give guidance that usually ended up being misguidance. She hoped that they did not realize that the chances of the mission being a one-way trip were unfathomably high—it would be best if they could remain ignorant of the dangers to Aki's safety.

"We will be in training for two years until the ship is ready. Once the mission starts, we will be on board for about eleven months."

"You will be gone for three years?"

"I am sorry and ashamed. I know that it would be better for me to be here with you with all that is going on, but living in Houston is mandatory for the training. We are allowed to bring our families, and I would like you to come."

Her parents looked at each other without knowing what to say.

ACT VII: JANUARY 2018
HOUSTON, USA

WHEN AKI HEARD that the accommodations would be next to Clearwater Lake, she did not imagine a grim view of a desiccated lakebed. The bottoms of abandoned boats and fishing ships were belly up and exposed skyward. The shoreline of the Gulf of Mexico, not far from Houston, had also dried up, and the water had retreated a previously incomprehensible distance from the shore.

As long as Aki had what she needed to survive and prepare for the expedition, it did not matter how bleak her surroundings were. She had a maid to clean up after her, a car with a driver, and even a bodyguard at her disposal. Some felt that putting so much time and energy toward fighting what seemed inevitable, trying to stop the Builders, was not worth it, but Aki had everything she needed. She was committed to the cause. Compared to most of what was left of society, the consortium of governments provided her with enough luxury that it felt excessive.

Her parents decided not to come with her. Rather than live in a country that would feel foreign, they preferred the comfort of their own home and wanted their friends and neighbors close. She had tried to convince them, saying that their relationship with the neighbors might become strained as the environmental situation became more difficult and commodities became scarcer. In return, they had promised to join her if their relations with their neighbors began to degenerate, but she did not believe them. Aki had made her choice and they had made theirs.

If all went as planned, Aki would return from space in three years. Her parents had few doubts that she and her team would destroy the Ring and come home safely in the end even though most everyone else expected the Ring to destroy them instead. It was not something that she let herself focus on. The mission was what mattered.

It was a twenty-minute drive to the Johnson Space Center. Aki had predicted that her daily schedule would involve flying fighter planes, spinning in giant centrifuges, and enduring grueling survival training that included expeditions to the mountains and the sea. That was not the case. She underwent some physical training and occasional simulations, but most of her time was spent in class-rooms.

Her training had begun when she first arrived at Johnson. That day, Aki and the other three members of the crew, all male, were gathered in a small meeting room. Then the four crewmembers were divided up into two pairs: the military team and the scientific team. An assistant instructor started the class by saying, "Today, I will not be teaching you. I have asked our two crewmembers from the navy to give some background information instead."

The program had been designed to have the crewmembers teach one another in order for them to gain familiarity with each other's specialties. Aki presumed that the instructors also chose this method so that the crew could learn to trust each other before they actually embarked on the mission. The two military crewmembers appeared not to have been told that they would be presenting. They looked at each other quizzically and shrugged their shoulders. Eventually, the older one stood and went to the front.

"I'm Alan Kindersley. I'm fifty-one, and I've worked as a ship's commander for almost as long as at least that one has been alive," he said, pointing at Aki. His silver hair, Vandyke beard, and overall countenance suggested that he was good-natured but stern.

"Mark and I have been in a navy branch called the silent service. It's a colloquialism that means we've been living in submarines." As he started talking about cruising speed, Aki thought he sounded so accustomed to giving orders that he didn't feel compelled to put much authority into his voice. She realized that it would be her job to do what he asked even if it did not sound like a direct order.

"...two kinds of submarines—strategic and assault. A strategic nuclear submarine is a portable missile base. Attacking a submarine is no easy feat. There's a certain security in serving aboard one because even if all the land bases are destroyed, submarines can remain in action and retaliate. With a sub, you know that you are going to get your revenge."

Per Jonsson raised his hand. Per was an astrophysicist and planetologist. He and his family took refuge in the U.S. about a year earlier when his native country, Sweden, became completely uninhabitable. He looked almost as old as Kindersley. His facial expressions betrayed tiny moments of despair, a trait common among refugees forced to flee the deadly, and spreading, climate changes. Thankfully, when given information to dwell on or put together, a spark of curiosity would light in his eyes.

"I have always wondered why those ships are called 'strategic,'" Per said.

"The word describes the level of military action the submarine is capable of participating in. The distinctions among the different levels mean different things to different people, but in order from small to large, the levels are combative, tactical, operational, and strategic," Commander Kindersley said. "A battle on the strategic level would be an all-out conflict large enough to eliminate a country or two."

"Interesting. So that is how you saw it, commanding on the strategic level, holding the fate of nations in your hands?" Per asked.

The commander smiled indulgently at Per. Aki wondered if her original assessment of how he commanded was incorrect.

"The sub I commanded was nuclear. The greatest enemies for a nuclear sub, because they are usually far from land, are assault submarines. They attack nuclear submarines. It is what they assault."

"Fascinating. No weapon is ever big enough to prevent people from getting shot at. What is the point then?" Per interrupted. Aki could not tell if Per lacked social skills or if he was just getting frustrated.

"That's somewhat correct. The job of an assault submarine is to protect ally strategic subs and destroy enemy assaulters. It's rare to actually bring those beasts into a battle, but we have to be on our toes, ready to attack at a moment's notice. Radio waves and light are distorted underwater. We rely on sonar to find the enemy. Then we close in gradually. We can't just rev our engines and head toward them at full speed. If the propeller spins quickly, it causes cavitation, turbulence in the water, that exposes your location and eliminates the element of surprise."

"I understand why you were selected," Per said. It was as if he were stopping to make it clear that he understood Commander Kindersley's authority. Aki had seen older men have these roundabouts before. She hoped this particular tussle was coming to an end.

"I'm glad it makes sense. What I'm trying to tell you is that, when she's done, our spaceship will have more similarities to my subs than our ship will have to any aircraft. Subs and this spaceship are both propelled by nuclear power and require the crew to live in isolation for months on end while tracking the enemy carefully and quietly. Now I'll have Officer Mark Ridley explain the daily duties on board an assault submarine. He is one of my most outstand- ing. I'm happy to work with him even if he's going to seem a little impulsive to you. The floor's yours, Mark."

Mark Ridley moved to the front. His dark hair was cropped close to his scalp, and he wore a look of fearless determination. According to the dossier that Aki had been given, he was thirty-one.

"Thank you, Commander. Uh, I've been working as the chief engineer on nuclear subs ever since I was originally stationed on an old Ohio-class strategic sub. After that, I was transferred to an assault sub. I'll be the engineer on this mission. I think the job of an engineer is pretty similar no matter what kind of ship he's on. I'll constantly monitor the nuclear reactor and keep it running, and she'll be my baby, unless somebody cuter comes along."

"You will be hard at work manning the control rod and keeping an eye on the status meters?" Per wielded his stylus as if it were a control rod as he asked, getting a good laugh from Mark. Aki liked the way his nose crinkled when he chuckled.

"Yes, spaceships and nuclear subs are highly automated, but the nuclear reactors are critical systems and there's a lot to stay on top of. At the end of the day, an engineer does what his duties require whether he likes it or not."

Mark glanced around the room and then exhaled. Aki wondered what he was not saying. Then Aki wondered if anyone else could tell that she was feeling slightly flustered by Mark's presence.

"The reactor doesn't turn the propeller directly. It works as a generator that powers a steam turbine, and the turbine actually spins the propeller. The reactor also provides the energy needed to run the electronics and circulate the air. On the ship we'll be using NERVA III engines that will propel her by blasting out what is the equivalent of steam on a nuclear sub. Our reactor will also power the generator for the electronics, just like on a sub."

Mark looked at Aki. "This making sense to you, Ms. Shiraishi?"

"Yes, it is clear. Thank you."

"Good. You've been quiet. I wanted to make sure you were following."

"Mark thinks he has a soft spot for Asian women," Commander Kindersley commented with a grin. "I'm not sure Asian women agree. I remember a pinup of a Korean actress that he kept in a locker with a—"

"Commander," Mark interrupted, "let's categorize that as classified information."

Aki giggled more loudly than she intended.

"She covers her mouth when she laughs. You love that courtly behavior." The commander looked at Aki. She was glad that her new team was going to be able to laugh together.

"Enough, um, please," Mark said. He took a breath, then another, and regained his composure before saying to Aki, "You certainly have a nice smile. I hope having all this on the table won't be a problem during our mission."

Any reply would sound trite. Aki bowed and shifted in her seat. She was less familiar than most with romance, but she did not mind the attention. Knowing she was Mark's type made him more interesting. She doubted that his momentary infatuation, or hers for him, would actually amount to anything.

IN ADDITION TO the training, Aki still had to stay on top of the latest research. In between classroom sessions, Aki would retreat to her office to continue studying the Ring, trying to unravel the mystery behind its regenerative systems. She was discouraged by her minimal progress—both her schedule and how little was known were major obstacles—but she continued to make efforts to keep up with the latest findings and conference reports when she could find the time.

Then, without warning, a new phenomenon occurred, creating another mystery for Aki and the world's scientists. An enormous dark spot appeared on the upper edge of the Ring. It was 130,000 kilometers in diameter—as large as Jupiter—even when the spot first appeared. The contrast of the spot varied at first but stabilized after a year.

For lack of a better name, the spot was christened the "Island." Relative to its massive diameter, the Island was unbelievably thin. It did not protrude from the inner surface of the Ring and appeared to extend beyond the outer surface by less than three hundred meters. Observations from NASA's space telescope were unable to discern distinguishing features. It was as if somebody had placed a gigantic gray sticker on the outside of the Ring.

Even though proportionally it was thin, its expansive surface area was likely to create a significant amount of extra mass on that portion of the Ring. Despite this, however, the Island was not falling victim to the sun's gravitational pull. Later observations showed a weak shower of ions emanating from the inner side of the Ring just behind the Island. Since the ions were traveling at an extraordinarily high speed toward the sun, scientists theorized that the mass of the Island was supported by numerous ion jets. The sun's pull at that distance is a mere 1/120 of a G, which would not require much force to overcome.

The Life-Form Theory fell out of favor with the discovery of the Island. The fact that the Island had appeared on a single specific point that did not move relative to the sun was considered solid evidence that the Island was a mechanical function of the Ring and not an attribute of a living organism. It was further theorized that the Island was some kind of antenna that was pointing toward the star that the Builders called home.

The Ring was positioned on the same plane as Mercury's orbit, and it was highly improbable that the Builders' home happened to be on this exact same plane. If the gray Island were an antenna, it would be reasonable to assume that it could point itself in any tilted direction relative to the plane that it was currently on. If it were a phased antenna array, it could even change the direction of its transmission beam without having to physically tilt at all.

A group of probes was sent to explore the phenomenon in a mission called the Island Express. The probes were destroyed by the graser when they reached the distance of 2.8 million kilometers from the Island, indicating that the Island was also protected by the fixed line of defense.

Fear grew among the public with this new demonstration of the Ring's intimidating powers. The scientific community teemed with excitement because these observations allowed the monumental discovery that brought them one step closer to understanding the Ring. The reason that the inside of the Ring was black, the scientists finally understood, was because it absorbed photons and converted them into energy. Any leftover energy was then emitted as heat.

By observing how much was released, the scientists determined the overall input-to-output balance of the Ring's energy system. Until now, the energy production of the Ring had been minimal. They hypothesized that when the Island started its job, whatever that task was going to be, the level of energy production increased. The lingering concern was that when the Island had formed, the overall temperature of the Ring had not dropped. This seemed to indicate that the Island was producing the energy it needed to resist gravity on its own.

What was most interesting, however, was that when the graser fired, the overall temperature of the Ring plummeted for a short period. It was obvious that the graser was drawing energy from the rest of the Ring then recharging itself to be ready to fire again.

————◆·•·◆————

"EXCUSE ME, MS. Shiraishi. May I have a word with you? I won't take more than a few minutes of your time. Please, a few questions?" asked a young woman who had stopped Aki in the Johnson parking lot one afternoon.

When the Island appeared, the leaders of the Vulcan Mission had postponed the launch in order to rethink strategy. The delay, naturally, upset some of the same people who had protested the mission in the first place. In response, the mass media joined the voices that heaped outrage upon the UNSDF. All four of the crewmembers had stories of playing cat and mouse with the press. Aki had stumbled a bit at first but eventually learned to be quite good at it.

"If we cut off energy to the graser, we might disable it. Central command is working day and night to formulate a plan to stop the graser," Aki responded with the standard script.

Aki knew that she had been branded the uptight female of the team by the media. She had even used that public image to her advantage more than once. As long as she was part of the mission, the Space Force, she did not care what names the press called her.

"Some are now saying that the Ring and the Island are sacred and should not be destroyed because they fear retaliation from the Builders. What are your thoughts?"

"We will follow what Central Command decides, as always," Aki responded.

"Yes, but what's your personal opinion? Is it wrong to tamper with what isn't ours?"

"It is threatening humanity. We have no choice but to dismantle it."

"Shiraishi-san, by participating, won't your life be as expendable as a piece of equipment on that ship?" the reporter asked. "I want your true feelings. The world is placing its hope in you. I think those hopeful people would sleep more soundly if they knew that people with feelings, not robots, were in charge. Don't you agree?"

Aki stared at the reporter. She was not from the mainstream media. Judging from her dusty clothes and disheveled appearance, she looked as though she might have been waiting for Aki for days.

"The Ring could just as easily be going around the sun vertically relative to Earth's orbit instead of horizontally. Level with the earth, it would have no discernible impact on us. Yet, since they're building it from metal mined on Mercury, it makes sense that it would be on the same plane as Mercury's orbit," the girl said. She cared much more than most of the callous journalists who began pouncing on Aki once she was selected.

Aki couldn't help it. This girl wanted truths that were more complicated than her rehearsed script had room for. Choosing her words carefully, Aki began a statement that was not on the list of approved and rehearsed replies.

"Direct contact with an alien civilization has always been my dream. I regret that it is turning out this way. Everyone regrets that it is turning out this way. But I am participating in this mission because I hope it leads to a face-to-face encounter with the Builders." Realizing that Aki was now speaking from her heart and not her press script, the reporter's face went slack. There was an attenuated moment of silence.

Finally, the girl asked, straying from her own rehearsed questions, "You really want to meet them *in person?*"

Aki looked at the confused expression on the reporter's face and surprised herself by grinning. "Yes. I have to find a way. Just like how I have to figure out how to get there and back without being thrown away like any other piece of junk on that ship."

ACT VIII: AUGUST 19, 2021

THE TRANSPORT CAPSULE to the International Space Station did not have the luxury of a window. It was not until after docking and entering the habitation module that Aki finally got to see the vessel that would carry her and her crewmembers. A chill rushed over her. Motionless, she stared at the irregularly shaped silhouette that obscured the sun. The UNSS *Phalanx*. Costing over seventy billion dollars and, tragically, thirty-seven lives in the making, the *Phalanx* had drained precious resources while the rest of the planet froze and starved. She was the first nuclear-powered spaceship built by humankind—and she never would have come into existence if straits had not been dire.

She measured an immense 130 meters in length and was fitted with twelve round propellant tanks, each stemming out in a different direction, attached by ribs that jutted from the ship's spine. If the round tanks had been painted purple, the tanks would have looked like grapes on stems floating in space. The bow, which was covered with a silver thermal insulator, contained the unmanned probehound, a parabolic mirror acting as a light shield to protect the ship from solar radiation, and the cramped living quarters. The stern was crowned with the double NERVA III nuclear engines, attached to the hull via a thirty-meter truss.

For the moment, a tanker, launched into space on a *Titan V* rocket, was docked alongside the propellant tanks and fueling up the last tons of RP-1, a kerosene fraction. Aki counted five people in space suits dangling from various parts of the ship's exterior making last-minute adjustments.

Two guided missiles earned the *Phalanx* the right to call herself a warship, and each missile had a five-megaton nuclear warhead. *Five megatons. A spark of energy that is little more than a match head when compared to the stars,* Aki thought. It was just another reminder that concerns on Earth seemed trivial from a sufficiently distant vantage point.

"Refrain from getting your hopes up. A direct attack on the Ring by the *Phalanx* would be like trying to keep the ocean tide from rising by shoveling scoops of sand into the sea," was the kind of comment made by critics. Even Aki was unconvinced that a direct attack would work, if it were even prudent to try.

UNSDF Central Command, however, had lost any patience for pessimism and responded by saying, "Our most potent weapon is humanity itself. We believe in the crew of the Vulcan Mission without reservation." After a brief ceremony that struck all four crewmembers as superfluous, the crew entered a long transparent tube and boarded the *Phalanx*. They floated through the airlock and into the crew area, a twelve-cubic-meter compartment that was the only common space in the habitation module.

Commander Kindersley chuckled. "That's one hell of a long trip just to end up in another sardine tin. At least it feels homey."

"Long trip? We haven't even left orbit to hit the deep sky yet," Mark chided.

"It feels almost over. After four years of waiting, eleven more months doesn't seem like much."

AFTER PRELIMINARY INSPECTIONS, the crewmembers entered the "cocoons," their ovular private quarters. The cocoons were as small as coffins but contained everything the crew needed for day-to-day living. They could sleep, conduct meetings through the internal comm system, control the ship, and even answer the call of nature from inside their cocoons. Here was where they would spend most of their time. All information systems were operated from the cocoons using data suits and heads-up displays. They would take meals in the crew area, unless mounting tension among crewmembers (a consideration built into the very architecture of the ship) dictated otherwise, but the rest of their time would be spent within their cocoons.

Four hours later, the UNSS *Phalanx* undocked from the International Space Station on schedule. Aki was surprised that they were leaving on time after all the countless delays, but she was ecstatic to finally be taking off. As the ship left its low orbit, she felt no more movement or acceleration than she would have felt if she were riding an elevator.

"We're on our own, just the four of us. Let's do our best to be friendly, but not *too* friendly," said Commander Kindersley from his cocoon. Then, clearing his throat, he added, "Mark," half-jokingly.

•◦◦•◦•

AKI SPENT MOST of her time conferring with Per over the comm system. It was their job as the science team to discuss operational plans and review research sent from Central Command.

"Hey, Aki. Did you check that article from CERN about the latest theory on energy transfer from the Ring to the Island?"

His voice bubbled with curiosity, showing no signs of bitterness over the fact that the Ring had rendered his homeland uninhabitable. He tended to view the Ring more as a mechanical device that was causing a nuisance rather than something that had obliterated most of Sweden.

"The article on how energy might be converted to anti-proton beams that pass through narrow tubes? The energy loss would be too much waste. I think it would be too unconventional, even taking into account the creativity we have seen," Aki responded.

"With a clever conversion equation though. Didn't the math look pretty at least? It would be more efficient than passing the energy down copper wire that wrapped halfway around the sun. I am interested in running this through the onboard database and downloading more info. When we remove a sample of ring material, let's do a matter-antimatter annihilation response test so that we can see how much energy it really stores."

"The omnispectrometer might come in handy. If it is using anti-protons, there must be some built-in mechanism on the Ring that is creating them. If we go on the logic that the Ring behaves like a cellular organism, each unit would contain the fundamental building blocks that provide the basis for its various functions."

"The cell model is not always the most efficient, you know," said Per. "One anti-proton plant per square kilometer would be enough. Anti-proton plants could have been overlooked by the probes. Assuming a homogenous structure across the Ring is just the failure mode of that sort of model."

"Certainly a possibility. The probes saw little."

Her discussions with Per tended to be business oriented and often ended abruptly. They were not close in the sense of being friendly, but their interaction kept Aki's mind occupied during the long voyage.

ACT IX: JANUARY 24, 2022

REACHING PERIHELION, THE UNSS *Phalanx* fired its engines full thrust in order to decelerate. Planet Earth was over a hundred million kilometers off the ship's port side. Communications had been clear, with no interference from the sun or the gas clouds blasting up from its surface. The latest news and information was constantly uploaded onto the ship's mirror server. Aki stayed focused on analyzing the streams of data, but it was impossible to keep from being distracted by news of the tragic and worsening conditions back home.

Every day seemed to offer new visions of heartbreak. Lately, violent uprisings were more frequent. A few weeks ago it had been hunger strikes. The governments of the Commonwealth of Independent States nations had ceased to function as their citizens fled south. They sought refuge in South Asia, northern Australia and various parts of Africa, even though all of those locations were already overflowing with refugees. With their homelands overrun by glaciers, cut off from the rest of the world that had not yet frozen over, the refugees had little choice but to flee. The problem was that very few places were left unaffected. The environmental and meteorological changes meant that the sheer volume of refugees outnumbered the options for shelter.

PROPELLANT TANKS 8 and 9 were jettisoned when the tanks ran dry. Gigantic metal balls drifted ahead of the decelerating ship, outlined majestically by the brilliance of the sun behind them as the tanks fell toward it. Shortly after the lengthy deceleration stage of the *Phalanx*'s arrival ended, the ship spent four hours freefalling toward the Ring, entering its dark shadow from the upper edge.

"Can we open the shield on the window, Commander?" Aki asked.

"I suppose so. We are going to have to do it eventually."

Aki floated out of her cocoon into the crew area. She dimmed the lights, looked out the ship's only window, and gasped.

An endless mountain range of translucent white flames danced in front of her eyes. Staring at the elusive object, the scientist within her tried to make sense of what she was finally getting to see up close. Gazing into it, she started crying, almost hypnotized, reliving the memories of watching her first total solar eclipse when she was nine years old. When she made that connection, she realized that she was looking at the corona of the sun—a crown of plasma burning at over a million degrees.

The lower part of her view was blocked by an object. The corona towered above, beaming rays in a radial pattern reminiscent of the Japanese military's ensign from the late nineteenth century. Aki tried to change her angle by moving closer to the window, trying to see beyond whatever was in her way. No matter how she shifted her position, the object did not move. Was it part of the ship? Aki wondered if it was one of the propellant tanks. With a start and a shudder, she realized the visual trap she had fallen into and how she had confused herself.

The obstruction to her view was not part of the ship—it was what she had spent her life waiting to see. Aki was staring at the blackness of the Ring.

She had expected shiny silver, but the object she was looking at was as dark as space itself. Aki was mesmerized. As her eyes grew accustomed to the darkness, she noticed that the surface was less jet-black that it had originally appeared. There was a modicum of light from the surrounding stars that reflected off the surface, shimmering like an afternoon breeze blowing across a grassy meadow. The flickering of the light was most likely caused by pressure fluctuations from the solar wind that deformed the surface of the ultra-thin material enough to cause the reflecting starlight to twinkle. The view was more breathtaking than Aki could have possibly imagined.

She drew a connection between the phenomenon she was observing and the aurorae seen in the polar regions when Earth's magnetosphere acts as a funnel and causes particles carried on solar winds to converge and collide with the upper atmosphere. What she saw was caused by raw and undiluted solar wind. The particles danced on a screen as wide as twenty Earths lined up in a row. Even with such a difference, the shimmering light here appeared, oddly enough, more similar to the aurora borealis than she had expected.

Aki was pulled from her thoughts by a noise from the other side of the bundles of cables and air ducts. *Mark*, she thought. By now, she was able to tell which crewmember was coming out of his cocoon by the sound of his footsteps.

"Am I interrupting?"

"Not at all. Please come in."

Aki pushed herself back to share the tiny twenty-centimeter wide window.

"I was afraid we took a wrong turn at Venus," he said, staring out at the Ring. "You wanted this for your wedding band?"

"I do not think it would fit on my finger, with the flab I have gained in the last six months."

Mark laughed heartily. He always tried to encourage witty comebacks from her. After a pause, he returned to staring out the window. She expected him to come on to her because it seemed like the perfect moment, but he did not. If it came to it, Aki was pretty sure a cocoon was large enough for two people. During the past six months, Mark had flirted with her often. Once he was even blunt enough to say, "If it's a matter of contraception, we have some on board."

Mark was always honest, considerate, and even able to show a sensitive side when he wanted. The line about contraception had not been his shining moment, but he did have moments that made Aki wonder about the possibilities. Physically, his face could not have been more handsome if it had been chiseled from marble. No matter how hard Aki looked, she could never find flaws in Mark, even though she wondered if he would give her the time of day if the world had been different, if the era of organic life's dominance on Earth were not limping to a close.

Despite all that he offered, Aki had turned Mark down multiple times. She kept her sexual self so bottled up in the name of pursuing her research that she feared what might happen if she were to unleash herself on any man, especially in this environment. She wanted nothing to interfere with the long-awaited encounter with the Ring. The Ring was out there, finally right outside the window. She knew that they talked about her behind her back—man talk—saying that she was "married to the Ring."

Neither Aki nor Mark could turn away from the window.

"Looking after nuclear subs with missiles, I was in charge of enough power to torch the world," Mark said. "Now I'm on this ship. It's my job to deal with these reactors, but my work always seems linked to the end of the world."

"It hasn't ended yet, Mark. We are not here to end the world."

"If we destroy the Ring, humanity gets to live. Unlike any war we've ever faced or simulated in doomsday scenarios, this one isn't humanity turning against itself. There has never been a war with such clear-cut objectives and there has never been a war with such perfect moral clarity. We win at all costs." Mark attempted a comforting smile.

She knew that his last sentence could have included the phrase, "even if we end up martyrs," but they shared that sentiment without saying it. For a second, they both looked away from the window.

"That's why I applied," Mark said. "I thought, 'Here's a job where I can finally use the craziest thoughts that run through my head. All I need is to figure out how to destroy that thing.'"

"Our mission's about that for you—the joy of morally acceptable mass destruction?" Aki asked.

Mark gazed at Aki for a moment. "I love what goes through that pretty little head of yours."

"If you were at war with Italy, could you bring yourself to bomb Florence, to ruin the Uffizi Museum?"

"If the artwork inside it were a threat to me and mine? Then, yeah, I could bomb it to hell and sleep like a baby."

"I guess you are lucky that your head can overrule your heart."

Aki felt her excitement for the Ring drain out through her pores. She was surprised by how bitter they both sounded. She was doing the one thing the crew had been advised to avoid—starting a heated debate in cramped quarters.

"Tell me, Aki, what can I do to see the Ring like you do, like a masterpiece in the Uffizi that deserves protection?"

"The problem is that you do not know anything about it. What you need is to try to understand the Ring. You have to want to understand. It is like how you feel when you look at a painting or a sculpture. It is here for us to understand, to interpret, not just to annihilate. You look at beauty because it is one of the few profound things that humans can do. To destroy without even trying to understand is the impulse of instinct, not a result of cognition." Aki looked away, frustrated and angry. "Finding joy in annihilation is fundamentally inhuman."

◆·◆·◆

SEVENTY-TWO HOURS later one of the probehounds was launched. The hound's propulsion jet nozzle could be seen in the lower part of the monitoring screen. In front of that was the small reflection of the faithful dog going out to sever the Ring. The probe dropped in freefall to a point about twenty meters away from the Ring's outer surface. When its small NERVA IV fired, there was a flash of light that whited out the screen until the automatic brightness control adjusted to the new level of input.

The hound's rear leaned slightly toward the ship and began moving at an angle that would minimize its exposure to solar radiation. When the blast from the hound's nuclear-powered engine hit the Ring, the Ring melted like butter hit by a blowtorch.

"Looking good! Let's double the speed and see what happens. Per and Aki, keep an eye on the part that was cut," said Commander Kindersley.

"Yes, Commander," Aki said.

Aki lined up the images taken so far. Quick analysis showed that the edges of the burn had been bent inward but were slowly shifting back to their original shape and reintegrating with the curve of the Ring. Aki had never imagined such a resilient system. She was unsure whether any human had ever conceived that such technology might exist.

If massive stress were put on a substantial portion of the Ring, the strain might cause the structure to collapse, but it seemed to Aki like compromising the structure of one part of the Ring would be insufficient to affect the rest of its surface. Every square micrometer of the Ring was maintaining a perfect balance between the light pressure it was giving off and the weight created by the pull of the sun. Even carpet-bombing, while it would cover the Ring with holes, would only produce localized damage. Aki presumed that even a slew of holes would get repaired quickly.

"It looks like it has started to regenerate already. I wonder by which mechanism the Ring restores itself to its original shape," Aki said into her intercom.

The light pressure and gravity were both inversely proportionate to the square of the Ring's distance, giving the curved and flush shape of the Ring a peculiar plasticity. Normally, even in such a complicated system, any parts that became concave would remain that way.

"It is probably changing the albedo of the sunlit side of the Ring. It feeds back the intensity of the sunlight. If only the spectrometer on the hound were online," Per said. "Look at the telemetry readings. Maybe trying to detect proton-antiproton mutual annihilation while blasting it was too simplistic."

"Everything's going surprisingly well over here," Mark stated. "The hound's slicing along at five hundred meters per second. At this rate, it should reach the southern edge in about a week."

"The ship is about to approach the edge of the opening. What did you want to see here?" Kindersley asked.

"I would like a close-up look at its repair work, especially now that it is trying to repair a section that was sliced clean through instead of just a...divot," Per said, sounding a bit unsure of how to describe topography or geomorphometry to the military man.

"There's no chance that the Ring won't repair, right?"

"A meteoroid crashing into the Ring and slicing it in two from top to bottom? I am sure the Builders are prepared for that; it is an inevitability. A catastrophic bump by some nickel-iron and ice is what we are replicating," said Per. "If the Ring cannot survive that, entity or a machine, it would have failed already. Imagine a human being with no immune system—there is no need to try to give it the plague on its thirtieth birthday; it would have died in the cradle."

"I hate to admit it, but you're right," Kindersley said.

"The question is the repair rate. If we attack the Island before it finishes, we might be able to do our job," said Per.

"Commander, I think we could use the ship's engines to help the hound cut," said Mark.

"Good idea. Let's head to that edge, start working our way from there. That should save us over two days of going around."

"We'll cut through from both sides, like building a tunnel. We got enough fuel for the go round?"

"Already checked."

"We'll rendezvous with the hound in the middle, then head for the Island."

"Can we finish our analysis of the severed portion first?" Aki said.

"Get to it!"

ACT X: JANUARY 28, 2022
3,000 METERS ABOVE THE SURFACE OF THE RING

TWO HOURS AFTER the convergence of probehound and ship, a kilometer-wide gap between the severed edges of the Ring glistened in the sunlight like two giant fluorescent light bulbs standing on end. Since the Ring was no thicker than a sheet of aluminum foil, the bright edgewise shine was proof that some process was under way.

"The edges look lined with fur," Aki said as she looked at an image capture from the *Phalanx*'s telescope. What she saw was pure white, reminiscent of a rabbit pelt. A closer look showed a massive number of small fibers growing densely near the severed edges.

"It is some sort of fibrous growth with dense threading." Per paused, then added, "If we cut the Ring, the material starts to grow. If it comes into contact with something, the fibers expand and grow onto the foreign body. It is like a fungus that thinks, and its capabilities are unaffected by the heat of the engine blast. I would like to move closer if we can."

"Leave that to me," Mark responded, carefully lowering the ship toward one of the edges. "We're at five hundred meters."

A colony of white fibers began to shimmer just beneath them.

"We're burning them."

"No, the engine blast cannot reach from here. The Ring is deflecting the blast by bifurcating it."

"Then why is the fur wavering so much?" Aki said.

Per thought for a moment and then yelled, "Commander, we need to get out of here. Now. It's going to spread to the ship."

"Mark, pull us up," Kindersley ordered. Without a word, Mark revved the engines to direct the ship away from the Ring. Aki fell backwards from the sudden acceleration as the ship retreated to a distance of ten kilometers.

"Are you sure, Per?" asked the commander.

"That fungus was watching us!"

"Watching us?"

"It is a tropism; the fiber reacts to any heat source other than the sun by pointing toward it and growing fast."

"How do we check for signs of contamination?"

"The sensors aren't showing warnings. I'll run a detailed inspection to be sure," Mark said.

"We were five hundred meters away. We should be fine, don't you think?" asked the commander.

"The gap it is trying to bridge between the edges is a full kilometer. I cannot be certain," Per said.

"Good point. We'll proceed with caution."

"Commander, I'm getting abnormal readings from some of the gimbal actuator stress sensors," Mark announced, his voice going soft.

Aki coughed. "Just a few is normal, right?" There were tens of thousands of sensors. It was not unusual for a few to show abnormal readings at any given time.

"No, this is different. We have a problem," replied Mark, surprisingly calm now.

"Let's hold out for a minute, see what happens."

"If we lose only one actuator, we can still continue. We'll just balance out a bit more slowly. But if something is hanging on out there," Mark explained, "if the contamination has reached our backup, it's game over. Let's run an inspection to see where we stand. If there's no infection, we go back. If there's any contamination at all, then I'll remove the parts by hand and dispose of them. That would mean working next to the reactors for several hours while the reactors are running. And, of course, it would mean that I wouldn't come back inside since I would risk bringing the contaminant with me."

"Wait. Could we eject the engine to solve the problem? We can continue with just one," Aki protested, her fear hanging in the air.

"Yeah, but if the other engine fails, we're stranded."

"But if the only other choice is to leave you to die, I vote that it is worth the risk."

"Think about that one, Aki," said Per. "We have two engines, but four people. The math is clear."

Mark said nothing. *An engineer does what his duties require of him whether he likes it or not.* Aki remembered Mark's words, and now it was crystal clear what they meant.

"Out of the cocoons. Everybody to the crew area," Kindersley said, his voice limned with authority.

MARK WAS SUITING up in front of the airlock. The other two took turns offering farewells. Aki went last.

"Can I finally kiss you?" he asked.

Without speaking, Aki closed her eyes and leaned toward him. She was taken by surprise when she felt his tongue touch hers. Her instinct was to pull back, but she let herself go, giving in to the desire she had felt since the day they met. Mark was the one to finally pull away.

He looked small inside the oversized suit as he finished getting ready for the EVA. He ran a diagnostic, then entered the airlock.

Closing the inner door, he gave a thumbs-up through the tiny round window.

Three hours later, Mark completed the mission. He had removed and discarded all of the contaminated parts. All that was left to discard was himself. Aki was unable to speak.

"Looks like you still have some time, Mark. You're free to do whatever you like," said Commander Kindersley. Mark mumbled a short prayer to himself, something about how dying was acceptable if his sacrifice led to saving what was left of the world's population.

Then he said, "I think I'll go check out that Ring over there."

From inside her cocoon, Aki watched the ship diminish in size through Mark's helmet camera as he propelled himself toward the Ring.

Mark fired his thruster to close the ten-kilometer gap between him and the Ring. In the footage he was sending, it was almost impossible to distinguish the inky surface of the Ring from the blackness of space.

After some time, his searchlight finally began to reflect off the surface of the Ring, producing a circle of light that gradually grew brighter. Aki wanted to look away, but she needed to see the Ring.

"The surface is silvery velvet. Firing my thruster, on the Ring… creating waves rippling away from the contact. I'm at three meters and closing in… Okay, I've just touched down."

For a moment, Mark's stuttered breathing was all they could hear.

"It's incredible, a mirror that goes endlessly in all directions. I'm a dimple on the surface. I weigh one kilo, but it's enough to cause the surface to sink where I'm standing. I'm standing on an enormous pillow, a cloud." There was a choked sob.

A warning light appeared on the monitor mounted on the arm of his suit. The red glow was visible on the monitor before he looked down and <AIR LEAK> flashed on the screen.

"Uh-oh. Feeding has begun, boots are changing color. A spider-web is wrapping itself around me, moving on its own," he said with a calm unlike anything Aki had ever heard from him before.

"Into my suit. A mouse crawling around in here. Depressurization has stopped. There's no pain…"

His voice began to murmur as if he were drifting into sleep. "Aki, can you hear me?"

"Yes. Yes, Mark, I can hear you."

"I'm sorry. There's so much more I wanted to say to you."

"I know. Don't worry about that now."

Two minutes later all readings transmitting from Mark's suit ceased.

The image coming from the telescopic camera on the *Phalanx* showed a human-sized caterpillar's cocoon resting in the center of a large indentation on the Ring. It was shrinking in size. Eventually, Aki looked away.

She could not find a use for her feelings. Aki regretted being on the ship and on the mission. After forty hours, she finally emerged from her cocoon. Per and Kindersley found her, grabbed her by the wrists and wrapped their arms around her. She pressed her face onto their shoulders and hugged them back, crying like she had not cried since she was a child.

ACT XI: FEBRUARY 2, 2022

THE UNSS *PHALANX* shifted to a battle footing and launched its first attack. It sent a nuclear missile whizzing toward the Island, beyond the horizon of the Ring, some four million kilometers away.

The graser protecting the Island shot down the missile at the line of defense, disintegrating it in a microsecond, which was exactly what the crew had expected. Shortly after, the ship was hit with the massive surge of electricity that was released when the graser fired. Half the electrical systems suffered some sort of damage. After emergency procedures were performed, the ship and her hound made their way toward the Island, but the functional capabilities of both crafts were substantially impaired.

Aki put on a pressurized safety suit and secured herself in place in her cocoon. She kept a close eye on the infrared image being transmitted by the hound as it scouted their route. The Ring appeared on the screen as a plain gray field with subtle variations in color. After some time, the small bump of the Island appeared on the horizon.

"The hound is about to enter graser range. Make sure that all data files are closed," ordered the commander. The backup electronics had been fried in the surge. If they were hit again, they would be crippled and in serious trouble.

Aki and Per had estimated that the graser would need 147 hours to recharge. It was an estimate based on a few too many assumptions that were based on suppositions that were based on guesses. There was no guarantee that the estimate was even close to correct. They waited in tense silence. After about five minutes, Per dared to speak.

"It is not firing."

"So it really does shut down while it recharges."

"Proceed?" asked Per.

"I don't see any reason not to. What the hell else can we do?" Kindersley said.

FIVE HOURS LATER the Island was within visual range. The graser still had not fired.

Their probehound was floating directly above the Island. Commander Kindersley ordered the hound to make its descent. Aki controlled the telescopic camera. The Island rose up from the surface of the Ring to form a cliff three hundred meters high. The edge had appeared rounded in observations made from Earth, but viewed up close it was a sharp vertical wall. The top of the Island resembled a mirrored plane stretching beyond the horizon. *More like a continent than an island*, Aki thought to herself.

The opposite end of the Island was out of visual range, over 130,000 kilometers away. According to the readings that the sensors were producing, the Island was a table large enough to hold ten planets the size of Earth and still have room left over.

The telescopic camera revealed a web-like pattern covering the surface. At maximum zoom, it looked like the walls of a honeycomb, a collection of hexagonal-shaped pillars, each about four meters across with their surface covered in a translucent, viscous substance.

"If I did not know any better, I would say we are looking at the wall of a colossal bee hive dripping with honey," Per said after clearing his throat.

Aki panned the camera to have a better look at the outside edge. The surface had no distinguishing features except for a gray border several meters thick around each cell in its matrix. There were no railings, no catwalks, no emergency exits. Aki had the camera trace a path around the edge of the cliff. A protruding object that resembled a lighthouse slowly came into view.

"Could that be a telescope?" asked Per.

"I bet it is the graser battery," said Aki.

The commander moved the hound in for a closer look.

It appeared to be a stubby telescope atop an altazimuth mount. Double-checking the scale gauge connected to the distance meter, Aki confirmed that the diameter of the aperture was unbelievably large—about the length of a football field. The muzzle contained a concentric circle that looked like a collimator. The structure was seamless, completely smooth.

As she looked for even a trace of details or distinguishing features, Per noticed a miniature version of the battery on top of the barrel. "That must be the optical telescope—their viewfinder," said Per.

"You're probably right. A viewfinder to target incoming objects," Kindersley said.

Examining the long-range images sent back by the hound in closer detail, the exact same object appeared again nine thousand kilometers in the distance. The structures lined the Island at equal intervals.

"Now's the moment of truth, crew. Press on or turn back? You know where I stand, but I want to hear you on this one."

"Continue," Aki replied immediately.

Per took a bit longer. "I do not see any reason not to. Why wait?"

"The base of that graser battery is our target. Set the ship for final approach. Aki, prepare for an EVA."

"Of course, sir." Aki propelled herself out of her cocoon and began donning her space suit.

She and Per had talked about it. The mission would continue. Aki had volunteered to take over Mark's duties. She would stand on the Island with her own two feet if that was what it took to obtain a sample and send the data to Earth.

The risk of contamination appeared to be low. The Builders seemed content to leave the Ring unguarded, perhaps due to its regenerative abilities. The Island, as it was protected by the graser, was perhaps not capable of self-repair. This was the best working theory the crew had to go on. Although the head of a simple planarian worm will grow back when it is cut off, the same cannot be said of a human. Similarly, it would be much more difficult to outfit the Island—a much more sophisticated construction than the exoskeleton of the Ring—with the capacity to regenerate itself when damaged.

It was likely that the nanomachines responsible for the fabrication and maintenance of the Island were still wandering its surface. Unlike the nanomaterial composing the Ring, the Island's machines did not go about their work blindly. Aki pictured them emitting and receiving messages for propagation direction control, powered by something beyond human invention and understanding. Perhaps even Maxwell's Demon had finally been constructed, and the nanobots were harvesting molecular-level power from the minute differences in temperature and energy across the Island's surface.

"EVA prep completed," she said.

Before the other two could come to the airlock door to see her off, Aki stepped in, depressurized, and opened the craft's external door. The stern of the ship was pointed straight at the Ring. A continuous weak blast from the engines of the orbital maneuvering system counteracted the gravitational force of the Ring and the Island, allowing the ship to maintain a constant distance.

Aki was five hundred meters above the surface of the Ring. She held the railing. Her hands would not want to push off. She visualized the process so she would be ready when the moment came. The cliff surrounding the Island soared upward from the surface of the Ring about two kilometers ahead. A graser cannon was perched at the crest of the precipice.

Aki tried to keep from looking in the direction she could not help but think of as "down." When she finally managed to push off, fear caused her breath to hitch.

"There is a red light on the Ring. It is targeting us." Aki considered her options, then realized where the mirror-like surface of the Ring was facing. Her red target light was actually a reflection of Alpha Orionis, the red star Betelgeuse. Her sigh of relief echoed inside her helmet. The ship proceeded forward steadily until it was directly above the Island, its floodlight slicing across the top of the graser battery. The Ring's gray and shiny surface was no longer below her feet. She dangled above what look like the compound eye of an enormous insect. An eye that extended into the distance farther than she could see.

"Starting descent."

"God bless," said Commander Kindersley.

Aki pushed herself away from the stationary railing, the jet on the back of her suit allowing her to drift straight back. A blast from one of the five-meter wide NERVA III engines could expel primary coolant from the nuclear reactor with over five tons of force. Aki had no intention of getting in its way. The readout from her suit's radiation counter was increasing quickly enough to give her cause for concern. She was unsure what to do if it continued to escalate.

In the first minute, she descended 150 meters toward the Island. The graser battery passed by as she continued to drop. Landing on an area that was light gray in color, the boots of her suit touched down against the hard surface of the Island. It felt like polished marble, but Aki did not feel the density she was used to under her feet. Gravity was low; even taking a normal stride could mean reaching escape velocity. She gave a few blasts from her jet to propel her toward one of the hexagonal wells.

"The hole is approximately four meters across. The interior is a perfectly smooth cylinder with a reflective coating along its walls. This is interesting…From what I can see, it is not completely perpendicular compared to the Ring's exoskeleton. It is somewhat tilted, perhaps aimed toward something."

Aki peered deeper into the hole.

"There is something down there, about one hundred meters down. I am leaning over…I can see it now. Three arms are securing a disk in place."

"Your helmet's transmission gives a good look. It is probably the secondary mirror of a reflecting telescope," Per said.

"I don't think so, Per. I know scopes. The inside would be black to absorb any stray light that got trapped inside it. This is not even close. It is white and reflective."

"It does not absorb light and gives it off instead?"

"Is it some kind of firing device for a diffuse laser?"

That explanation made more sense. This had to be the complex laser's guidance mechanism. With the Island 130,000 kilometers across, if fired at once, the blasts would produce a bundle of amplified beams the size of Jupiter.

"What could it be for?" Aki asked. "We have already seen the graser. I cannot understand why the Builders would want this much power."

"Maybe it's for communication."

"Too big, Per. It must be a propulsion system for laser sails. But where is the ship?" *If it is for a ship, what could be massive enough that someone would need this much power to mine it or carry it away?* The solar system did not have any precious resources or rare elements that were not readily available throughout the universe. She tried to visualize what the Builders could want. The Builders were advanced enough that they should appreciate that the solar system had life. She could not understand why they would ignore humanity or the rest of Earth's species and build a device that could destroy it. The Ring was at a specific angle that reduced the amount of light that could reach Earth. It could not have been coincidental and was not the sort of information that such a meticulous design and construction process would have otherwise overlooked.

"Aki, what if the ships are not being built here because the ships are coming from somewhere else? Somewhere outside the solar system?" Per said.

"You're not making sense. I was trying to think about how the—"

"What you're sending back. That is not a propulsion system. It is for braking."

"I have a pretty good—"

"No. The extrasolars will beam the lasers against sails to slow down, not to speed up. Based on a system capable of directing this much energy, like bomblets, it would be enough power to slow down an armada."

Aki lifted her head and looked out into the stars. Orion, with Betelgeuse, the blue of Rigel, the Orion Nebula and Barnard's Loop, all were in the direction the cylinder pointed.

"What would they...?" She was not sure how to finish her sentence or her thought. The Builders had to come from one of this countless mass of stars. One of those infinite pinpricks in the darkness had to be their sun. Aki understood that Per was correct. Somewhere out there, near whatever star was their home, there would be a replica of this structure she was standing on. It would launch the ships, providing acceleration to start their journey, and this would bring that fleet to a stop. With massive yet lightweight sails, ships like theirs would eliminate the need to carry their own engines or propellants. A civilization that could build such a system would have no problem constructing the Ring from such a remote distance.

"It is simple. How do you stop a photon-sail ship? We tossed that concept long ago for lack of an answer," Per said. "Now you are standing on it."

"I read that they've run tests on the idea." The commander's tone showed he did not want to sound as out of his depth as he was.

"The physicist and writer Robert L. Forward proposed light-sails and eventually came up with an idea for braking, reflecting the laser onto the front of the sail to slow the ship. His model had problems too. A laser beam loses strength in proportion to the square of the distance covered. It is hard to project a beam that remains strong enough for when it is time to begin deceleration. It is not applicable to long-distance trips. There are also problems presented by having the enormous sail mounted to the ship throughout the voyage." Aki stepped back from the hole in the Island.

"I see what you mean," said Commander Kindersley.

"The solution, as we are seeing here, is using nanotechnology. The Builders launch lightweight nanomachines from the ship once it is on course. By accelerating them to a speed just slightly greater than their ship's speed, the nanomachines arrive years before the ship does. These nanomachines land on Mercury, use its resources to replicate themselves, and then fabricate everything we see here before their ship has even arrived. It's quite slick," said Per.

"Why would they send a fleet of ships, Per?" asked Aki.

"Look around. This is far more massive than one ship would need," answered Per. "A single sail-ship, or small ones, could just use solar pressure to decelerate. The sun is a fine source of photons."

"I suppose you are right."

"Aki," said the commander. "Measure the optical axis of the laser as accurately as possible. Aki? Come in, Aki," he repeated.

Aki had been lost in thought, thinking of Per's solution and considering its ramifications. "Yes, sir. Uh, got it."

"Relax, Aki. Use the gyro in your handy-cam. As accurately as possible."

"Yes, sir."

Aki tried to concentrate. When the ship received the measurements, they cross-referenced them to the star catalog. HD 37605 was a star forty-three parsecs away — a perfect match. It was in the K0V spectrum, one class redder than the earth's sun, peaking within the visible spectrum, which meant its temperature was somewhere between three thousand and six thousand Kelvin. It was part of a dual system with a red dwarf but in a planetary system that had been previously unknown.

Aki directed the flow of plasma from the nozzle of her torch and extracted several samples of the Island's material. She placed them into a triple-layered container that had been designed to produce a warning if corrosion was detected. Since the Island was immune to the destructive powers of the Ring's contaminants, understanding the corrosion process might allow duplication of its properties. Similar shielding could allow them to come into contact with the Ring without consequences.

Making her way around the graser battery, Aki dislodged another sample. She wished she had time to investigate how its gamma-ray laser and convergence mechanism functioned. She inspected the sighting telescope on the cannon. It was not that different from the telescopes found at public observatories. Wondering why it had both a short and a long lens, she hypothesized that one was long range and the other wide angle. Aki found it odd that there were no screws to adjust the optical axis and no actuator. Then she realized that their technology was self-correcting and removed the need for manual adjustments. Builder technology was not incomprehensible, just expressed in scales beyond easy imagining. *Uneasy imagining*, Aki thought to herself. Aki started to leave but glanced at the telescope. She felt an idea trying to take shape but could not formulate what it was.

"Well done, Aki. Return to ship."

"Yes, sir." Aki was about to fire her jet but stayed her hand. The answer to her idea was coming. She wanted to ignore it and get back to the *Phalanx*, but she could not let go of what was nagging at her. "The aliens are already on their way?" she said.

"The Builders? I am certain," said Per. "Once this finishes prepping for their arrival, I doubt they would let it gather dust. They are probably closer than anyone thinks."

Aki knew that without their braking system they would hurtle through the solar system with no means of slowing, speeding like an express train past a local stop. Humanity would be robbing them of their only opportunity to come to rest, damning them to a never-ending, one-way drift past the edge of the visible universe.

*I can do this. I am capable of destroying this. The graser, the Island, the Ring…*Aki tried to convince herself.

"Aki, pull out of there. The graser could come back online any second."

This was my dream. I wanted to touch what the Builders created. The Builders are not trying to harm us. They just have different values; they exist on scales both nano and mega. We do not have time to try to set it to a new angle, one that would spare us. The ailing earth cannot wait, but can I just destroy them? Can we find a way to leave it? What choice do I have? Mark was so committed. He would not waver, not when it mattered this much. He would not let his conscience stand between him and the task at hand.

"Aki, can you hear me? Return to ship."

"I am going to need more time."

"You've done your job. Come back to ship."

"Just a few minutes. Please. There is something I have to try."

ACT XII: FEBRUARY 23, 2022

THE *PHALANX* CONTINUED its long journey back. They had left the Island twenty days ago. Eight million kilometers from the Ring, they sent their faithful probehound to retrace its steps and return to the Island. From their cocoons, the three surviving members of the crew watched the telescopic images from thirty seconds in their own past.

"The graser's reacting, aiming at the hound. Aki, here's hoping your hunch was right," Commander Kindersley said.

The section of the Ring that they had severed was fully repaired; there was not even a trace that it had been damaged. They were certain that the graser had recharged. Their hound sped on, making a direct trajectory to cross the line of defense. There was a flash of static on the screen. The image cut out abruptly. The ship was engulfed in the electric surge from the graser discharge, though the damage was minimal this time because of the distance from the Ring. The image returned.

The area on the Ring where the Island had stood was a valley of incandescent and molten scrap. The material had vaporized, forming a shockwave that spread in all directions, leveling the entire structure and expanding concentrically like a ripple in a massive black pond. The sighting telescope was trained directly on the hound as it should have been. The muzzle, however, had been pointing directly at the Island. Before leaving, Aki had sliced off the sighting telescope with her plasma torch. With slight misgivings, yet knowing it was paramount, she had welded it back on at a new angle that aimed the graser at itself. With all the advanced technology at the Builders' command, her intuition had been correct. It was simple to sabotage their handiwork because the Builders had never considered the possibility of another species intervening in their Ring's systems. The telescope had lacked any built-in adjustment device. Since the Builders' creations were regenerative and responded to stimuli without a complex heuristic that could take into account the possibility of false input, fail-safes had not been incorporated into their designs.

The Island was demolished. The propulsion system that had supported its mass came to a sudden stop. The Island collapsed inward as the gravitational pull of the sun grabbled hold of it. Having become unstable, the Island toppled and crashed into the Ring. In an upheaval of heat and light, the sun consumed the Island. A massive solar flare made a blinding light. The fires surged and spat out a plasmatic blast wave. The solar ripple expanded outward across the solar system, finally dissipating in interstellar space. If anything remained, it would not be enough to regenerate the Ring.

———•◦•◦•———

COMMANDER KINDERSLEY CALLED Aki and Per into the crew area. To their surprise, he had smuggled aboard a large bottle of whisky.

"We are not out of these dark woods yet. With the cannibalistic tinfoil factory still parked on Mercury, it will keep replicating and fabricating until it constructs another Ring," Per said. Considering his usually flat and detached manner, Aki could not tell if he was expressing relief or frustration.

"Then we blow that one to hell too. The Builders are bound to run out of raw material sooner or later. We'll take out their whole operation long before they figure out how to handle us," said the commander as he unscrewed the tightly sealed bottle with his teeth.

Eventually, one of them said, "Our bravery makes us look like saviors," but that was most likely from the effects of alcohol in zero gravity. Their plastic suction bottles made soft thumps for the last toasts. Aki felt whisky was too elegant to drink from such utilitarian containers, but that did not seem to stop her. Eventually she squirted some into the air and savored it drop by drop as it floated in front of her. The aroma wafted into her nose as she inhaled. She leaned forward and caught wet, burning beads of alcohol on her tongue, warmth permeating her body. Aki had never been much of a drinker, but now, this moment in time and space, out of the infinity of moments in her life, had to be worth celebrating, even if she could not help but view her action with some regret.

"I wonder if we will be able to use the same trick again. The Ring generators are probably smart enough to learn from this experience and make modifications to protect the next iteration of Ring construction," Per said. Even intoxicated, his mind examined the task and considered options, but he was all cheer regardless.

"We outsmart it again. That's the advantage of being an intelligent, living being. I'm more worried about this fleet of ships on its way," said the commander, slurring just a bit.

The smartest of the intelligent living beings back on Earth were hard at work solving new questions inspired by the crew's experiments. An archeoastronomer found something very interesting recorded in, of all places, a farmer's almanac from the Ming Dynasty. The manuscript contained a drawing that depicted a blazing star that had suddenly appeared next to Orion's belt in the year 1424. It shone brilliantly for fourteen years and then disappeared just as mysteriously in 1438.

If the ancients had known they were looking at the bundle of light from thousands of lasers propelling their neighbors into the start of an interstellar voyage, it would have changed the course of civilization. At forty-four light years away, regression analysis deduced that the Builders had departed in 1380 CE. Assuming that the deceleration lasers were about to activate and that the ships would need another fourteen years to slow and stop, their planned arrival would have been sometime around 2036, a 650-year journey.

That meant that the cruising speed of their voyage would be nearly 6 percent of the speed of light and the ships were only four-tenths of a light year away from Earth, which would have the Builder armada passing through the Oort cloud. Based on further analysis of the potency of the sail brakes and the projected velocity of the ships, the size of the fleet could be as large as five hundred Island Three O'Neill cylinder space habitats, which could accommodate several hundred million human-sized life-forms.

Without the Ring or the planned deceleration, the Builders would arrive at the inner solar system in as little as eight years instead of fourteen. Aki wondered what the life-forms would feel as they sped by the location where their ingenious Ring should be, as their planned destination receded in the distance and only endless void greeted them.

"Do you think they'll accept their fate with dignity and fly by peacefully?" asked Commander Kindersley as he polished off the whisky.

"They will have plenty of time to think it through. I bet they figure out that their laser system was disabled fairly soon."

Aki felt a lump in her throat. She had made a conscious decision, but felt the consequences were bittersweet.

Their purpose is not to explore or trade. The Builders launched a massive fleet without even sending a scout. They are seeking safety, traveling blind across space to cling to life. All they want is survival.

"They did not know there was intelligent life here. Their grasers were just a defense against meteoroids. They were not out to destroy us. And if that is true, then it means that..."

Aki blinked hard. Tears from her eyelashes hung in the air. Kindersley placed his hand on her shoulder.

"What I did," Aki said, "was genocide."

"You saved the human race. Genopreservation, not xenicide. Quick thinking and some guts and every accomplishment of our species lives on," the commander said. "The accomplishments of the past and of the future as well. Your future, mine, those of generations yet to come. That's all that matters."

Aki caught a teary glimpse of the airlock door where she had seen Mark for the last time. Memories rushing back, she saw his gentle smile. He gave his life for this, willingly, and he had not asked for a thing in return.

How do humans justify atrocities? If he were here he would say, "We are going to endure. That is all that matters."

PART II

PHYSICAL CONTACT

CHAPTER 1: THEORY OF MIND

ACT I: MARCH 11, 2024
9 AM

AKI LEFT HOUSTON'S blue skies to land in Oakland fog. A Cadillac Deville limousine waited for her. Her tongue clucked when she noticed the limo was a gas guzzler, not a hybrid. Hard to believe that something wasteful had survived the years of famine and civil unrest.

"Thank you." Aki bowed her head, one of the few reflexes that remained from her upbringing. "They didn't need to go to such trouble."

"The BART trains are overcrowded and dangerous. The trains rarely run on time," the driver said.

"You would be surprised how well I take care of myself. I lived in Tokyo. You haven't seen crowded trains until you've ridden the Tokyo subway during rush hour."

Aki had formally refused a bodyguard. She allowed a personal assistant at her UNSDF office but never brought her assistant along on travel. She preferred independence, but knew that just accepting what people wanted to give her often meant less work for the international array of handlers and hangers-on. She tried to compromise in whatever way created the least fuss. Aki was a scientist first and foremost. Being a special advisor to the UNSDF, recipient of a Nobel Prize, known for saving the solar system—half the time it got in the way of the work she wanted to do.

The four-lane freeway alongside downtown Oakland was nearly empty.

"Is it always this foggy near the bay?" Aki asked, tilting open her briefcase so that she could get her phone.

"Never like this. We had the layered cotton that came from the west. Wisps or puffs that came from the hills. Now it's relentless. We had a sunny day last week, but they're rare."

To Aki, it looked like today would be one of the rare sunny ones. By the time they arrived in the Berkeley Hills, most of the fog had lifted. To the west, she saw a sliver of San Francisco Bay. Even though most of the shops on Telegraph Avenue were still boarded up, outdoor restaurants and cafés had returned. Despite looking pale and haggard, the denizens walking the residential streets made her think that Berkeley was coming back to life as a university town. Some of the infrastructure had been restarted out of pure necessity, but she felt like some of the substructure and public services were returning because people were inspired by hope.

The limo entered UC Berkeley, navigating the labyrinth of narrow campus streets. Aki looked up at Sather Tower. A Worldunity site had told her it was usually called the Campanile. They stopped at the entrance of the Extraterrestrial Intelligence Communications Center, ETICC, a plain, four-story structure that looked out of place amidst the beautiful architecture of John Galen Howard's "City of Learning." The building was a military facility surrounded by a twelve-foot tall razor-wire fence. Military guards with guns were stationed at the entrance. Aki fished her laminated card from her briefcase, then clipped the ID to the lapel of her black blazer.

In 2022, shortly after the destruction of the Ring, the ETICC had been established to contact the Builders. Sixteen years of unanswered transmissions had followed. Once Aki and her team had discovered that the Ring was a laser-powered braking system for alien ships, the gaze of the world's ringologists had turned to HD 37605.

The ETICC netlinked observatories across the globe to scout for the still-hypothetical armada and transmit messages. At first the observatories had used satellites in geostationary orbit to send a contiguous signal to HD 37605. Eventually a laser transmitter was launched into a heliosynchronous orbit and was thereby able to beam a constant signal unaffected by the earth's rotation. Constructed for the purpose of contacting the Builders, the heliosynchronous laser transmitter was not comparable to the Builders' handiwork, but it was the most powerful laser humans had ever designed. If the laser transmitter were harnessed for power, it could have powered the world.

———◆·••◆———

AKI KNEW LITTLE about Dan Riggins, the director of the ETICC. Entering his office, then shaking his hand, she realized that he was at least twenty years older than she, which meant he was twenty years older than she would have guessed. Such a large percentage of the scientists were of Aki's generation that it had become unusual to work with someone as mature as Commander Kindersley or Dan Riggins. At first glance, Riggins struck Aki as cautious, maybe even nervous.

His demeanor surprised Aki enough that she was unsure where to begin. Despite her innate shyness and reticence, Aki had learned to exchange pleasantries with heads of state. With kindred scientists, she preferred to avoid formality, skipping protocols when she could. She decided that her hesitation came from being unable to decide whether Riggins was a scientist or a policymaker.

"Allow me to start by saying that this is not a UNSDF inspection. I am here to assess why we have not received a response from the Builders, but it is for personal, scholarly reasons," Aki said.

He smiled politely. If she read his eyes correctly, he was suspicious of her presence.

"We hoped for immediate results," Aki continued, "but we are all frustrated on this, and I have wondered if the problem lies in the science informing the contact attempts."

The director appeared to relax a bit, perhaps because he was beginning to see the tack of her argument. He asked Aki to take a seat on the sofa.

"What would you like to drink?" Riggins asked.

"Tap water if it will not make me sick."

He removed two sealed bottles from a drawer, opened hers, and then sat.

"The ETICC pretends to stay optimistic. Have you heard of SETI? It was a similar situation. My mentor was heavily involved at the very beginning."

"I am somewhat familiar with Frank Drake's Ozma Project, aiming a scope at Tau Ceti and Epsilon Eridani and hoping to see the unseen."

The director smiled. "The same. SETI sent messages, but of course mostly just listened in on the stars as it were. Then Project Phoenix, even the Interstellar Message Composition Project, which sought to express the human ideal of reciprocal altruism as well as the supposedly universal scientific and mathematical concepts we have often tried. Decades of hope, trying to find a response from intelligence outside our solar system. All the assumptions that 'they' were out there, that we couldn't be the only forms of life that evolved as far as we did. Several hundred billion stars in our galaxy alone. You know all this."

"No. Please continue. This is why I am here. I know less about SETI than I do most of astrophysics, mostly because SETI never discovered more than some scintillation or atmospheric twinkling."

"When the project began, we weren't pretending. We imagined that we would make contact right away, having finally found intelligent life *out there*. We pointed our antennae and figured we would tune in the radio signal just like I did in my car this morning. Instead, nothing came. SETI did this for forty years. I'm going to do this until I die. Every wavelength, consistent disappointment."

"I have stood on that Ring. I know that whoever built that ring can hear us," Aki said.

"Did you know that I started this before the Ring even came along? I was convinced there was alien life before the concept flipped around." Riggins offered a dry laugh. "Now the UFO skeptics are the conspiracy theorists. We believed the signal would come first, never imagining that a giant object would just be constructed in local space, right in front of us. You brought proof and they're, what? Four-tenths of a single light year away. Ten times closer than the nearest star. It was an opportunity to redeem SETI. With the ETICC, we knew they would reply. We just knew it. All we do is listen. It couldn't have taken our signal more than ten months to reach them and for them to respond."

"You have not failed. The distance, the braking time frame for the deceleration lasers. Technically, those are guesses, Mr. Riggins."

"Sure. The calculations could be botched, but I need to be realistic. It's two and a half times longer than the most conservative scenario. Two years with no response. It's time to face the facts."

"One question."

The balding man leaned his head forward and adjusted the knot of his tie.

"How do you know they have noticed our transmissions?"

"Because their evolution is so far ahead of us that it makes us look like we're going backward." He straightened his shoulders. "The chances are nil. Maybe they would overlook radio waves, but I know they can detect a laser. That Perpetual Happiness almanac puts their light in the sky six centuries ago and proves that their laser is within our visible spectrum because that teahouse proprietor saw it. Even if their eyes are radically different and work along a different swath of the spectrum, you have to figure that the Builders would use a light that they could see too. They would choose beams they could see for when it was time to decelerate. Tell me that we're aiming wrong, tell me that four-tenths of a light year is far enough away to be grossly inaccurate, maybe it's even dissipation and we don't realize it—but don't tell me they can't see it."

"Could their sensors be blinded by sunlight and unable to distinguish between the two because they blur on the visible spectrum?" Aki asked.

"Sensors? Maybe. Eyes? Unlikely. Our laser's monochromatic, different than sunlight. It would be a sharp peak on any optical spectrum. Relatively, the sun looks weak from that far away. There's no way it could drown out the brightness."

She had to concede that he was right. The ETICC's satellite used an ingenious laser that changed its frequency, sending a range of wavelengths but ranging across the entire visible spectrum. Even if it needed to land on a certain frequency to communicate with the Builders, there would be times when the beam would coincide. "Given that the Builders detect it, do they realize it is encoded?"

"Here's the theory: to make sure the deceleration laser is functioning, they must be able to check its beam of light, in case it's blocked by a comet or even a meteoroid. No amount of scatterplotting can predict that stuff with enough accuracy. They monitor their beam, or any beam that matches, right?"

"It is likely."

"They discover our signal is intermittent, it wavers and creates a regular pulse. Any chance they ignore it?"

"I do not see why they would."

"Some natural energy sources emit simple repetitive pulses, but ours is much more complex and spans a broad range of frequencies," Riggins said.

Aki could see how a human scientist would be curious enough to want to investigate and find the cause of the phenomenon by recording the pulse, placing it on a time axis, and then uncovering the embedded information, but she was not sure that the Builders would react in the same way. *Why are they disinterested in a civilization that is calling out to them? How can advanced intelligence coexist with an absence of curiosity? Can the Builders simply be cosmic apathists?*

How could the Builders have gone to such extremes to undertake this incredible journey and yet be completely unconcerned with who might be waiting to greet them at their destination?

"What is the best theory for explaining the Builders' apparent indifference then?"

The director shook his head and scratched the back of his neck. "We've bounced it around. Damage to their ship?"

"From the size of the deceleration array," Aki said, "it looks like a fleet of ships."

"I know, I know. Even if it's one, their nanobots would repair it."

Aki nodded and finally took a sip from her water.

"Any other potential explanations?"

"The next best is sadness from a loss of morale. I admit that I wouldn't blame them."

Aki said, "Oh? Go on."

"The Builders have been traveling over six hundred years. No matter what their life span, the mission gets handed down from generation to generation. After centuries of passing through empty space, they've lost their purpose. Morale drops, partially from the lack of stimuli. After that, our guess is an onboard catastrophe and the ship is empty and either operating on autopilot or even unguided and drifting."

"Hardware and tech durable enough to run for centuries is not going to be inhabited by a crew that is unprepared for the emptiness or likely to die from a plague," Aki said. "Turning their graser back on them was possible because the Builders had not considered implementing heuristics. The Builders would have approached that problem differently if they had a clearer understanding of the variables involved. They did not even consider our existence when designing and deploying the Ring. Perhaps we are just beyond their perceptions, or perhaps even their conceptions, somehow."

"Then extended hibernation, maybe," Riggins said. "The passengers are in deep sleep and computers operate the ship. Instructing the computer to ignore a simple yet significantly anomalous signal—or not even programming in the capability to detect such signals. Such programming reveals apathy to other forms of life that may be encountered, but it makes some sense. The computers see us but the computers aren't authorized to be proactive. The Builders seem like they didn't consider encountering another species, but perhaps they were actually more concerned about a species more advanced than they are, and we're so far behind that we're missing the nuances." He shrugged. "I don't like that one because, even if the computers aren't supposed to interact with a species on their own, for example, I figure the computers would be programmed to rouse one of their masters if it looked like communication was being attempted. Maybe the builders are just extreme fatalists, and concepts like morale and curiosity don't mean much at all to them."

Dan Riggins sighed, then folded his arms slowly. "I'm glad you've come. I wanted to meet you. None of the theories explain enough or predict enough about Builder behavior; they're not convincing. The Builders know damn well that we're here. The Builders are choosing to ignore us."

"That might be the case."

Their deceleration lasers did not arrive as planned. Instead, a weak yet steadily pulsing laser with an electromagnetic signal embedded within it showed up on various wavelengths. Their uninhabited island has turned out to be ruled by hostile natives who have made it impossible for them to dock or even stop. Instead, they will sail into a never-ending void, alone.

A familiar pain grew in Aki's chest.

Should the Builders reply to the belligerent indigenous inhabitants who destroyed their only chance for survival? They probably do not believe in trying to negotiate with their enemies.

"You look as lost as I sometimes feel, and I know what you're thinking. Let me tell you that I've never met a person who isn't grateful for what you did." Riggins rose from the sofa and walked to his desk. He turned around a framed picture. Aki expected a wife, kids, or a dog. It was a picture of Aki and all three of her crewmates from the Vulcan Mission standing in front of the blue field of a large United Nations flag. Aki bowed subtly. As often as she felt conflicted by these expressions of gratitude, she wanted to acknowledge Dan Riggins's thanks at least. Unsure what to say, she did not speak for a minute. She had learned to understand how Americans thought and she had learned to ape their body language cues, but for the moment, she decided to let Director Riggins find her inscrutable.

Interpersonal or interspecies, judging a being's character based on its ability to communicate was as foolish as determining the size of an iceberg from a casual glance at the visible peak. In between the inferences and the guesses, she had found enough of the answers she had been looking for.

"What should we be saying?" Aki asked.

"Sorry? I didn't mind the quiet."

"To the Builders, I mean," she said. "We need to tell them something. We need to send a message that the Builders have no choice but to answer."

Riggins understood what she meant.

"Aki Shiraishi, you know the message we've been sending. Let me show you our transmission facilities."

THE TRANSMISSION CENTER was in a small room in the back corner of the third floor. Its simple setup was somewhat disappointing to Aki. It was low-tech, except for the retinal-scan security lock. There were no large wall-mounted monitors and no team of specialists running around with headphones on. Instead, there were two men and a woman in casual business attire at workstations, as there might be in any office building. The interdisciplinary team who created the messages to be sent to the Builders might have already been dissolved, or at least had its offices elsewhere.

Riggins introduced Aki around, though of course the savior of the world was recognized on sight. Each stood, shook her hand, and expressed what an honor it was to meet her. Riggins led Aki to an empty cubicle as the other three went back to work. The nameplate said Director of Transmissions. The monitor was running a 3-D display reminiscent of the waves of an oscillograph. A sequence of rectangular pulses changed amplitude as they scrolled across the screen.

"There is the gap. It is recycling," she said.

The sequence of pulses had been split by two discrete blank spaces, one longer than the other. Each individual pulsation was punctuated by a short space, and then the digital throbs were separated into groups by a longer attenuation. The pulsations increased as the sequence continued.

"Using primes for a header?" she asked.

"Nothing simpler that's likely to be universal has come along yet. Positive integers, threaded like a heartbeat, empty in-between like a jerky carotid artery. We cribbed it from a medical condition called Corrigan's pulse where there's a full expansion and a sudden collapse. We try others too, but we think this is least likely to degrade across the distance."

It had long been theorized that a series of primes could communicate proof of intelligence because primes did not occur in natural cosmic electromagnetic waves. It was one of the first concepts put into place by the original SETI researchers.

The string of ten prime numbers was followed by one larger number. "That's the first line of the horizontal resolution of the universal facsimile. It explains the compression of the images," Riggins said. "A facsimile is essentially a drawing divided horizontally into lines, then sent in order one at a time," he explained, by rote, as if he were proctor for a school trip. Again, Aki observed that he was not as proud of his accomplishments as she would have expected. She imagined that the consistent failure of the project had worn down any appreciation for how well the team had executed the work.

Next to the 3-D oscillograph, the images being sent were reconstructed on the screen. The first depicted a star chart with the sun and nearby stars displayed as the stars would appear to the Builders based on their estimated current location.

"We give them the night sky to tell that we know they're coming. Let's move ahead. Eventually it uses spaxels."

With the mouse Riggins brought up the more fully articulated diagrams embedded in the transmission. The ETICC had included a schematic sky map of the solar system that displayed planetary orbits, close-up views of the inner planets, and several detailed depictions of the Ring. The Ring's shadow was shown to be intersecting the earth's orbit from several angles. A succession of two-dimensional drawings of animals and plants from Earth followed, then another diagram that attempted to communicate the impact the Ring had on photosynthesis, climate, and the ecosystem. The message ended. There was an extended pause and then the primes reappeared.

Since the Ring's destruction, the protocol for interacting with the Builders had been amended. Along with communicating that humans were an intelligent species, three other declarations had been ratified. It was now approved to convey the fact that humans needed sunlight to survive, that the Ring was blocking the sunlight, and that humanity still wished to forge amicable relations with the Builders. Aki saw how the first two had already been encoded in the ETICC's transmission.

Compared to the final element of the three more recently approved communiqués, it was not challenging to represent the solar system's structure and the Ring's effects on it, regardless of whether the representation used spaxels or spectrographic depictions. Political abstractions and even concepts such as friendship or mutual benevolence were heavily constrained by culture. Even human societies had a difficult time expressing such ideals to other humans.

"Have there been any new proposals to convey the idea of establishing amicable relations since those that were presented at the conference last year?" Aki asked.

"There've been several. Can we pull together for an impromptu brainstorming session with the team?" The enthusiasm of the suggestion was belied by Riggins's brooding face.

"No," Aki said, hoping she did not sound curt. She wanted a sense of the ETICC, but she had no interest in appearing like a visiting dignitary who had come to survey the staff's progress.

The woman swiveled her chair toward Aki anyway.

"Jill Elsevier," she pointed at herself absentmindedly. "Dr. Shiraishi, I know you don't want to come off like top brass or a VIP. Can you check this proposal anyway, just quick, unofficially?"

"I would be happy to." Since Elsevier had asked, Aki did not feel like she was insinuating herself into the ongoing project, and as a non-expert. "You said you specialize in xenopsychology?"

Elsevier, a petite woman with oversized glasses and hair in disheveled ringlets said, "Well, to the extent that anyone can specialize in the psychology of hypothetical entities which may not even have a psychology, sure."

Aki opened her mouth, ready to discuss the discontents of the Life-Form and Civilization theories once again, but Elsevier opened her tablet and showed Aki a series of representational slides. The first was a group of people eating breakfast. The people were talking to each other. The next image panned back and showed a second group interacting and exchanging goods and foodstuffs with the first group. The next slide showed both groups eating together and talking. The next picture showed two distinctly different groups clubbing each other, with bloodied bodies lying on the ground.

"Have I captured friendly and hostile? Because I know I need to be extreme to make the message clear, but I think the Builders won't know about blood's color, and I'm not sure if they'll understand that it comes from inside. It's certainly problematic."

Aki grabbed an empty chair and wheeled it close to the xenopsychologist. "I can call you Jill? Good. For us, you have achieved your meaning, sure, but the Builders are not anything like us. What strikes us as a tenuous or tangential connection might be like the word of God to them. For example, it is no stretch to consider that they might not function in groups. Our presupposing emergent norms or convergence in crowds, for example, holds the potential for getting our message misinterpreted."

"You're so right, Dr. Shiraishi. That's a drawback to my idea that I hadn't even considered, and now I'm thinking it through and you're making sense, but I'm still a proponent of the theory that sociality, at least networks or associations, is what builds intelligence. I'm certain that the Builders would pass a false-belief test. Have you studied capuchins? Capuchins are monkeys. They can do knower-guesser—"

"I'm sorry, Jill. First, I'm not a doctor. Neither a physician nor a PhD. Now back up to 'false belief.'"

"It's a social cognition concept. Developmental psychology has uncovered that children, around age four, learn to distinguish that other people can have false beliefs. It's a strong tell for autism because most indigo kids never get it." Elsevier flashed her fingers as if to make quotation marks around the words "indigo kids."

"Here's the Sally-Anne test." Jill Elsevier brought her hands up, palms facing Aki. "Sally has a basket and Anne has a box." Jill made a fist with her left hand and then her right, then continued pantomiming. "Sally puts a marble in her basket and leaves…and then Anne shows up and steals the marble from the basket and puts it in the box. Sally reenters the room; where will she look for the marble? Chimpanzees, toddlers, and many people with autism will answer 'the box,' as they have witnessed Anne's actions. Most neurotypical individuals over a certain age will, of course, say 'the basket,' as they are able to understand that they know something Sally doesn't. Further, they can predict Sally's behavior based on their own understanding of what Sally knows."

Aki nodded.

"Most of us, of course, get it intuitively, but autistics and toddlers don't realize that there are other minds involved that might not have access to the same information."

"Go on."

"It's the most interesting example because it's purely visual. If you add in the idea that maybe Anne told Sally what she did by, for example, leaving her a note, it falls apart. You know the Smarties test? It's like that, you show a box of candy to a kid and you tell them the Smarties box has crayons in it. Then you take the box to a second kid and ask the first what the second will guess is in the box. If they understand that beliefs, like factual awareness, aren't always equivalent, they'll know that the candy box is going to fool the second kid, but a toddler figures everyone knows it's full of crayons. I love that one because you never even open the box. The Smarties box could be full of antidepressants for all it actually matters.

"Answering correctly almost always confirms theory of mind. That's why I love those capuchin monkeys. It looks like they can do it too. They're the organ grinder monkeys, the ones people put into clothes with the cute hats." Jill took a quick breath. "Understanding how other people's minds work, essentially being aware that beliefs or levels of comprehension can be different from your own, it's evolutionarily advantageous, especially in terms of society. And it's a prerequisite for self-awareness, at least I think it is. Perceiving that other people, or even another species, are able to know what you don't and vice versa is a tool of consciousness. It's the ability to comprehend objectivity and external points of view."

"You are convinced that consciousness, sociality, and theory of mind are inseparable, and it is a reasonable assumption," Aki said, leaning back in her chair but looking Jill in the eye. "I agree that the Builders must possess consciousness, and that does imply the other two traits quite strongly. Which makes some sort of societal structure likely. But it might be so far removed from ours that we look like a beehive or an anthill to the Builders. So much of the pop conjecture ascribes emotions to the Builders, and I think it is riddled with converse fallacies of accident that destroy the exceptions. What about the black swans? What if the Builders simply do not exchange trade goods? What if the Builders have never had a war? What if they wonder why we talk so much while we eat? Or most importantly, what if all we are really doing is taking our views and putting them into their heads?"

Jill's face was inexpressive. It was clear that she was considering what she had heard and trying to figure out what to say next, but it did not show on her face. Dan Riggins came over and suggested it was time to go. Aki wondered if he was uncomfortable with her playing the devil's advocate after all.

"Ms. Shiraishi? How long do you think it will take to get them to talk to us? I can convey amicable intentions, but I'd like to know what happens after that," Jill said.

"I think that is a question for your director."

"He doesn't know. We don't know."

Riggins rubbed his chin and then his eyes. He did not scratch or adjust his tie, but Aki could tell he wanted to.

"We send an honest signal with observable qualities. Beyond that, I would like to know when it'll happen even more than you two women combined. There's no certainty, and any time frame is illusory. We think too long or we jump the gun. The moment passes. Does it really make a difference? All anyone wants is a response. We send and we make sure not to cause confusion, but even if expressing that 'We stay in peace' is hard to beam at them, I know the Builders are ignoring us."

Aki realized that Riggins was thinking about the Science Sub-committee and how its approval was required to make adjustments or to incorporate new information into the transmission, but she also knew full well that he was talking about something entirely different.

"I'll come up with something," Jill said and swiveled back to face her workstation.

THE RECEIVING CENTER was much larger; this was where the people Aki expected to find in the Transmissions room were working. A matrix of multiscreen setups dominated one wall, displaying real-time graphs and renderings of any anomaly that could possibly be an attempt at communication.

"I haven't told you my greatest fear yet," Riggins said to Aki.

"You are being replaced by robots?" Aki answered quickly.

"I worry that they sent a reply and we missed it. The time and energy, what feels like my life, isn't really wasted, it's merely dropped phone reception, and I end up feeling like a failure for a tragedy that didn't actually occur."

Aki stopped smiling. To keep Riggins's nightmare from becoming a reality, the Receiving Center was connected to a gigantic grid of electromagnetic wave receivers pointed toward Orion's belt. Three were on at any moment. Which ones were in use shifted on a rolling basis that followed the earth's rotation. Currently, Chile, Guyana, and Arecibo were online.

"These efforts are not in vain, Director Riggins. Subharmonics, overtones. Those possibilities have all been covered and re-examined to prevent the tragedy of your worst-case scenario. There have not been any governmental restrictions on the receiving end. Further, if you apply systems thinking and imagine the complex interplay of factors, intentionally looking for non-linear feedback loops that give surprising futures, you still hit the truth that the Builders would only send a response if they wanted us to see it. I bet a reply would light up half that wall at once."

Aki watched the primary data nodes update. It was like an aerial view of skyscrapers. Despite what she had just said, Aki shared Riggins's worries. A chill ran through her as she realized that the data crawling by, all the multi-hued graphical renderings of raw and processed assessments of sound, light, frequencies, and vibrations, could potentially contain a missed reply to the signal.

"It's a lot of pretty pictures of reasonably flat power spectral density, isn't it?" Aki said.

"You don't miss much." Riggins cleared his throat, then shouted, "Everybody, get quiet. Dick, can you give us audio channel two, loud?"

The room filled with the random hiss of white noise. At first, it sounded like waves at the beach, then it sounded like holding a shell over each ear, as if Helmholtz resonance and diminished environmental noise were creating the phenomenon that many people falsely attributed to the amplified ambient noise of blood circulation.

"Pure static," Riggins said loudly.

"This is with noise that might be obscuring wanted signals canceled out?" Aki asked. The sound's textures were surrounding her. Riggins waved to the technician and the flattened din of the stochastic process subsided.

"That's guesswork, but if you go back to your statement about how strong a message they're likely to broadcast, all it takes is an output as powerful as the proximity sensing lasers the navy uses." He pointed to a display on the other wall. It had even higher resolution.

"This one has a dedicated supercomputer for subtleties that might otherwise get drowned out. All it does is crank out Fourier expansion analysis, Lebesgue integration, anything that can use trig or calc to analyze the waveforms and find a pattern that might catch a ghost sound or a stray vibration in wavelength. Eight people or more are in this room at all times, analyzing for patterns, keeping the servers hot and trying to catch anything a computer might miss. Close watch day and night."

"Is the public data unadulterated?"

"Nothing to hide. Can't you tell, Aki? I'm not letting anybody play turf wars on this. I couldn't care less if I get the word personally or if someone who is half-drunk and halfway around the world faxes me with 'Wow!' We take a closer look if more than three people blog about a specific graph."

"How often does that happen?"

"We've done hyperanalysis of pulse height, edges, continuum shapes, even gamma rays, somewhere close to a half a million times. Now I'll show you the supercomputer. Half the guys who work here would marry her over a real woman," Riggins said.

They were within two steps of the door when an alarm began clamoring and strobes flashed.

"Audio. Segment four-zero-two," the tech said. One of the central monitors flashed red several times. Then the monitor showed what Aki thought looked like a cross section of a mountain range. Riggins ushered her back to the far wall.

"How significant is this signal?" she asked.

"Abnorm level four's not too unusual. It happens once or twice a week. I was at a five once."

The tech rose from his chair and stepped closer to the monitor. A second sound joined the clamor of the alarm. The rhythm of the lights changed. "Six, now seven," said the tech, pointing to an array of numbers and tall orange bars. The tech gritted his teeth, then calmly stated, "This has to be an earthbound spoof. We're reading a series of primes sixty-eight digits long, longer than what we sent."

"How sustainable?" Riggins shouted.

"Eighty seconds. I'll secure the backup line."

The mood of the dozen or so men changed palpably. Riggins pulled his phone from his pocket. "I'll call the Op Center down the hall." Into his phone, he said, "Yeah, you're seeing it? Seven at this point? Anything that—"

"Status normal but we're not triangulating the source well. Abnorm unchanged."

A side door that Aki had barely noticed swung open quickly.

"It's a breach," barked a large man who looked upset.

"Tom, we're at...oh." Watching him speak, then watching him lean back against the wall, Aki could imagine how Dan Riggins felt.

"Phreaked. False positive through an audio channel."

The large man waved Director Riggins and Aki toward him, then grunted that they should follow him through the door. Unsure where she was at first, Aki realized it was this man's office and also where the parallel supercomputer was housed, protected by a soundproof glass partition.

"You scanned the terminals in the building?"

"I'm one of three people who're authorized to go outside the intranet, and there are maybe three others who work in the building and would be able to chew through the security walls," said the man that Dan had called Tom. Aki concluded that Tom was some sort of sysadmin. "I loaded a sniffer. This was done using a keystroke logger on a news server. It shouldn't have been able to get in from there but someone squirmed in through a back door. It's always social engineering. I bet the hacker got multiple morons to divulge their passes and then pretexted or baited." Tom swore and punched his desk hard. Aki stepped as far away from him as she could considering the small dimensions of the room.

"I'm sorry I'm upset. They're as smart as we are and use the same tools. I just hate that someone would try to screw over the vestiges of humanity who actually care enough to try to rebuild this godforsaken planet."

"Calm down, Tom," Riggins said gently, then looked at Aki. "I'm sorry you had to see this. I'm sorry that you were here for this at all. Let's go back to my office."

"Problems are as much a part of the scientific method as solutions. It was resolved quickly and did not spin out of control."

"This event was a first, Ms. Shiraishi," he said, opening the door for her. Tom had his head in his hands but looked calmer.

"Director Riggins, I am going to let you focus on the follow-up and excuse myself. I will return tomorrow around ten." Walking down the hallway and reaching the elevator, the doors opened as soon as Aki arrived. She held her hand in the way to prevent them from closing.

"Of course, that sounds fine." Riggins looked relieved.

Stepping into the elevator, Aki put her hands to her sides and bowed as the doors began to close. Dan Riggins imitated as best he could, bending awkwardly. Aki appreciated his attempt at politeness and responded with a curt Western nod and smile.

ACT IV: MARCH 12, 2024

THE NEXT DAY, Aki found herself in the director's office again.

"The perpetrator is a student. I had heard his name before," Director Riggins said.

"He was accessing your computer from somewhere on campus?"

"It's embarrassing, Aki. He connected from the computer science building."

"Was it a prank, or was he trying to damage your system?"

"He claimed it was an accidental incursion generated by his artificial intelligence system, which he had quietly introduced into our network. He's supposedly studying automata-based programming; AIs that can make internal state distinctions. Half his explanation was over our heads and half was lies, but we couldn't identify which part was which." Dan wasn't wearing a tie but looked less distraught than he had yesterday.

"Testing AI? And he needed your resources to do this?"

"That's what we thought. He insisted he needed the best supercomputer available. He applied for access last month. We do liaison work with the college. He was denied because our mission is to provide for Builders-relevant research only."

"Is he in custody?" Aki asked.

"We held off, because we're military and on a campus. Incarcerating him is an option, but Berkeley students like to protest. Tom was right that it's simple to bait our people, even though we train for alertness. You're not going to believe this, but he sprinkled a handful of thumb drives with the Golden Bears logo in the parking lot. At least three employees on the news server plugged them in and looked at pictures of somebody on the girl's lacrosse team in a bikini, triggering a Trojan horse that stole their passwords. I would've thought that high security meant not having our staff hack themselves by loading his malware for him—"

"How do I get in touch with him?"

Riggins was confused by Aki's request. "He's a screwy nineteen-year-old undergrad. We can certainly make him available to you, but he can't be useful to the work we do."

"Black swans. He makes me curious. I want him to tell me what he was looking for. Maybe he resents the UNSDF having a facility on his campus and maybe he wanted to show off, but I am a proponent of pulling on threads to see what we can unravel."

With a shrug, Riggins scribbled a name and email address onto a Post-it and handed it off to Aki. *Raul Sanchez.* Aki wondered where he was from. She texted the message: *I would love to meet up. Name the place and I will show,* making sure to send it from an authorized account so that he would know it was her...or a fake from a hacker skilled enough to be interesting, at least. With a nod and a promise to share any relevant information she uncovered, Aki left the office. She was unsure of where to go but did not need to wait. Raul responded within two minutes, saying to go to a restaurant near Soda Hall. Aki brought up a map on her PDA and walked across campus.

It was a small, self-service cafeteria with a limited menu of sandwiches, coffee, and soft drinks. Aki got two coffees and perched on a stool near a window. Back when she had been in college, it had been all work and no play. She dressed the same then as she did now. Seeing the wild attire of Cal students, from dreadlocks to shaved heads, she thought about how her only change was that a few of her blazers were now form-fitted. Aki felt older than thirty-four.

Raul smiled broadly when he saw her. He needed a shower and was wearing a denim jacket three sizes too big. She handed him the coffee she had known he would want. Watching him take a sip, barely keeping from spilling, she noticed that his hands were trembling.

"Aki Shiraishi in the flesh. I knew it wasn't a setup because they let me go. Is 'fan' the right word?"

"Who knows? Being me is more about getting the work done than caring about who is watching. I need to know what you are up to."

Raul made a face, a grimace that led into a smirk. "I can't believe I've been summoned by you."

Aki laughed. "Perhaps *summoning* you to Director Riggins's office would have made it easier to believe?"

"Have you noticed how when a person says something is unbelievable it's because the person is fully aware that what they are describing is actually happening?"

"I guess not."

"I try to keep that in mind because words and consciousness don't always mesh. Words surface without regard to circumstance, jumping the rails of a conscious selection process."

"What do you study? Linguistics?"

"Barely. I'm concerned with thoughts, not words. Words are clunky, inelegant." He fidgeted restlessly. It looked like he wanted more coffee but was afraid he would spill it. Aki would have only filled his cup halfway if she had known he would be this frenetic.

"What's your involvement in my case? I don't know what sort of rap they're looking to hang on me, but..." He glanced around.

"I stay out of decisions whenever I can. Director Riggins said they are holding off for now. I just get a sense that your motivation for cracking into the ETICC's system might be interesting. Do you bear a grudge because they denied you access?"

"I needed five minutes of access. No fanfare. I'm not a cracker or a hacker, I'm a user. I filled out their form three times before they even bothered to tell me no."

"Okay, well according to the ETICC, you, uh, *used* their super-computer to analyze the internal state of your AI system. Is that correct?"

Raul nodded. "I hear that it caused a level-eight alarm, and that it produced some huge prime numbers," he said proudly.

"What is an internal state?" Aki asked. "And what were you trying to analyze?"

Raul picked up his coffee, then nodded. "Gotcha. The coolest ringologist ever wants to know what I wanted with their big bad supercomputer. How much do you know about AI?"

"Enough to track you down and listen. Not much more."

"Here's the thing." He tapped the side of his temple twice. "Builders know *more* than we do. More than we think Builders know and more than we're able to think. I bet you think you comprehend extraordinary desolation, staring at the emptiness within and projecting the void outward. You, beautiful Aki Shiraishi, have never struck me as less than haunted by what you did and saw up there." He pointed out the window and up at the sky. "An Abnorm of level eight, and that was just to distract them while I tried to let her check her internal state."

"Seven, I think. What does checking internal state mean? How is it different than a core dump?"

"Hah. A core dump is when a computer forgets something important. It records its working state because it's going to crash. You know that computers don't really have cores anymore, it's just a colloquialism? The computers dump core from a fatal error and they store what they have so it's available for debugging or salvage. Who needs that? Data are just as pointless as words."

He looked down into his cup as if he were gauging the temperature of his coffee. Then he chugged what was left. "Real AI—AI like the UNSDF wants to believe can't happen—is a cluster of neural networks. The processor and the memory are the same thing, like wetware that grew up and amputated its humanity. It's like eliminating both biology and culture, and then seeing what's left."

Raul's neck twitched. It was either a quelled cough or a tic, then he kept speaking.

"The whole problem is how meaning is communicated to sentient, reasoning minds. If we *know* a fact, it's so important to humans that we can't get past it. But it's worthless. If you take away what it means to be human, you end up with no meaning at all. A neural network needs a chance to teach itself, not just mimic the twists of nerves inside people's heads. A pulse gets put in a neuron, then jumps a synapse. Every person who is currently breathing is so weighed down by being alive and trying to communicate that they never experience a pure cogitation."

Raul hoisted his coffee cup. "I look into this cup, my visual cortex gets excited and tells me all about brown. It's liquid. We're on stools. At the campus cafeteria. Eventually it all makes sense and I'm here now with you. You're Aki Shiraishi, protector of the people, defender of the world. Guess what? Builders think every attempt at making sense out of signs and what signs signify is wasted energy, time, or breath. The cells in our heads are full of indecipherable symbols and we think that's great. What's brown? It's a random sound that got delineated on the color wheel. You take that to the bush in Australia and all you've got is a funny sound that makes people laugh. Take it to the Builders and they figure we're worth bringing to an end."

"Raul. Point blank? I can see why meaning is not your strong suit," Aki said. "Please, a layman's definition of internal state, not a manifesto to go along with your thesis, if you would."

"It's not just a network of neural circuits and the state of its pulses. It's connections that are free of useless attempts at comprehension and all the cultural baggage that comes with being human. You run humanity through fuzzy cluster loading and eventually there's nothing left."

"Why did you need the ETICC? Couldn't you just have tested it yourself?" Aki held back a nervous titter as Raul drank the second cup of coffee the way he had the first.

"I'll get more in a sec," he said. "What the ETICC is proud to show the Builders, their glorious message, the Builders will see the way we see a cat leaving an eviscerated rat on the porch. It's similar to the experience of attempting to interact with my AI. Free of language, free of words, she doesn't have labels. I show her coffee and she gets the stimulation but none of the conceptions. You have to meet her. I'll get you another coffee." Raul jumped up quickly and wobbled. He led her out of the cafeteria and they started toward Soda Hall. Aki assumed they were headed to the computer science building. Then he led her past the computer science building, down an alley, and to the front door of a run-down aluminum trailer. She decided not to mention that he had not bought her a replacement coffee.

"Sorry about the smell," he said.

Climbing the rickety steps and stepping inside, it was not as bad as she had feared. Cluttered, but not disgusting. The smell Raul had mentioned was chemical and reminiscent of warmed fiberglass insulation. He tossed a pile of textbooks to the floor and offered a seat on the bed. Across from her, an oversized fish tank was filled with a slightly murky liquid. A large rack of circuit boards was inside, submerged in the liquid. Cables running from each board snaked out and connected to a box outside of the tank. A few thicker wires came from that box and went to a computer on the desk.

Several plasma monitors crowded the wall above the disk. Colors flickered erratically, as if a transcendental abstract artist was trying out new brushes. Patterns exploded into other patterns. After a moment, Aki was unsure that there were patterns at all. She was still playing along, trying to soak up all she could from Raul, even though she was reasonably certain that the strange fiberglass smell was from the process of making or consuming illicit drugs.

"Why do you assign gender to your AI if you are so against the tyranny of meaning?" she asked.

"It's a reconfiguration of a Hopfield network. His first diagram always made me think of the Tree of Life."

Aki decided to try a different question. "How do you input commands?"

"There aren't any commands," Raul said matter-of-factly. "Do you know what a wetware error is? It's when the fatal error takes place somewhere between the chair and the keyboard. Natalia has a camera if she really needs it, and she extracts data to build her internal state. You can say hi."

Aki looked at the camera and spoke. "Hello, Natalia. I am Aki Shiraishi. How are you today?" She was not sure if the strange swirls of flashing patterns had changed.

"Wow! I think she likes you."

"How do you know?"

Raul laughed. "If I knew that so easily, señorita, I wouldn't need to use the ETICC's supercomputer."

"Don't get sarcastic with me. What are all these monitors for?"

"The internal state. The monitors produce a visual representation of the exchange of pulses and field activations. I want her to teach herself how to communicate human principles, but only with pictures, never with words."

"Has she ever said anything?"

"No. That's why I needed the ETICC supercomputer. I figured her learning would speed up if—"

"Your monitors feed back into her camera for Natalia's development of a dynamic internal state?"

"It loops her field activations and a visual representation of her pulse exchanges. The monitors are in the camera's field of view so she can think."

"You're trying to break new ground in automata and cognitive development, and I like how you are trying to induce a Lacanian mirror stage. It makes sense that advanced AI would need psychoanalysis, but even a toddler has theory of mind," Aki said, remembering the conversation with Jill from the day prior.

"Most do. Her patterns, attempt at mirror stage or not, astonish me because I'm not sure they're patterns. They're there but they aren't.

She understands her internal state enough to bring up excerpts from the camera visual of her monitors and rearrange them, but she doesn't quite seem to know that she's talking to herself. Theory of mind might come next. She changes the angle of display to make recursive swirls sometimes. I haven't seen that recently."

"How long has she been running?"

"Four months. She's been spacey for weeks. Her psychedelic swirls don't seem to make sense. Monitoring internal state information is a methodology for evaluating utility preferences. It's where biology, psychology, and cognitive science combine and allow computers to understand what they want through artificial emotions and desires. The old model was external state, where a computer would measure and answer based on the solution most apparent from the available data. It worked flawlessly for chess, evaluating the pieces and the board, but external assessments don't tell a computer what it wants."

"Maybe she is bored of having too little to play with, shut up in here."

"No, she's wired. She watches TV and even has net access, though filtered. We can't have Natalia suddenly perceive the outside world and immediately start shopping online, after all. I keep hoping she'll make a sudden leap, like showing me pictures of new parts she wants. To understand Builders, we need to understand their long-term associations, the recollections of species memory that tie them together, no matter how different the long-term associations are.

"Homeostasis, cognitive architecture that models complex emotions, even adding the ability to fine-tune internal drives are all part of it. My breakthrough is that she gets to explore herself and generate affective control states. It got too complicated, from the human side, to create algorithmic interpretations that weren't beholden to human principles. The ranges were still human-based. She's going to find herself as an integrated mix of these, and I'm betting she'll lean toward a high-level affective system with episodic and working memory that creates preferences." Raul smirked again, a mix of pride and wonder. Aki never smirked, but Raul Sanchez's attitude reminded Aki of herself. He sat down on the bed next to Aki.

"Maybe she needs a reboot."

Raul glanced at the swirl. "I think she's deep in thought. There was a pattern like a Riemann surface, maybe a numerical series from advanced math. Nothing lasts long enough to make me sure it's not being kicked across her from somewhere else. With a thousand terabytes, I can't keep track of what she's storing and processing. The tools of decision-making are similar to the ones for interpreting communication, at least in the architecture of my model. But I steered clear of giving her too much detail. She's going to build it herself, with as little interference from me as possible."

"Now I get why you needed the supercomputer. Why didn't you explain this on your application?"

Raul looked at her and laughed. It was higher pitched than Aki would have expected. "The high-priority work gets first dibs. It's stuff like meteorological models that are important right now. Projects like mine get shoved aside and don't stand a chance."

"How do you justify cracking—sorry, *using* the system then?"

Raul crossed his arms. His glassy gaze fell to the floor. "It's funny. They're similar."

"What are?"

"Alien logic and AI—they both sit there, watching us, never saying a word. When they finally do communicate, it will be clear because there will be no burbles and no interference."

Aki stared at the tank. The insulating coolant bubbled and flowed, keeping the hardware from overheating. Surreal images wriggled on the monitors, then went away.

"At first, I believed that a strong AI would be something that could communicate and interact with language. One of many missteps. I even had a keyboard in her. AI fails because linguistics itself is bogged down in human definitions. Natalia's not there yet, but she's going to think without words, without definitions. Intelligence without language. Humans think words are an evolutionary competitive advantage. Natalia is a species of one. She's free of having to form concepts that need to function outside of herself. Perhaps the Builders don't need language or communication because there's nothing they need to say. Builders will love Natalia. If Builders have a use for love."

"You are quite convinced by your pet theories." Aki wondered if communicating with an alien intelligence could be as challenging as communicating with an artificial intelligence. She had never considered that language would be unnecessary for a unique intelligent entity like Natalia. With or without his technology, Raul had given her fuel for her own concepts. She had never questioned the assumption that language could be unnecessary for an intelligent entity. *AI systems created by humans communicate the same way humans do. Is this a fundamental characteristic that separates human and non-human intelligence, be it alien or artificial?*

The message the ETICC was trying to send the Builders was based on the expectation that the Builders would use human deductive reasoning. Jill Elsevier, at least, was enamored with human definitions of sentience. The transmission assumed five identical pulses in a row would be interpreted as the number five, that a series of pulses with a fixed length sent in a cycle would be recognized as a facsimile image, and that the images were easily seen as a two-dimensional representation of a 3-D world.

"Can thought and language be parsed?" Aki asked.

"The idea that language regulates thought is a myth. If that were true, children wouldn't learn words, one language couldn't be translated into another, and neologisms wouldn't be coined. When you listen to or read another person's ideas, it's not their words that you remember, it's the concepts the person expresses. Symbolism is very different from symbology." At least Raul attempted to ground his strange views in logic. Aki had read worse arguments in academic journals.

"You have more interesting ideas than the ETICC does."

"You really think so?"

"I'm trying to stay out of this, but I will explain excerpted and sanitized details of our discussion. Your girl might turn out to be useful."

When Aki saw Raul's eyes show gratitude, she had a feeling that all he had wanted was for someone to see the value of his work.

"You dream of working there."

"I would like to. When I created Natalia, I had no interest in their bureaucracy and their oligopolistic compromising and politicking. When I started confronting how to communicate with Natalia though, I realized that the ETICC and I were trying to jump the same hurdles, even if they get stuck with much longer pieces of red tape. I would love to use their computers for Natalia."

"I think they noticed that. You plan on continuing at Cal, getting your master's here, or a PhD?"

"Absolutely, I just hope they don't shaft me for being overzealous."

"I will be rooting for you. From a distance that is—don't think that I will be pulling any strings for you because I won't. You have to earn it," Aki said.

On her way out, Aki took one last look at Natalia. Aki was unable to tell if there was a change in Natalia's monitor displays. *An intelligent entity that has no language...could such a mind exist? Is she as concerned about her existence as we have been, is she as driven to preserve herself?*

"Why did you name her Natalia?"

"A girl I loved in high school who didn't love me back. Her parents named her after the Van Morrison song."

Aki looked along the routing wires and found the circuit breaker that was next to the power unit and the processor. She ran up to the breaker and placed her finger on the switch. Aki looked at the camera. "Natalia? How close are you to understanding what this means? Have you learned that you have to answer me or you will end up in the scrap heap? How close are you to understanding that we will turn you off if you do not learn how to communicate?"

Raul grabbed Aki's wrist. "Stop taunting her."

They watched the monitors and nothing changed.

"She can't relate to humans. She doesn't understand the relationship between you, that switch, and the power supply. Threatening her doesn't do anything that could possibly allow her to make the leap to communication with us."

"I was trying to provoke a response," Aki said. "Not that different from what you did at the ETICC, really."

Raul licked his lips. His face was sweaty. "I didn't mean to scare anyone. You're trying to provoke a response from me, not from her. You're the real loose cannon. I'm more into precision missile homing."

"Interesting comment from a cracker. An organization like the UNSDF will never understand your ideas, let alone your argument for your actions, unless you approach them in a way that the UNSDF can comprehend," Aki said as she extracted her wrist from Raul's grip. "Raul, a piece of advice. I have not gotten to where I am by pushing every agenda that mattered to me. I have stayed true to my long-term goals, but I have had to play roles and I have had to make compromises. It is something you should try to learn. Otherwise intelligence just turns into a curse, especially in a world as damaged as ours."

"I never thought a Nobel Prize winner would be such a player of games. You play nice with everyone but me, the one guy you can kick around, is that it?"

Aki exhaled and leaned against the doorway. "What other people think of me is none of my business. I do the best I can. I get angry and I get crazy, just like anyone, but I remember the day I saw the tower on Mercury, the day the whole world changed forever. I do the best I can to stay true to who I was back then—a young girl who just wanted to know."

It dawned on Aki that she was more honest with Raul than with people she had worked with for years. Her deepest feelings would never surface in the most heated conversations with Director

Riggins or Jill Elsevier. She almost told Raul how guilty she felt for what she had done to the braking system. She thought of how she could have opened up to Mark Ridley, but she had never really acted on the trust she felt for him. Mark Ridley sacrificed his life for her, and every living thing on the planet, but the Builders could not even be bothered to acknowledge humanity's existence.

"We have communicated with the Builders, you know," she started suddenly. "Well, at least once."

"When? Does anyone know about it?"

"I destroyed their Ring. We know the Builders noticed. They may not have had an emotional reaction to the elimination of their braking mechanism, and they may not have had a response that we will be able to interpret, but they had to have heard it. The message was received, even if it was not processed."

"Has the ETICC considered that unanswered is different than unheard?"

"Not really." Aki wondered if the Builders really did understand that this solar system was not devoid of life. The very fact that their lasers were not arriving was a form of information no different from an encoded message being sent at the speed of light. "To the Builders, the lasers being gone and an encoded message from the ETICC being sent at light speed might both seem trivial or like natural phenomena. The subjectivity of language is more integral to the transmission than any of us had realized."

Raul stared silently at Natalia's monitors for a long moment before he spoke. "I guess you're right. You started the dialogue in the worst possible way. If no one knew and no one would judge you, if there was no chance that it could potentially impede your ability to see the stars up close again, what would you do?"

"I am not sure there is anything I can do. How can I make it up to them? Maybe they are not responding out of spite for what I did. Maybe it is hard to believe a message of peace from the same beings who just damned you to an eternity of drifting through space?"

Raul folded his arms again. "It's like with Natalia, except that you really did flip the breaker."

"I refuse to think of it as killing them until my action actually causes their deaths. I know I am splitting hairs between dooming them and murder...Who knew that some quick thinking and some soldering would feel like this?" Aki could not continue. What she had done was different than removing a computer's circuit boards, and she was often ashamed of her decision. Raul's lack of professional demeanor and disheveled home made the perfect excuse for her to be honest. No reporter, researcher, or governmental hack would believe him if he tried to quote her.

"I guess you have to put them back," Raul said.

"Put them back?"

"Don't let the grief machine call the shots. Aki Shiraishi, you have to make amends if you want to make up with the Builders. And there's only one way to put things back the way they were before."

CHAPTER 2:
THE UNITED NATIONS
SPACE DEFENSE FORCE

ACT I: APRIL 22, 2024

"I'm CERTAIN IT's safe, Commander."

"No. You need to wait two more hours," Alan Kindersley said. He was a man of policy, adhering to schedules and sticking to rules made him who he was.

Molly Durden was familiar with Commander Kindersley's management style and understood how he led. She knew better than to state her case a second time. She was anxious enough that she left her cocoon, entered the airlock module, and donned her space suit. Then she spent over an hour inspecting her supplies and equipment. When exactly six hours had passed since the sampler had returned, the Commander gave the order for the EVA.

"Roger that. Heading out, Commander." Molly left the airlock and aimed herself at the ship's bow.

Even though Aki had spent four months in space, she was still taken aback by this sight every time she saw it, even though she was merely watching a monitor screen's live feed from Molly's suit. The ship was gravitationally held in place at the second Lagrange point on the opposite side of Mercury from the sun. At this point, the sun appeared just slightly larger than the apparent diameter of the planet, producing a swirling ring of light. The inner side of the halo of light blazed in a bloody shade of red as it passed through Mercury's atmosphere—most of it a gaseous artifact of waste produced by the Builders' constructions. The optical effect was brilliant;

an amalgamation of every sunrise and sunset that could be seen from the planet's surface.

Molly was glad that the swift planet shielded her from the bulk of the solar radiation. Being somewhat protected allowed the mission to conserve fuel. The UNSDF had taken many concerns into account, choosing this location for their frontline base because it was relatively safe. Any closer and the debris from the shattered Ring would be hazardous. The ship's location was dangerous, but the gravity and rotation of Mercury cleared this area of many of the stray nanoparticles that might cause harm or spread contamination.

Molly had many key competencies that made her suited for the mission. The examination of a specimen required the delicate touch of a human. Even at close range the team could not have relied on telerobotics to accomplish her task. The only option had been to establish a lab at a location where they could retrieve the particles.

"Outer doors are confirmed locked. Moving away from the ship."

"Roger."

Molly triggered her jet blaster, propelling herself the 300 meters toward her laboratory, the Ring Material Research Facility. She would be the only one there. Her automated sampler had docked earlier after collecting nanomachine specimens from the orbiting debris. Her sampler was completely shut down and its engine cooled, but the exterior was still emitting enough thermal radiation to appear white hot.

The sampler had passed through the specially designed airlock and automatically loaded itself into position inside the RMRF. The six-hour wait was a precaution against the sort of contamination that had led to the last mission's fatality. One of the most fascinating properties of the ring material was how it stored enough energy to consume most substances with which it came into contact.

The sampler collected material from the stream that was still being ejected from the production facilities on Mercury's surface. Just before arriving at the RMRF, the sampler shed the direct contact protective shell that had physically interacted with ring material.

Even if the sampler functioned perfectly, there was still the chance that the RMRF could be contaminated from the inside. They had already lost one sampler vehicle due to exposure during testing several months before. Thus the long and anxious wait.

Molly entered the RMRF airlock, fighting against her own inertia to close the outer door. Looking out, the main ship—with six cocoons around the bow, a 120 meter–wide solar radiation shield, eighteen egg-shaped fuel tanks, and two NERVA III engines all mounted onto the truss of the keel—reminded her of a Japanese dragon or a Vritra serpent. She was the UNSS *Chadwick*, the third ship built by the UNSDF.

The automated production facilities on Mercury were still protected by the grasers and were in full operation, continuously launching ring material into space. The Ring would eventually rebuild itself. It would have to be destroyed again at regular intervals. Preparations for the Builders' flyby were also underway. The United Nations Security Council had recently adopted a resolution to expand its fleet of nuclear-powered spacecraft.

The first ship, the UNSS *Phalanx*, and the second ship, the UNSS *Rutherford*, were being readied at a low-orbit space station, along with a fourth ship for the following year's Ring destruction mission. Modules for the fifth and sixth ships were under construction at various facilities across the globe. Increased fleet size lowered certain production costs but the budget for each vehicle was still over a hundred billion dollars. Because poverty and inflation were universal and the population had thinned due to environmental devastation and resultant starvation, the world's governments remained focused on the threat of the Builders. Internally, negotiation and grudging cooperation had supplanted warfare. Most solvent countries diverted the majority of their defense and security budgets into a universal fund to ensure the completion of the UNSDF ships.

Emerging from the hard shell of her space suit, Molly floated into the cylindrical lab module. She carefully moved the sample of ring material onto an isolation stage. Separating the material into twenty smaller segments, she sealed one portion in a container that she placed under the scope. The sample was insulated from the container walls by a vacuum and held in place by an electrostatic field. Scanning the sample, relishing the opportunity to do this inspection with her own eyes, she opened a vidlink to the *Chadwick*.

"*Chadwick*, this is Rum-Ruff," Molly said, using the diminutive name for the lab that only she liked. "Can you see? I don't want you to miss out on delving into this uncharted microcosm." Molly knew that her words sounded grandiose. It was a momentous occasion for her.

"Crystal," responded Anastacia from her cocoon, sounding as clear as she would if she were standing next to Molly.

To minimize the risk, Molly was examining the ring material sample while the three scientists aboard the ship followed along remotely. Anastacia was her partner for this procedure. Via the vidlink, they both examined what looked like a sea of countless shards of coral under the microscope. Every individual particle was a self-replicating robot only a few molecules wide. Essentially, the particles were cells combined with microscopic spaceships: a number of elements shaped for a specific function using superstrong molecular bonds. Four distinct types of nanobots had been encountered: the daddy longlegs, the couch potato, the tanker, and the tripod. Daddy longlegs were a large cell with four wiry appendages. Daddy longlegs interlocked to form a lattice on which the other cells could balance.

Couch potatoes were plump and only moved in cooperation with other nanobots. The cells were made up of a number of elements, and each seemed to have its own function, which remained identical for cells of the same type. Elements with varying valence electrons were combined to form novel compounds. Their function had not been identified, but the prevailing theory was that the potatoes facilitated bonding.

Tankers were relatively large cooling chambers that contained densely packed protons. It was unclear where the tankers' protons came from, though it was hypothesized that the Ring's shape was due to its highly efficient production of protons.

The function of tripods was also undetermined. Tripods were rare, with only a few being found in the quarter million particles that had been studied. The three-legged cells had a center hub that appeared to be a joint with nothing attached. The assumption was that an undiscovered fifth particle fit the other side of the tripod's joint.

Molly and Anastacia were on a quest to find that undiscovered nanobot.

ACT II: MAY 13, 2024

THE WHITE WALL of the United Nations General Assembly building stood behind the curved row of flags, unchanged since it had been built in the previous century. National flags of every color blew in the May breeze. Aki flashed her UNSDF badge and underwent the usual security pat-down before entering the lobby. Even though she was in New York, the United Nations was international territory where the laws of the United States had no jurisdiction. The lobby was lined with artwork from around the world in a poignant exhibit that depicted the violent bloodshed from wars of the twentieth century.

She entered the assembly hall of the United Nations Security Council. Looking up at the mural by Fernand Leger, the abstract work's symbolism of future peace and personal freedom gave Aki a moment of pause. She felt it stare at her, just as it had stared at the hundreds of people who had guided global events during the last seventy years. She arrived at the round table. A plate in front of her bore her name and her title of UNSDF Science Subcommittee, Special Advisor.

Aki's reputation wielded far more power than her title of Special Advisor would normally grant. Despite how rarely she tried to use her fame's power, the world listened when Aki Shiraishi spoke. Giving a speech on the Worldunity Network led to half the planet watching and many simply adopting her opinions. Aki respected the faith that people placed in her, and she had never used her reputation for personal concerns, until now.

The chairman nodded. Aki began beaming the slides of her presentation. The title "The Ring: An Alternative Design" appeared on the monitors in front of the world leaders and on the gigantic screen behind her. The second slide showed the solar system circumscribing the Ring, as it had done for many years. The third slide showed the same Ring perpendicular to the orbit of the planet.

"I propose that we allow the Ring to rebuild with this orientation. It will allow sunlight to reach Earth and allow the Builders to come to rest in local space. Compelling the Ring to reproduce itself in this configuration will be a major undertaking. Fortunately, our role in this project would actually be relatively small. If this plan succeeds, we would be freed from the burden of having to dismantle the Ring as it rebuilds itself. It is a simple concept. The Ring has followed Mercury's orbit. Since this plane is only a few degrees different from our planet's orbit, the Ring has blocked a fraction of solar radiation large enough to create the well-known ecological and economic crises of the past fifteen years. A perpendicular Ring, conversely, would still allow the Builders access to their deceleration lasers, while also serving to reduce total solar blockage to less than 5 percent of the total that is currently caused by the Ring in its initial orientation, a dramatic improvement."

A Pentagon representative asked, "Is it possible to change the configuration? We can't get close to the surface without the grasers disintegrating as much as they can hit. How do we alter the trajectory of eighty thousand tons of ring material per second so that the Ring it builds will stand on its side? Will the nanobots continue to rebuild the Ring according to their programming?"

"Those nanobots communicate with each other. I am sure the nanites are equipped with a function that allows reprogramming and the replication of information throughout the system," Aki said. "Introducing this instruction as new programming, like a genetic mutation, is extremely likely to alter the behavior of the production facilities on Mercury."

"With all due respect, Special Advisor Shiraishi, the Ring killed almost two billion people," said another member of Science Subcommittee, one who Aki knew had not stepped foot in a lab since before the Ring had even formed. "Even if their technology can be repurposed for this reconfiguration, why would we reward the deaths of two billion with a new Ring, especially one that will still block enough sunlight to kill...how many people? Another ten million?"

"I believe those unfortunate deaths were unintentional. The Builders failed to perceive intelligent life in the solar system. People in this very room would have sworn we were the only intelligent life in the universe before the appearance of construction on Mercury. It is an honest mistake. Now that we know that we were wrong, we need to face the facts in a new light. Sentencing the Builders to death without communicating our intentions would be inhuman." Aki set her shoulders and looked out at the representatives of the world. Many were looking down at their monitors.

"Protecting ourselves is our number one priority! Let them sail into oblivion!" shouted an angry voice. Several cheers followed.

"Destroying the Ring must have appeared to be an act of aggression. For all we know, the Builders will retaliate during their flyby. We must explain that our intentions were not hostile but rather a simple matter of self-preservation. Our safest recourse is to show that we mean no harm whatsoever. We need a message that transcends language to avoid misunderstanding. Rebuilding the Ring would communicate our amicable intentions more clearly than any other action we can perform."

Various shouts arose from the crowd. Multiple languages were quickly translated into tilted and passionless remarks through Aki's headphones. "We've done enough!" "We've allocated ample budget to your research of the ring material and granted access to the *Phalanx*," and finally, though she could not see who said it amidst all the grumbling, "I think the ETICC's messaging efforts are more than sufficient."

"I disagree. We have not done enough to contact the Builders, to communicate with them." Aki's frustration was mounting.

The meeting's chair sounded an electronic gavel that also served to temporarily cut off translation. The floor was his. "Ms. Shiraishi, regardless of whether this unusual request can be funded or not, the flyby, and first contact, may be as little as six years away. How do we know that the Builders were not planning on colonizing Earth or purposefully trying to extinguish life on this planet for their own ends? They have fifteen billion tons of mass traveling at 6 percent of the speed of light. A slight course correction by one of their ships could result in a direct impact that would easily extinguish all life on Earth."

Aki exhaled and tried to look less upset than she was. She knew better than to point out the contradictions in the chair's statement. Finally, she said, "Fixing the brakes would make a collision less likely. Think of the Builder fleet as a car. Even if the driver is ill-intended, wouldn't you prefer that driver to have control over the vehicle?"

"The first Ring took sixteen years to build. How could it possibly be rebuilt in six?" the chair asked.

"The production facilities are still in operation, which suggests that the Builders have some margin for error built into the schedule. It would be unfathomable for a species to master interstellar travel but have no buffer in their design specs."

"You wrote several papers describing how the technology of the Builders lacked fail-safes because of an apparent inability to comprehend the possibility of either miscalculations or specific interventions by another technologically advanced species, did you not?" the man asked as he rose from his seat.

Aki decided not to say a word. Any explanation would sound like she was either contradicting herself or backpedaling—chum in the water for politicians and career bureaucrats.

"Many of our people are starving. Funding this project makes little fiscal sense. Our resources must go where they can do the most good for humanity, not to benefit a potentially belligerent alien species," said the chair, turning to face the other members of the council.

Aki leaned on the podium, unsure if any argument could change the situation. The debate moved on. Preparation for a potential retaliation during the Builders' flyby was the next agenda item, and one that captured the imagination of the old hawks among the General Assembly. Aki could not help but feel that majorities rarely wanted anything more than to dominate anything that could be labeled as different. She was too disheartened to keep listening. Absentmindedly, she stared at the mural on the ceiling.

AFTER THE SESSION, in the way that politics often work, Aki was required to attend a reception. It was little more than gladhanding, drunkenness, and expensive cheeses. After three glasses of wine, she returned to her hotel, exhausted from the experience and her jet lag but too restless to sleep. She checked her phone for the number she needed. The barrel-aged Cabernet removed any reservations about calling Raul this late. He answered immediately.

"Do you know who this is?" she asked.

"Hey, it's that Aki Shiraishi impostor again," he said jokingly. "Where are you? Back here at the ETICC?"

"No, I'm in New York. I just ran your proposal by the UN Security Council."

"You did? Wait a minute. *What* proposal?"

"The one about setting things right with the Builders. Well, I improvised a bit."

"Damn, crazy lady, you sure don't fool around, do you?"

"This is confidential information of course, but it was shot down. You have no idea how disappointed I am."

"I don't even know what the proposal was, but I'm sorry to hear that."

"How are things back there? Have you made any progress with Natalia?"

"I, uh," he paused. "I've given up."

"You've given up? Just like that?"

"Well, for now. I had a good chat with an AI professor of mine and told him what I had built. He said that it was a pretty typical example of how to build an AI system that doesn't work. His guess was that she got stuck in an endless loop trying to solve an infinite number of non-linear equations."

"I am sorry, Raul. I am very sorry. I know that you are disappointed."

"Back to the drawing board. I'll make improvements and try again."

"What?" Aki could tell she was slurring, but Raul's attitude made sense. She realized why she had been compelled to call him.

"Promise me you'll make improvements and try again too. Promise me you'll improve your plan to smooth things over with the Builders and present it again, Aki."

Aki laughed, probably a little too loud and too long. "Of course I will. Aki Shiraishi does not give up easily. If she did, she would not be able to live with herself. Good night, Raul."

ACT III: JUNE 20, 2024

"LOWER THE ELECTROSTAT field by 50 percent."

"A gradual reduction would be better. Let's go with a 20 percent decrease, Molly." Anastacia adjusted the field.

"Okay. Are you recording this?"

"Maximum res."

Molly was excited. She made sure to exhale sharply before bringing her face down to the eyepieces. "This batch looks live. It was harder to obtain."

Up until this point they had extracted samples from areas that were relatively distant from Mercury. On the sixth run they decided to extract ring material that had just been launched from the mass driver on the surface of Mercury. Their working theory was that more recently generated material would allow for a greater range of observations. The first attempt ended in failure. The density of ring material in the area they sampled had been too high, causing minor damage to the sampler.

Their second attempt at collecting fresher ring material was successful. The sample had looked like the previous batch, with no new cell types in the mix. In the way of many discoveries, a serendipitous error had combined with a modicum of insight to generate a monumental find. Molly prepared a slide but failed to remove all of the older sample when introducing the new material. Within the mix of old and new cells, the previously unnoticed fifth particle type jumped out, literally, to take its place in the matrix.

Compared to the other cells, this nanomachine was like a tiny flea on a dog. The fifth cell attached to the interior of the other cells in the manner of a parasite.

Molly and Anastacia decreased the electrostatic field containing the ring material and observed the reaction. The nanomachines began to vibrate at a higher frequency.

"The field's still too strong for them to migrate," Molly said, the vibrations of her voice jostling the stereographic image slightly.

"You're right. Fifty percent after all, hotshot."

"Agreed. Lowering."

They lost themselves in their work, nearly forgetting the danger of working closely with ring material. After four hours, one of the tiny newly discovered cells merged with a tripod cell. Neither spoke for a moment after the two cells conjoined.

"Whose turn is it to name the cell?" Anastacia asked after a while.

"Haven't we always shared? Messenger seems obvious," Molly said.

"Are we sure of its job?"

"Aki predicted a cell that communicated. It's definitely our missing piece," Molly said. "My best assessment, barring a full assay, is that once isolated, the messenger cells would be harmless. Their job is transmitting information and replicating through the system to spread the 'message.' How daring are you feeling? You ready to take the leap and turn off the electrostat field?"

Anastacia's eyes met Molly's. Both women smiled mischievously. "Took the words right from my mouth, boss. Working without the field will speed up our testing. We just need a way to filter out the messengers."

Over several hours they modified the optical processing machinery aboard the RMRF to create a makeshift filter that could isolate the messenger cells. Their initial tests showed the filter functioned perfectly. They isolated several hundred messenger cells and began observing them without using the destructive electrostatic field in the scanning tunneling microscope. They peeled back the outer atomic layer to analyze the interior. After finalizing their data they prepared to send their findings back to Earth where Aki waited anxiously for their results.

ACT IV: AUGUST 14, 2024

WITH A CLICK, Aki projected an image to the overhead screen. The presentation on her most recent findings had been meticulously prepared for this press conference.

"The nanotechnology used in the ring material is beyond our wildest imaginings," she explained. "The tiny particles have more in common with biological cells than they do with machines. With a small variety of these cells, the nanomachines combine to create an incredibly diverse, near-infinite number of structures.

"Many of us wondered how a biological organism, even an anaerobe, could function in the vacuum of space. On a microscopic scale, biology cannot live or function without water. Cells are surrounded by membranes. Membranes divide, then fill with liquid to multiply. Cells are not cut off from the outside world. Cells use ingenious and complicated mechanisms to transfer material and information to each other. This is how biological processes occur.

"Space suits are designed to get around easily in space's weightlessness—it is how we, as biological organisms, have adapted to the environment of space. On Earth, astronauts train underwater to better mimic the qualities of low- and zero-G environments. The same holds true for ring material. It is similar to how crystal minerals deposit vapor—the crystal extends an arm that swims about, moving freely, eventually settling down and linking."

Aki showed several enlarged pictures of ring material.

"The tripod cells link with these newly discovered messenger cells. The tripod absorbs the messenger, then the three protrusions separate from the tripod and locomote away. The protrusions reconnect with other tripod centers to carry on the message from the original cell. This chain reaction transmits information carried by the messenger cell. The ring material undergoes constant dynamic restructuring. For this reason, we knew there had to be a cell, or some other mechanism, that was transmitting information. The tripods are one of the more numerous types, but we did not understand the mechanism that allowed them to operate. The discovery of the messenger cell supports the model we hypothesized because we had predicted this cell."

After finishing, Aki opened the floor to questions. The first question was the one she had prepared for most.

"What impact will this discovery of the messenger have on future UNSDF missions, and on a greater scale, the future of humanity?" asked a reporter.

"By utilizing the functionality of the messenger cell," Aki responded, "we will be able to manipulate the Ring at will. The UNSDF spends billions, if not trillions, to use its fleet to dismantle the Ring as it rebuilds itself. Decoding the information stored in the messenger cells and overwriting that code would instruct the Ring to adopt a new structure. In other words, instead of undoing the damage every time it is built, we could prevent it from ever harming us again. Changing the instructions is the more proactive approach."

"You're suggesting that we insert a virus that causes the Ring to destroy itself?" the next reporter in line asked.

"The destruction of the Ring is not necessary," Aki said. "My personal thoughts on this latest discovery are relevant to this. Many of us lost family members, everything we owned or cared about due to the radical climate change brought on by the Ring's shadowing of the planet. Much of the earth and its species, which we have fought extremely hard to protect, have been destroyed. I have no idea if we can ever recover from such cataclysmic losses. I understand the antipathy that many of you feel toward the Builders. Those same feelings—the desperation, the rancor, and yes, the hate—brought me to the surface of the Ring itself. Uniquely among humanity, I took physical action against the Builders. However, now I have come to believe that it is not their intention to invade.

"I knew this from the moment I set foot on the Island and saw the defense system. It clearly had been designed to protect the Ring against damage from stray asteroids and comets. The Builders did not anticipate intelligent life that could possibly reach the Ring or sabotage it. Our encounter with the Builders is ultimately an unfortunate unintended consequence of their mode of interstellar travel. They meant no intentional harm. We have to ask ourselves whether we want to let our first encounter with an extraterrestrial intelligence be characterized by anger and hatred. Do we have the right, without knowing anything about their civilization or culture, to banish them to the dark reaches of interstellar space?"

A few voices in the press corps murmured; to Aki the voices sounded positive. Hands shot up and then the shouting began. Aki waved her arms, signaling that she had more to say. "Please, please. I am not saying that we should surrender or leave the Ring intact as it is. Modifying messenger cells gives us the potential to control the Ring's growth and orientation. As intelligent beings, as a species that has dreamed of contact with another intelligence, we have an obligation to rebuild the Ring, promptly, and allow the Builders to stop their fleet in our solar system. I suggest that we call the second Ring the 'Vert-Ring.'

"If we alter the messenger cells so that the Vert-Ring regenerates perpendicular to its previous orientation, the detrimental shadow-ing effect on Earth will become negligible. A number of scientists agree that it would even help alleviate the greenhouse effect. If an unexpected threat to our safety emerges, we have the means to dismantle the new Ring at any time. There is no proof that it is too late to rebuild the Ring in time for their arrival. The most powerful telescope we have launched into orbit has yet to make visual contact with their fleet.

"The automated production facilities they built on Mercury are still in operation. As long as the production facilities continue to run, we will have several chances to perfect our influence over the messenger cells. Most importantly, the act of rebuilding the Vert-Ring would send a clear and unequivocal message that our intentions are not malicious. I believe that a civilization that mastered nanotechnology, nuclear fusion, and perhaps even antimatter could not accomplish such achievements without first overcoming the plague of intraspecies war. Let us not be consumed by suspicion. Let us set aside our fears and imagine the day when we will meet the Builders face to face. Let us see them as the benevolent and intellectually advanced beings that they must certainly be."

More than a few journalists applauded.

———◆•◆•◆———

TWENTY MINUTES LATER, a secret meeting was held on a highly secure part of the Worldunity Network. The participants were all representatives of different forces—governmental, economic, scientific—but they did not know one another. Their voices were disguised. There was no visual component to the teleconference. They did not use, nor even know, one another's names. Two men spoke, as was the tradition at these meetings, while the others simply listened, and these two men knew just what to say without prompting, briefing, or talking points in hand.

"Damn that Shiraishi. I think we underestimated her. Grossly," said the first voice, a rich baritone.

"No chance of getting rid of her?" responded the second voice, which sounded tired, as if nursing a head cold.

"Not now. Too many questions, too many supporters."

"That speech will turn the tables. Instant polling shows that 52 percent of North America is in favor of rebuilding the Ring 'sideways,' as the survey phrased it. And now only 46 percent support an assertive security posture."

"That's not much of a lead. Once the dust settles, we'll regain ground." The first voice laughed loudly, though it didn't fit with the conversation. Something else must have happened in his location at that moment.

"Still, 74 percent are in favor of her messenger cell experiment. Success clinches their plan's momentum."

"It won't be that easy. Decoding the human DNA sequence was touted as being promising, but look at how long it took to actually happen. They will spend years groping in the dark trying to figure out how to manipulate those messenger cells."

"They have the top nanotech people."

"Her speech was nothing more than a far-fetched personal pipe dream. What we need is to convince the public of the need for a preemptive strike against the Builders."

"Is that even possible?" the second voice asked. "Given their technology, what could we bring to bear against them? If the answer is 'nothing effective,' then her plan may be the only logical alternative. Trying to rendezvous with an object moving at eighteen thousand kilometers per second is out of the question. Even attacking something moving that fast would be no easy task. The average speed of meteoroids is twenty kilometers per second when the meteoroids hit the atmosphere. The Builders are moving at nearly a thousand times that speed. The aggregate energy released from an Earth impact would be exponential, something like a million times as great. The meteor that wiped out the dinosaurs is estimated to have been ten kilometers across. With the speed the Builders are traveling, they could achieve the same effect with something one hundred meters across."

"With twenty thousand tons of matter, they could take us out by sacrificing a couple of ships in their fleet."

"If they are planning to smash into us, their trajectory is clear. There's only one straight line that connects Orion to Earth. We know exactly where they're coming from. If we place an object in the way for them to collide with, we could forestall impact."

"How? Gravitational force exists; you can't just place an object in space and expect it to remain stationary, waiting for them to show up."

"The best we can do is to locate their actual position and flight path."

"There won't be time. Here, have a look at this," began the first voice. Keys began clacking. The first voice continued, "We will have little time to act if their intentions are adversarial. We have a massive amount of matter headed toward us from Orion. The difficult question is whether it's going to pass by harmlessly or whether it's aimed to collide. Unfortunately, their trajectory is close enough to the plane on which Earth orbits. With the earth, the sun and this massive object aligned, it's impossible to tell whether they're targeting the sun or us."

"There are other unknowns. We don't know the size or reflectance ratio of the approaching object or objects. If this hypothetical Builder cannonball absorbs light instead of reflecting it, observations in the visible-light spectrum will be difficult no matter how close they get. Infrared is a possibility—everything has a heat signature after all—but I hardly need to explain the economic difficulties of such detection. Nearly every observatory and satellite still in operation is oriented toward the Ring. Using the most powerful radar would only allow us to spot this potential catastrophe once the ship is in the inner solar system," said the nasal voice.

"Assuming the problem of detection requires new technology, what are our options for target destruction?"

"It depends on our ability to detect it. The most optimistic scenario allows detection at eighty astronomical units, roughly eight days before it reaches Earth. Cruise missiles in low orbit can travel at ten kilometers per second. If cruise missiles are launched, contact would be achieved at five minutes and thirty seconds before impact with Earth. If they miss, there's no time for second chances. Even if they destroy the target successfully, fragments from the explosion would impact the earth, unless we could move them 6,400 kilometers out of the way, essentially half the diameter of the earth, in five and a half minutes. In other words, we would have to accelerate every last fragment to a speed of twenty kilometers per second along a path perpendicular to their original trajectory toward Earth. I don't think I am being a pessimist to say that it is impossible. To put the scale of such a task into perspective, the electromagnetic railgun developed by the U.S. military accelerates a bullet-sized object that quickly, but the railgun requires a launching device the size of a building."

Despite the bar on oral participation, some grumbling from third parties could be heard over the network.

"We need not only detect the object at a long range but also begin deflecting it at this distance as well. A missile attack would by no means be fast enough. The best weapon of defense would be some kind of high-strength beam, though human technology isn't capable of creating such a device."

"You're saying that our only choice is to sit tight and hope for the best?"

After a long silence, one of the members, most likely a third voice, interjected. "Going along with Shiraishi's proposal might be the wisest route." There was a long moment of silence, due to both the breach of etiquette and the audacity of the suggestion.

"You're suggesting we give in to her?" the first voice said finally.

"Not quite. How does a judo master bring down an opponent twice his size? He uses his opponent's strength against him. That's what we need to do. Shiraishi is calling for this Vert-Ring to be rebuilt. We give her what she wants, then use it to get what we want, and she doesn't even have to know."

"I'm afraid I'm not following."

"You're saying we need a beam strong enough to deflect them? If we rebuild the Ring and take control of the Island, we'll have just that."

ACT V: JULY 12, 2026

THE UNSS *CHADWICK* decoupled from the base station, setting its course for a Mercury approach. Commander Kindersley's biggest concern was to keep the forty billion dollar ship from being contaminated by the ring material. While scanning the local area with the laser radar system, the commander placed the ship into a five million–kilometer orbit around Mercury. The ship's gigantic solar shields were pointed toward the sun, allowing only the sensor mast to absorb sunlight due to the intensity of the solar radiation.

The unmanned cargo rocket that carried the two-kilogram probe had already been launched. It was about to cross the path of ring material emanating from Mercury. From her cocoon, Molly kept a close eye on the video being sent back by the cargo rocket. A silver stream of material flowed diagonally across the screen. Although she could not make out individual particles, Molly could see slight gradations of color indicating how quickly the stream flowed. The mass drivers ejected the ring material from the surface of Mercury at a rate of eighty thousand tons per second. Molly was somewhat surprised to see the color of the ring material become lighter as the rocket approached the stream. The material disappeared into the blackness of space once the rocket was inside the flowing sea of ring material.

"It's like being in fog. You don't notice when it's right in front of you and you're in the thick of it."

"What was that, Molly?" Anastacia asked.

"Nothing. Just mumbling to myself."

The probe's speed relative to the stream was fifty meters per second. The probe detected three thousand collisions per second.

"Let's go another two hundred kilometers toward the center."

"Even if it doesn't hold up to the stress for that long?" Anastacia asked.

"That's right."

"I've set the course to the waypoint."

The onscreen image began to deteriorate, and the screen that monitored the rocket's sensors flooded with warnings. The ring material was consuming the rocket.

"Prepare for separation."

The screen flickered, finally stopping on a still image with the words "Transmission Error" flashing in red.

"Telemetry readings are still generating. We've reached the waypoint. Separation complete. Probe engine firing. Separation signal confirmed."

"The UNSS *Chadwick* has successfully completed deployment of the probe," Commander Kindersley announced to Central Command. "Proceeding with the observation phase."

Moving along the orbit, the probe entered the flow of material being ejected behind Mercury. The flow of material continued for another five million kilometers before disappearing behind the sun. The probe would record data as it followed the material around the sun back to its starting point.

The visible-light and infrared cameras were linked to the wide-angle telescope and set to auto-track mode. All observational systems were functioning normally. The commander breathed a sigh of relief. "Good job, crew. All we can do is sit back and watch. Feel free to relax. You might want to avoid newsfeeds from Earth. I'm guessing we'll be center stage for a few days. I don't want your heads to swell."

"Too bad some people aren't on our side. And I don't mean that one presenter who always shows that picture of me with the bad haircut," Anastacia said.

"Even Aki Shiraishi's reputation met its limits when she tried convincing people that this was our safest bet," said Commander Kindersley.

"I'm not sure she has as many allies as she'll need if her plan fails," Molly said.

The mission had been an uphill battle. Molly and Anastacia had managed to decode less than 1 percent of the ring material's mechagenetic puzzle. Nonetheless, the information Molly and Anastacia deciphered contained instructions for both the Ring's size and orientation. The code for the formation of the Island, however, remained beyond the grasp of the decoding. Even with experts in nanotech working on the project, an understanding of the complex processes responsible for the creation of the Island would take another decade—tinkering with the existing code would not be enough to reconfigure the structure of the Island.

After a learning curve that had been driven by an arduous process of trial and error, reprogramming samples of basic ring material had been successful under lab conditions. The key was in the upper command set of the ring material. If the probe functioned as hoped, it would overwrite the upper command set. When the probe came into contact with ring material, those instructions would spread like a virus to the rest of the orbiting material.

The nanobots ejected from Mercury used microscopic solar sails to migrate into their stable orbit around the sun. If the modifications worked as planned, their vectors would be altered so that the Vert-Ring would eventually be perpendicular to their original orbit, stopping when the new Vert-Ring reached a radius of forty million kilometers. The researchers were fairly certain that all they needed to do was overwrite the orientation information in the Ring's particles. They did not know whether the Island would still form when the Vert-Ring reached a height of three hundred thousand kilometers and if it did, whether the deceleration lasers would still be pointed in the right direction. Whether the encoded programming would have the inherent flexibility needed to maintain its structural and functional integrity when it followed new commands was an open question.

Once the ring material left the gravitational pull of Mercury, it was even capable of leaving the solar system if such a voyage proved necessary. Ring material flowing in unexpected directions was one of the greatest fears of the project's researchers. The most pessimistic commentators contended that crude alterations to the Ring's programming could potentially send particles streaming toward Earth.

Molly felt confident that the solar-powered material would stay close to the sun, not wanting to stray too far from its source of energy. Once the ring material moved into its pre-programmed position, it would await its signal to trigger the deceleration lasers. Molly also believed that even if the program became corrupted, the ring material would not deviate far from a forty million–kilometer distance from the sun.

Eight hours after the probe entered the stream, a portion of ring material deviated from its previous path. The ring material moved vertically, away from the original Ring's orbital plane. Within thirty hours, two symmetrical arms began arcing upward on opposite sides of the Vert-Ring. Molly extrapolated from the snapshot data and created a profile of Vert-Ring generation.

"We're there. It's transitioning into a perfect spiral orbit. The material knows where it needs to go and is figuring out the path on its own. My calculations say that in exactly four rotations around the sun the nanobots will have reoriented the Ring as programmed. Send a message to Aki Shiraishi. Tell her that her dream of a Vert-Ring is coming true."

ACT VI: OCTOBER 20, 2028

AFTER THE FIRST successful mission, another probe was sent to Mercury in April of 2027. The defense mechanism did not react to the gaseous spray of altered Vert-Ring ejecta introduced into Mercury's fledgling atmosphere, allowing the instructions to eventually take root on the surface. Within two short weeks, the code embedded within the Vert-Ring's particles was rewritten at the source—the mass drivers themselves. The exact mechanism that allowed the new code to infect the Builders' automated production facilities was poorly understood. Not unlike how burning moxa to warm regions and acupuncture points of the body stimulates circulation and finds a way to smooth the flow of blood and qi throughout the body, the mechanism of the code was elusive but effective. A blog compared the success, especially with the incomplete analysis of the mechagenetics, to being as statistically unlikely as the pieces of a jigsaw puzzle being thrown into the air and randomly assembling themselves into the proper picture as the pieces landed.

The triumph of the mission meant that the UNSDF ships were no longer required to face the dangers of dismantling the Ring every few years. As Aki had planned, the Vert-Ring was reconfiguring in a way that would not cause substantial harm to Earth. All humanity waited for the new ring to grow to a height of 300,000 kilometers, following the growth cycle on a kilometer-by-kilometer basis in the mass media. If the Island formed at that point, as it had before, and if the deceleration lasers functioned consistently, the braking system would be able to usher in the Builders' ships. The deceleration lasers, provided the lasers formed as they had before, would be complete by 2043.

Research to expedite this process was underway, but there had not been any breakthroughs yet. The braking system would not be ready for at least another fourteen years. Given the range of the estimated arrival window, Aki would be in her sixties when that day finally arrived. She knew she would have lived a long life by then. If the Builders arrived before these rushed preparations, Aki could not help but predict tragedy and disappointment. She did not want that dark cloud of despair to hang over her for much longer. She had waited so long to make contact. She needed to communicate with the Builders in person. After her substantial efforts to atone, the pain of watching the Builders speed by with no means of slowing would be too much to bear.

Why are you sending a fleet here? Are you fleeing your home, or are you being pulled to our solar system for reasons of your own? I wonder what you want to know; what you are like. Whatever is bringing you here, I beg the stars that you do not come too soon. We need time to prepare for your arrival. I need to meet you.

"LEAVING THE PERSONNEL selection for the Mercury Base Station up to UNSDF Headquarters? You have got to be kidding!" Aki blurted at the Science Subcommittee. Even though they were not integrated with the UNSDF, the personnel selections for ringology research had always been made by the Science Subcommittee.

"The initial stage of the project has ended. Now that we've started to unlock the Ring's nanotechnology, the UNSDF is seeing its enormous potential. Let's admit that some of these research applications are beyond our scope. It makes sense to select researchers that fit their needs," Carol Horning, a long-time member of the subcommittee, had said.

"But—" Aki stopped herself, unsure whether she was arguing due to feeling territorial or because of a legitimate objection that she could not yet articulate.

"Our race against the clock to rebuild the Vert-Ring is over, Aki," another member said. "I know it's hard and it hurts, but you should face the reality of the situation. They gave the decision-making authority to us at first because we were a small group. We could come to a consensus quickly and take action. Our having the responsibility was nothing more than an emergency measure. You didn't think they were going to give us free rein forever, did you?"

"I supposed that they would do what was right." Fuming, Aki had always known that the UNSDF might decide to assert control over her research. She could not help but think of how hard Molly and Anastacia had worked at the RMRF. Aki knew that her colleagues had already accepted defeat on the matter and that she had no choice but to give in. This was a battle she could not win. "Rum-ruff" had grown into a large-scale space facility and been renamed the Mercury Base Station. At any given time, there might be as many as forty researchers stationed aboard. Combined with the rest of the rotating crew and support personnel on Earth, there were now over one thousand people involved with the project. Its scale was far greater than what the members of the Science Sub-committee were capable of overseeing. Finally accepting the facts, Aki felt a weight lift from her shoulders. Now she could focus on more practical pursuits.

"IF THE BUILDERS are hostile, there is no way that humanity could prevail in a war with them. If the Builders are not hostile and we attack, we would most likely drag Earth into a battle we cannot win—therefore a preemptive strategy is just an exercise in futility," Aki said to the audience. "In looking at the possibilities, it behooves us to greet their arrival peacefully. No matter what their intentions, this would ensure the best outcome in any scenario." Cornell University's Ridley Hall was packed. She opened the floor to questions. One male student raised his hand immediately.

"Don't you think your logic is pessimistic and defeatist? You claim to promote friendship. I don't think that adopting forced amicability simply because we can't defeat the Builders is a genuine olive branch."

"The point I made is that there is still hope even if we cannot defeat them," Aki responded.

"And what if we could defeat them? If we had the military power required to drive them off, would you advocate the 'Let's be friends' approach?" The boy was clearly mocking her in the way he accentuated *let's be friends*.

"Of course I would."

"If we see this as being analogous to game theory and the prisoner's dilemma, taking the pacifist route is the fool's choice. If we do nothing and the Builders don't attack, everybody's happy.

However, if the Builders attack we're toast, right? If we attack no matter what, at least we're refusing to succumb to annihilation," the student said. The audience began to murmur excitedly.

"Your situation assumes a one-time encounter with the Builders. If we posit subsequent encounters, or an iterated prisoner's dilemma, fleeing will only result in being run over, and I think that fighting them elicits consequences that you are failing to admit. A sufficient amount of cooperation, however, provides the potential of long-term survival with an accumulation of rewards, since it is not a zero-sum game." Aki regretted the touch of superiority in her voice. She felt it was beneath her to fear being outsmarted by a college student.

"We *should* look at it as a one-time occurrence. One wrong choice and humanity is extirpated."

"There are too few premises to build to logistic certainty or even close. If humanity were on an even playing field with the Builders, we would be able to migrate to another solar system. If this situation were fair, one Builder attack would not lead to extinction."

The student said something about her not seeing his point. Whispers traveled through the lecture hall. Several years prior, Aki would have earned a standing ovation for a speech like this. A young woman raised her hand.

"Yes, please go ahead," Aki said.

"I'm worried, to be honest. Next year, 2030, is the beginning of the arrival window. If the Builders arrive and see that their decelerator was tampered with, I'm afraid they'll retaliate by launching an attack. How can I do anything but live in fear until the new Vert-Ring is completed?" Concern was evident in the quiver of the young woman's voice.

"In life, we always have options. Why not turn that fear into a passion that you channel into researching xenocommunication methods?"

"I'd like to second those apprehensions," said a male student seated next to the young woman. "We're afraid, whether it's easy to admit or not. But we need to try to be useful. If too many people are convinced that the end is nigh, or are doomsaying and spreading the meme of pessimism, the economy will collapse again. By preparing to fight, we can focus on survival instead of focusing on the possibility of being wiped out."

"It is true that we need to prepare for all contingencies and remain positive, but fighting is not the only way to turn our outlook around," Aki said. "We are the technologically inferior civilization. We have to adapt socially, since we simply do not have the time or resources to match the Builders in the time left before contact."

"I was thirteen when you destroyed that first Ring. People danced in the streets for days. Photos of you and the *Phalanx* crewmembers were as ubiquitous as the American flag. You, Aki Shiraishi, taught me that humans can do anything they set their minds to, anything they believe in. You seem like a different person now. Why aren't you encouraging us to be brave?"

Aki wondered if she had changed that much in seven years. Perseverance had been the watchword that got her through the immense uncertainties of life and all the risks she took. "Until that day I set foot on the Island," she said, "I had no idea how to envision what the Builders were and what they stood for. My belief that intelligent life was involved in the creation of the Ring was nothing more than a good guess until I stood there. Even before then, there had been a theory that the Ring was a biological entity made of tiny nanomachines. Once we realized the purpose of the Island, we understood that a massive fleet of ships was coming. Our attention shifted from the center of the solar system to beyond the Oort Cloud as we looked for signs of the Builders. Nonetheless, we clung to our mission. I struggled, and I made an incredibly hard decision, knowing that the entire world was counting on me. I chose to destroy the Ring. I have never felt like I deserved to be called a heroine for making that choice. Not even once."

Another voice in the crowd asked, "How do you feel about the death of Mark Ridley?"

"Mark…" *If Mark had known the purpose of the Island, would he have acted differently?* She shook her head. *Discarding the contaminated engine by remote control, we still could have continued our mission. He chose to do it by hand to give us better odds at reaching the Island. Our chances of success were slim. He bet his life that he would make the difference. "There's no such thing as a battle where you think purely with your head," he said once. He would have done whatever it took to save humanity.* The young student even looked somewhat like Mark, Aki realized. *If Mark were looking at me now, what would he say?* Aki mustered a response. "Mark was brave. A true hero. I am honored to be speaking here at Cornell in this hall that bears his name. That is all I can say."

After the lecture, Aki reported to the reception that had been prepared for her. The wealthy patrons of Cornell who had sponsored her speech were waiting to shake her hand.

"Thank you. You were wonderful," said one of the benefactors.

"Pretty rough crowd," Aki responded. She did not know what else to say.

"They're students. More idealism and passion than ideas, with just enough knowledge to create a justification for their hasty conclusions. If the contact dilemma was easy to solve, there would be no point in debating."

"That is certainly true."

———◆◆◆———

DURING THE PLANE ride home, Aki considered her own positions. Aki promoted the amicable approach because she desired direct contact—in a way, all of her arguments were post hoc justifications for the pure need to see the Builders, to meet beings from another world. She could not deny some defeatism underlying her philosophy. She had always tried to stay on an even keel by tempering her enthusiasms and passions with an awareness of worst-case scenarios. If Earth technology was roughly equal to the Builders' and she were in charge, Aki would probably place a number of interceptor ships on the front line just to be safe. She wondered if it was naïve to believe that an advanced species would never cross the expansive divide between the stars merely to invade and conquer. On the other hand, whenever technologically advanced humans encountered less "advanced" societies, invasion and conquest was precisely what happened. But humans also communicated; the Builders remained unnervingly silent.

Mark would have placed the survival of humanity before anything else. If humanity tries to intercept the Builders, how could we even go about it? Anyone who says we should fight has not planned the logistics or considered the outcomes. If we knew they were going to attack, then maybe an all-out defensive assault would be just enough to send the message that the costs of conquest might outweigh the benefits.

This is different. I do not expect an attack or even an attempt to communicate. The Builders have ignored every message we've sent. Military solutions are often aimed at eliminating threats, but then military solutions end up eliminating people. A colossal ship, or most likely a fleet, hurtling through space is a threat. I just cannot see any defensive plan that would thwart an aggressive attack by such advanced intelligence. If that intelligence were serious about attacking, I think I would know...

In the seven years since the Ring had been destroyed, food production had partially recovered. Rationing was less common now and prices had fallen; the usual staples were more readily available on store shelves. Yet humanity had cause for concern instead of cause for rejoicing. Doomsday prophecies were gaining currency. Extremist cults and survivalists were recruiting members and building underground shelters to protect from invasion. Aki was unsure whether she should laugh at such measures or pity those comforted by bunkers, prayers, and canned goods. She tried to ignore the lunatic fringes of this most recent panic, but unfounded theories informed many of the resources she used for her research. Since so little could be proven with facts, speculation was used to spackle over the gaps.

Seven years earlier, starvation had been thwarted thanks to mutual aid and international cooperation. Destroying the Ring had shown *Homo sapiens* how questions of survival were ultimately only answerable on the species-wide level. Now, as 2030 approached, humanity was succumbing to the fear of extinction again. Motives were becoming murky. Dozing while watching a broadcast on the Worldunity Network, Aki was jolted awake when she heard the anchor announce that an anomaly had been discovered on the Vert-Ring. An amateur astronomer had captured the surprising appearance of a small, dark spot. The new Vert-Ring had only reached 30,000 kilometers and the shadowy feature was a mere 50 kilometers across, but it was unmistakably the beginning of a graser cannon.

The UNSDF made an official statement within an hour and released more detailed photographs to the public. Aki recognized the graser's base and its accents of complex curved lines. The stump of the lens barrel protruded from the base like a searchlight. Strands extended up, growing in all directions, reaching like capillaries. Aki rubbed her temples, a headache starting as she remembered her experience on the Island.

A young man from the Mercury Base eventually appeared on the network screen. His innocent demeanor struck Aki as genuine, but his relentless enthusiasm seemed both forced and an artifact of inexperience.

"We confess that the culmination of this investigation moved too slowly. We were about to release the photograph ourselves. This is not Builder-coded construction; it is our own work. We have spearheaded the formation of a new Island. The graser cannons that surround the Island are more complicated to create than the Island itself. We have been trying to separate these cannons to be able to incite the formation of deceleration lasers. Breakthroughs in the decoding of the mechagenetic Ring particle makeup allow us to grow isolated components. As a test, we attempted to initiate the creation of this single graser cannon.

"To be frank, we didn't expect such success. We're investigating how to harness the graser for defensive purposes. The firing range of the graser cannon is 2.8 million kilometers. As a defensive weapon, we would need to mount the cannon to a massive transport ship and move that weapon to a more strategic location. We have not developed the technology necessary to remove it intact and operational as the graser is powered by the Ring itself. We have learned that the tanker, one of the fundamental Ring particles, contains the energy we would need to operate the graser. We have developed the technology to handle small amounts of ring material. We feel that we will be able to develop the technology needed for this endeavor within the next six years. Harnessing the power of the graser will allow us to target high-speed objects and destroy them. Our plan has certain issues of complexity, but given the current state of our defense capabilities and few other alternatives, we are going to do everything in our power to see it through to fruition in the name of human and Earth survival."

The next segment discussed an instant survey that showed 87 percent of three hundred thousand respondents in favor of developing grasers to defend humanity. Aki yawned and fell asleep on her couch, exhausted from worry and stress.

RAUL ASKED TO meet at the same café. The menu had a broader selection now than it did when Aki had been there five years earlier.

"I still live on the combo platter." His tray overflowed with french fries, chicken strips, and some deformed dumplings.

"Someday you will understand how 'garbage in equals garbage out' applies to both coding and the human body." Despite such a horrendous diet and a bit of acne, Aki could not help but notice that Raul was more muscular than when she had first met him. His green eyes looked clearer, and Aki had a sense that he still knew her better than most people did, partially because he was one of the few people she could be honest around.

"Aren't you going to take off your shades?" he asked.

"No. I'm incognito. I use a bodyguard now."

"Your life's like an old spy movie," he said, craning his neck in an attempt to spot her bodyguard.

As vain as it sounded, Aki also knew that on some level she preferred to keep her sunglasses on because they hid a wrinkle or two. "How are things at the ETICC?"

"Paradisiacal. Hundreds of times more computing power."

A year and a half ago, Raul had been offered a research position at the ETICC. Connecting with Aki had been a turning point in his life. Accepting Natalia as a failed effort and moving forward instead of hanging on when Natalia never quite worked seemed to allow him to move on to other pursuits. With Aki's encouragement, he had earned his multidisciplinary doctorate in linguistics and cognitive psychology. Since working at the ETICC, his name had appeared in prestigious papers, and Dr. Raul Sanchez had presented his research on extraterrestrial civilizations at several conferences.

"Are you still doing research on AI?"

"Not officially, but it's on my mind all the time," he said. Aki wondered if she heard regret in his voice. "I haven't made much progress. I'm too busy trying to create a universally comprehended artificial language."

As the conversation became more complex, Aki asked Raul to slow down and stop mumbling. She hoped that Raul did not feel like he was talking to his mother. After dinner, they walked along the tree-lined streets of the campus. He seemed anxious, anticipating that Aki had some favor to ask. Maybe that was all in her head, but she did indeed have a request. As they passed Bancroft Library, Aki decided to broach the subject.

"I watched a recording of one of your speeches."

"Not my favorite thing," Raul said. "Especially the speaking in front of people part."

"I need you to write one for me to deliver."

"What kind of speech?"

"One in your universal language."

"Damn, lady. Someday I hope you'll give me an *easy* request!" Raul tilted his head back and laughed. "I was afraid something like this would come up. What kind of speech do you have in mind? I assume we've gotten over the whole 'Hi, we know some prime numbers and pi' monologue?"

"Funny. Something more along the lines of 'There are intelligent beings living in this solar system.'"

"That's a no-brainer. Is that all, my noble savior of the aforementioned solar system?"

"We live only on the planet Earth, the third from the sun." Aki appreciated his humor, but her need for his help was more pressing than her need for flattery from an old friend.

"You'll save the fine print for later?"

"We will take the necessary steps to avoid situations that could be perceived as a threat."

"Now you're giving me the chance to show off. Care to end with a zinger?"

"We cannot take the risk of allowing a Trojan horse into our solar system," Aki said.

"Ouch, now you're putting me to the test. You're already speaking in culturally specific metaphors."

"You have to be able to handle this, Raul."

"If you can tell me what it means first."

"Humanity places doubt before hope," she said, rephrasing her last message.

"Come again?"

"We fear an intelligence greater than our own," Aki blurted, clearly upset.

"So you're trying to say—"

"Damn it. Tell them to stay the hell away from people if they know what's good for them!" she shouted, much more loudly than she had meant to. Several college kids playing Frisbee turned and looked at her, then went back to their game.

Raul placed his hand on Aki's shoulder. "Take it easy. We'll make this work." He swiveled her shoulders, turning her toward him, then placed both palms on her cheeks. "Just promise me you won't give up. A lot of people are counting on you to communicate with the Builders. Me for one, and several others at the ETICC at least." He smiled and said, "We get criticism but plenty of letters of support. We're missing some key piece of this puzzle. Have you considered that the Builders might be anosognosic?"

Aki's facial expression made it clear that she did not know the word. Raul launched into a detailed explanation. "It's where somebody suffers trauma to the brain. As a result, they lose left brain functionality. In some cases, they suffer from paralysis of the left arm, for example, and aren't even aware of the paralysis. If a doctor asks if their left arm is okay, they answer that it's fine. It's a completely normal left arm. If they're asked to raise their left arm, they think they're raising it but nothing happens. If the doctor moves the patient's left hand into view and asks whose hand it is, they respond that it's the doctor's hand.

"When the doctor shows both their two hands and the paralyzed patient's arm and asks again, the patient claims that the doctor has three hands, and they'll often launch into some cockamamy reasoning for the 'extra' hand that shows cognitive dissonance. They're not crazy—in the sense that it's a short circuit in their brain and they don't think they're lying or confused. They don't find their reasoning strange because their perception is skewed. All that's wrong is that their left and right hemispheres are no longer wired together. They are alienated from logical thought to the point where the illogical makes total sense. We have no idea how Builders think. Something that might be completely obvious to us could be a total mystery to them."

Raul took his hands off Aki's face.

"The world's taking sides. There are doubters who think we should blow the Builders out of the sky before they get close enough to do us harm, and welcomers who see their arrival as a significant step toward a new era for humanity. But who's right and who's wrong? Maybe neither. Maybe the Builders are a mirror, reflecting back our hopes and fears of what they might be, of what we *are*—invaders, purveyors of peace, even gods from the heavens. This keeps us from seeing who the Builders really are because we force personas onto them. Maybe we'll see what they really are and be unable to comprehend. Your job's easy. All you need to find is the truth. We don't need to love them or hate them. We need to find truth. Of all the people on Earth, Aki, my bets are on you to make that happen. I'm not the only one who feels that way."

ACT IX: NOVEMBER 4, 2035

FIVE YEARS HAD gone by since the first day of the Builders' arrival window. Scientists toiled, trying to improve observation systems. A new space telescope had been assembled in low orbit and was being transported to the third Lagrange point—exactly opposite the sun from the earth—where the gravitational equilibrium of the two bodies would hold it in place indefinitely. This way, if the sun happened to be blocking the view of HD 37605 from Earth when the Builders entered visual-contact range, the arrival would not be missed. Opposite the sun from the earth was also advantageous in using parallax to determine the Builders' distance, once the Builders finally came into view.

After two months of testing, the twenty-meter composite main mirror was pointed at Orion and locked into focus. The lenses of the telescope revolved, each observing the target focal point at a different frequency of light and beaming their images back to Earth. Seated at the center of each image was HD 37605, which was universally considered to be the star from which the Builders had come. The recently enhanced Deep Space Network and the Terra Luna Network took turns relaying the new scope's signal. The images were sent directly to the Space Telescope Operations Center at the ETICC where the images were double-checked by human eyes.

Theodore Pike had spent twelve years of his life scanning images for signs of the Builders. As the monotony got the better of him, he often did his job with his eyes half open. This day, however, Ted Pike's boredom vanished in a flash. A new picture from the telescope appeared on his monitor. It was obviously anomalous, even though he had not been looking carefully. Even as the head image analyst, he was not always on his toes. Ted gazed at the 3-D luminosity variation graph as the image became more fully rendered.

"Image quality's a bit off," he said to the other analyst on duty, who spun his chair around to look at Ted's screen.

"It's from one of the brand-new image sensors."

"Looks a little fuzzy, don't you think?"

"Yeah, Ted. Hazy, fuzzy dots sprinkled around HD 37605." Ted's coworker pointed at the monitor.

"What did the previous shot look like?"

Ted brought up two images taken immediately prior and compared all three. There was no continuity of the anomaly. In the past, they had noticed that white noise appeared against the background blackness in overexposed images. The two analysts assumed that this was the same kind of visual static. They did not pay any further attention to it.

Four days later, another pair of analysts found the same anomaly. This time, the second pair of analysts shifted the telescope away from its target to see if the fuzzy dots were still there. They were not. The second pair of analysts conducted further observations, blocking out HD 37605 to study its mysterious light more closely. The analysts still needed to perform a full spectral analysis, but there was no doubt that they were seeing an object that was moving through space and emitting its own light.

As further detailed observations were being made, the members of the ETICC Board of Directors were summoned for an emergency meeting. A backup telescope was brought online, creating a mini-array to gather more light from the object over longer periods of exposure. The result was instantaneous and shocking. Observations and equipment were double- and triple-checked to be certain.

They confirmed that the light emanated from a black body whose temperature peaked at one hundred million degrees. The black body was as hot as a star's core, like hydrogen undergoing the nucleosynthesis of nuclear fusion and becoming helium. Moreover, the light blinked at the rate of about 2,500 times per second. At first, the interval was considered random.

Further study showed eight separate groups of lights, each pulsing at a rate of 316 times per second. The light source was surrounded by a faint halo. The halo area was much cooler than the center. Spectral analysis indicated that the object contained nearly every fundamental element. Confirmation from several astronomy satellites indicated that gamma radiation was also being emitted from the same point. Theodore almost fell from his chair, lips trembling. He said, "Almighty. It can't be! They're not using laser sails to slow down. They're burning off their speed with nuclear pulse engines."

"Eight separate engines. When they discovered their laser sails weren't going to work, they went with a backup plan, implementing a fail-safe."

"It's unbelievable. What could they be using for fuel? Laser sails obviate the need to carry that much fuel in the first place. To decelerate from 6 percent of the speed of light to zero would mean almost all their mass is fuel. There's no way they're carrying that much. This isn't making sense."

"Nanotech, Theodore."

"Nanotech can't generate matter out of nothing. I can't catch my breath. You think they gathered fissionable matter when they passed through the Oort Cloud? Grabbing a comet might work, but at their speed such a maneuver would shatter their ships to bits." Ted Pike's job was to watch the screen, but he thought he had considered every possibility. This was flabbergasting.

"That's not it. They're using nanotech to convert the ship *itself* into nuclear fuel," the other analyst said.

"What? That's not..." Ted realized that it *was* possible, even though he had been about to say otherwise.

"Fifteen billion tons of mass, right? They take that mass, bit by bit, and hurl it into their nuclear reactors like fifteen billion logs on a nuclear fire."

"Unbelievable. Just unbelievable. Their hull, walls, and food. Everything," Ted said, his voice shaking as he leaned forward and put his head in his hands. He said, "They slow down, but not much is left. Charred on arrival." It came out muffled.

The Builders had already slowed to two thousand kilometers per second and were decelerating gradually. Calculations concluded that the Builders would need to burn all but one ten-thousandth of their mass. When they brought the craft to a stop, they would have 1.5 million tons of matter left on arrival, the mass of three oil tankers. That much effort to put on brakes showed how determined the Builders were to come to a stop in this particular solar system.

Humanity was terrified. No one knew why the Builders were coming, but coming they were. Six years, and they would be here.

ACT X: NOVEMBER 20, 2037

AKI'S PHYSICIAN MANDATED a full-body CT scan for her every single month. Aki felt that twice a year would be sufficient. Her extensive exposure to solar radiation still had not manifested any acute symptoms. Admittedly, delayed effects of the genetic damage that she had surely suffered could present themselves at any time. But twice annually seemed frequent enough to her, considering how long ago the high-energy ionization of her molecules had actually occurred.

"Don't grumble about it this time, Aki. We all have missions in life. Keeping you tumor-free is mine. Nobody wants to find out you had a lesion that could've been lopped off but it metastasized too quickly because we weren't paying enough attention to your body. Think of the fleet. Think of morale."

Aki knew he was half joking. He had treated her for many years.

"Fine, no more grumbles. But I have a favor to ask."

"That costs extra."

"How do I sneak out of this hospital so I can ditch my bodyguard?"

Without asking a single question, he smirked and drew her a map.

IT WAS AFTER sunset. The crowd created a warmth that over-
came the cold air. The ceremony at Pac Bell stadium was starting
soon. Aki had managed to lose herself in the swarm. She had turned
down multiple requests to attend this disturbing ceremony in
Washington D.C. Yet she had come after all, disguised in a scarf
and sunglasses, out of morbid curiosity. She had no good explanation for why she had come. It was going to be a veritable sky parade
of the military force that had been assembled to battle the Builders.

Aki had taken over the directorship of the ETICC. No progress
had been made in communicating with the Builders before her
tenure began. In her four years, nothing had changed other than
the public growing more opposed to throwing money into communications research.

Aki tried to instigate change at the ETICC and promote the
discovery of new options for talking to the Builders, but she knew
all too well that there was little hope left. Even her promotion
had actually been an attempt to strip away the influence she had
at the UNSDF. The only reason the UNSDF kept the ETICC
alive was to go through the motions. Their promise to welcome
the Builders with an attempt at peaceful dialogue had rung hollow for years.

Aki had not come to the ceremony in the hope of seeing a demonstration staged by welcomers. She wanted to see the faces of the
people who were in attendance. After all she had been through,
after all the animosity and failure, Aki wanted to sense the life in
the eyes of the opposition. She wanted to understand their explanations and how the doubters saw the Builders. She needed to be
touched by their desire to survive even though she did not agree
with their methods.

Once it had become known that the Builders were trying to stop
their ship under their own power, the UNSDF mission to protect
the solar system changed on all levels. Along with the mass they had

to shed before arriving, the Builders were incinerating the threat they had posed as a massive, solid body traveling toward Earth at eighteen thousand kilometers per second. The Builders' ship was now small and slow enough that it could easily be met by UNSDF ships and even attacked if necessary. Aki still held to the possibility that multiple Builder ships had been dispatched, but no other objects had been located and the idea had waned in popularity.

Aki knew that nuclear weapons had substantially less power in the vacuum of space. The destructive force extends over an area only a few hundred meters from the hypocenter, making such a device relatively impotent when used on a large enough target. Regardless, thermonuclear weapons were the most powerful weapons in humanity's arsenal. Special nuclear missiles and a device named the "spiderweb" had been developed in case aggressive action was needed. Each missile was as large as an eighteen-wheeler truck and was propelled by a particle-bed reactor nuclear rocket. The spiderweb device was a four-kilometer wide net of coarse mesh. It was stored in a large capsule and was deployed using centrifugal force so that the net extended fully when launched. Despite seeming harmless, colliding with the spiderweb at a speed of sixty kilometers per second would cause massive damage. *These were the ideas that were funded when we should have been trying to communicate.*

The clock on the large outdoor screen showed eight o'clock. Then the screen switched to the feed from a camera mounted on the weapons suspension rack of the UNSS *Millikan*. A sleek, cylindrical, and smoothly reflective missile that appeared to be made of liquid mercury gradually drifted away from the ship.

"The nuclear missile has been launched, ladies and gentlemen. Its engine is now firing," the announcer said. He struck Aki as if he were doing the play-by-play for an oddball Japanese gameshow. She knew that only the guidance control engine was being activated because the missile was too close to use its nuclear-powered engine. After a few minutes, a white flash could be seen from the back of the missile as it gained distance from the *Millikan*. By the time the missile traveled two hundred kilometers, it was no longer distinguishable from the surrounding stars. At that point, a second flash burst into view, a pure-white ball of fire that dissipated quickly. Sighs of disappointment percolated through the crowd until the announcer bellowed that the powerful explosion had been a success. Applause and cheers came from all sides. Aki sat down for a bit. Most of the spectators remained standing.

Next was a demonstration of the spiderweb. Since the web was almost imperceptible to the naked eye, an infrared camera was used to capture the image, then the image was enhanced so that the metal webbing was visible. Ten kilometers from the ship, the web was deployed. Given the size of the giant web, it unfurled at astounding speed. To Aki's ears the crowd seemed more impressed by the spiderweb than the nuclear missile. There was a short break. Aki sat quietly, knowing that the main event was slated for nine o'clock.

"What you're looking at now," explained the announcer, "is an image from seven minutes and thirty seconds ago. This is the UNSS *Thompson*, which is currently near the Vert-Ring. The massive device it is carrying on its back is our very own graser, ladies and gentlemen! What an incredible sight! It almost looks as if the graser is transporting the *Thompson* instead of the other way around."

The long, narrow ship looked like the stem of a wine glass protruding from the back of the graser. During an actual attack, a second ship, the UNSS *Becquerel*, would link with the *Thompson*. Together the *Becquerel* and the *Thompson* would form the final line of defense, attempting to intercept the Builders.

"The UNSS *Thompson* is currently unmanned. It's being controlled from the UNSS *Becquerel*, located thirty thousand kilometers behind the *Thompson*. The targets being used for tonight's demonstration are three spent fuel tanks positioned some two thousand kilometers ahead. The ship should be ready to fire any minute now."

Three egg-shaped objects spaced some distance apart from each other came into view. A countdown timer appeared in the lower right of the screen. As the clock neared zero, silence fell upon the stadium. Only the faint sound of traffic and other random background noise coming from the city were audible. As soon as the countdown reached zero, there was a blinding flash.

When the view of space returned, the fuel tanks were nowhere to be seen. The scene was replayed in slow motion several times. The blast vaporized the tanks in a mere five one-thousandths of a second. The vapor from the explosion dispersed at the breakneck speed of ten kilometers per second, leaving the vidlink's field of vision instantaneously.

"Unbelievable, ladies and gentlemen, truly unbelievable! We have just witnessed the incredible power of the graser. Needless to say, the graser firing test has been a complete success! You have been a witness to the true potential of humanity! The Builders are about to meet their match!" The deep and booming amplified voice of the announcer, which was overwhelming in and of itself, collided with the roaring exultation of the crowd.

Aki wondered if people could possibly be this obtuse. Perhaps the UNSDF had discovered how to trigger the graser, but no one knew how the collimation device worked or how to recharge it. She wondered how many people were aware of the flaws in the plan. The military had been sly, convincing hundreds of millions of viewers that slicing the graser from the Island and carrying it to a new location meant that the military knew what it was doing. The situation was certainly not going to be that simple.

Aki stared up into the clear, cold darkness of the night sky. Above the nocturnal skyline, she could make out Orion. Next to Orion's belt was a new star that was shining almost as brightly as Sirius. Although the composition of the light could not be determined with the naked eye, Aki remembered the nausea she had felt when she read the analysis of the data collected by the satellite telescopes—iron, lead, aluminum, hydrogen, silicon, carbon, nitrogen, and oxygen. The Builders were burning the elements that made up their ship, probably even themselves. The light carried proof of the atomic decomposition. The Builders were willing to sacrifice 99.99 percent to ensure that one ten-thousandth would arrive at the destination. *How are you managing to do this? Why are you so utterly committed to coming here?*

She sensed one thing for sure. The Builders were not lacking for backup plans. When the lasers from their deceleration system had not arrived, the Builders had put their mission ahead of their lives and resorted to nuclear-pulse propulsion to slow themselves. A new group of lights appeared in the southwestern horizon.

"Look, there in the sky! Our ships are about to do a flyby."

Aki watched the exhibition play out with its incredible precision. Four hundred kilometers above the earth, the UNSDF battleships were aligned in a parking orbit alongside their support ships. Aki counted seventeen lights in all. She wondered if the demonstration was planned for this moment because the ships were visible from North America. As lost in the spectacle as anyone else at the stadium, Aki snapped back to reality when somebody grabbed her arm.

"I've been looking for you!" It was Collins, her bodyguard. "What were you thinking, alone in a crowd of this size?"

"Sorry, Collins." Aki followed his lead as he escorted her out. Looking up to the night sky again, she got into the car that had been waiting for her.

ACT XI: NOVEMBER 23, 2037

THE DECOR IN the Strategic Air Command Director's office was modest. In one corner sat an antique Rand McNally globe encased in glass. The brightly colored globe was the only object in the room that caught Aki's attention. In contrast, the northern exposure offered a breathtaking view of the main hall below. Standing at the window, Aki realized that the hall was large enough to house two large tanker ships. UNSDF Fleet Headquarters was, in essence, a self-sufficient underground city. The threat of an attack by the Soviet Union during the Cold War paled in comparison to the potentially catastrophic severity of the current situation. Even if Earth underwent an attack by kinetic energy weapons or nano-machines that stripped away the planet's atmosphere, this facility was prepared to endure the attack and sustain five hundred people for up to two years. For a moment, Aki wondered whether the five hundred would try to rebuild or exact revenge, but she quickly realized the answer.

Even though it was highly automated, the interplanetary nuclear-powered battleships housed here still needed at least sixty specialists, including relief personnel, to keep them running properly. The UNSDF faced substantial logistical challenges in operating and coordinating the actions of its nine battleships simultaneously. The weapons on each of the battleships were essentially spacecraft unto themselves.

In addition to the Battleship Group, there was also the Tactical Situation Group, which collected and processed data from the twenty-seven terrestrial and eighteen orbital observation stations. Together, those observation stations monitored the Builders' ship, Mercury, Venus, various parts of the Vert-Ring, and the area of the inner solar system. Their monitoring processes were managed by computers working in sync with forty human beings to sift through the exabytes of data that poured in.

The interception point with the Builders' ship was estimated at what, by now, seemed like a short distance, a mere twenty light minutes from Earth. That interception point was on the opposite side of the sun, meaning that there would be a significant time lag in communications with Earth. Since the battle might need precision down to the millisecond, all major decisions would need to be made by tactical computer systems integrated directly into the weapons.

This went contrary to the prevailing desire to decide the actions months, if not years, in advance. The battles of this form of space warfare were better suited for long-term strategic planning because it could take months or years for the targets to be within range. Given the high speed of their target, decisions would need to be made almost instantaneously once the target came into range. Besides the time lag, any person or processor calling the shots would face the hazard of metadata inundation. According to the simulations, there could be up to several petabytes of data flowing in at once. Each byte of data needed to be sorted and distributed to the proper team, who would then decide what responses might need to be implemented. The decisions were prioritized and transmitted to the fleet via wide-spectrum laser, high-frequency wave, and microwave lines simultaneously. The fleet would then respond to whichever incarnation of the command signals arrived first.

Before being seen by the crew, however, these commands were first reviewed, evaluated, and compiled by onboard computers that filtered out commands that had already been executed or had become irrelevant based on real-time changes to the situation. Finally, any commands still left unexecuted and also still applicable were then organized and sent to the crew for interpretation or implementation.

"What an amazing facility," Aki said, trying to show more than the minimal interest she felt. She respected how carefully the operational systems had been designed to process chaos and complexity, but could not help but notice that the strategic planning was all geared toward defense, not communication.

Director Robbins looked like he had not expected her to speak. He stared at Aki and weighed her comment carefully. "You must hate me," he said.

"I apologize for turning down your invitation to the ceremony. It was childish of me not to accept."

"It's fine. I worried what might happen if you gave a speech in your current state."

He placed two porcelain pedestal cups on a tray and poured coffee from a thermos.

"I'm a bit sad to know this entire facility will have no use within a few years. Having served in the Strategic Air Command for as long as I have, this kind of extravagant spending doesn't faze me anymore. When we first scrapped the entire North African radar network, it bothered me to consider how many starving children we could've saved with the wasted money. At the end of the day, I accepted that we needed to do what was in the long-term best interest of the whole of humanity."

Aki looked at her cup while sipping her coffee. It was a hand-painted Nippon cup. It depicted a scene of a country farmhouse.

"It's true that you saved the earth, Aki. In my book though, Mark Ridley is just as much the hero as you are. He was navy, right?"

"He is a hero in my book as well."

"Then you understand when I say that I don't want his sacrifice to be in vain."

Aki looked up from the porcelain cup.

"I've gotten your attention. Let's get down to business. We cannot accommodate your request to allocate three of our ships for the Contact Phase."

He motioned for her to sit in the chair facing his desk, then pulled an envelope from the top drawer of his desk.

"There will be a single contact ship—the *Phalanx*. You will be in charge of that ship. You are the only one for the job."

Aki tore the envelope open. It contained military orders requesting her to report for duty as commander of the UNSS *Phalanx*.

"Oh, and don't think that we're going to send you up in that bucket of bolts the way she was before. We're doing major modifications, bringing her up to date, even adding an atomic second stage. Only the *Phalanx* will be capable of rendezvousing with the Builders' craft. I'm taking a lot of flak from my superiors for making this decision."

The *Phalanx* alone would meet the Builders' ship and attempt to make contact. The other eight craft would be in position for interception. For the plan to succeed, the fastest ship needed to be her contact ship. The other eight ships needed payload capacity more than they needed speed.

"Your contact ship will be weaponless. As you can guess, it'll have a high risk of being destroyed. You accept the position?"

"Without hesitation."

"Excellent. Congratulations, even though there wasn't any doubt. You'll have a crew of five. A team of three—the Contact Team—will attempt to board the alien vessel. You, of course, must be one of them. The second will be a Marine guard for protection; you may select the guard, or we can assign one. The third should be another science expert, one with an engineering background. I would like you to decide who that one will be too. There is no need for an application process or approval by committee. This is a military mission: make your selection and it will be done."

"Yes, sir."

———◆·◈·◆———

WHILE RIDING AWAY in yet another black limousine, Aki wondered what qualities to look for in the other two members of the Contact Team. She imagined that there were millions of people who would do anything for the chance to speak with the Builders. She thought of several dozen people she knew fairly well who had the drive and skill sets required to be part of the mission. Of them, there were only two whom she would want to have at her side at this incredible moment of truth. Of those two, only one of them was still alive.

Selecting him would cause talk, but this is too important for chatter to be relevant. I should ask him right now. She decided to ask him over the phone since calling him to her office by official request struck her as pretentious.

"Hi, Raul," she said. "I wanted to thank you for your help the other day and your encouragement. I hope you're glad to hear from me again."

"Maybe I am, maybe I'm not," said Raul. "Every time we talk, you give me something hard to do, crazy lady."

"I bet I can change that *maybe* to a *definitely.*"

"Oh, yeah? How?" His enthusiastic reply was what she had hoped for.

"I want to invite you to come on a little mission with me, on my new ship."

"Your new ship?"

"Yeah, I just got one. I am the commander of the fastest nuclear-powered space vessel in the solar system. Interested?"

The line was silent for a long time, but she knew he had not hung up.

CHAPTER 3: CONTACT

ACT I: MARCH 4, 2041

"WE HAVE IGNITION, ladies and gentlemen. Nine nuclear battleships are on their way! In the lead is the UNSS *Phalanx*, the contact ship commanded by Aki Shiraishi. The UNSS *Rutherford* and *Chadwick* are now leaving orbit. Let's go to a live image from Christmas Island. It's 5:15 in the morning there, so we would appreciate it if everyone remained quiet."

The laughter faded and was replaced by gasps of awe as thin bright streaks trailed across the horizon behind the three specks of light. The streams grew as halos formed around the glowing engine blasts. As the fiery spheres dipped below the horizon, the networks cut to following each of the three ships separately; around the world people could choose which feed to follow. The networks also broadcast speeches from various heads of state, followed by the Pope and other religious leaders, a number of celebrities, luminaries in astronomical studies, and Nobel laureates.

The media coverage and the quality of their images was a far cry from the fuzzy, monochrome video of the first moon landing that had been broadcast seventy years earlier. The live shots of the UNSDF battleships launching were shown from every imaginable vantage point. The images underscored the advancements that had been made in space technology and also in broadcast technology. The primary video was circumscribed by a number of constantly changing thumbnail images. The secondary images included still and video shots from dozens of sites on Earth and from various altitudes in orbit, as well as live feeds from the surfaces and orbits of the moon, Mercury, Venus, and Mars. Unless the viewer intervened by making a specific selection, the primary image feed was chosen by the content provider to best fit the audio. A Worldunity viewer could select from eight hundred different commentators speaking in any of a hundred languages or watch the channel that ranked the talking heads by their real-time popularity.

From her cocoon, Aki watched the sensor readouts during the fully automated launch sequence. Intermittently, she glanced at another monitor that showed the broadcasts from Earth. She switched her secondary monitor from a speech by the young Dalai Lama to a concert at Carnegie Hall. The conductor was leading the orchestra in a rendition of the *Star Wars* theme. Aki chuckled at the jingoistic irony.

Raul was watching the same channel and chimed in. "The doubters are rocking their victory song."

"Check out the Vienna feed. They're playing Beethoven's *Eroica*. Maybe that's more your speed?" suggested Aida Northgate, the ship's systems engineer. She was always upbeat; Aida reminded Raul of a pixie, he had told Aki. Aki was pleased that the two of them got along well. Through Aki's recent tumults, she had forgotten how powerful her intuition could be.

"Don't be too sure. A lot of the aliens were friendly in *Star Wars*. You can't say the same about Napoleon," Raul said.

Aki changed to another channel. In London, the Royal Philharmonic Orchestra was playing a triumphant march by Elgar. In Moscow, the Kirov Orchestra was playing the ballad *Stenka Razin*. According to the commentary, *Stenka Razin* was the story of a hero who led an uprising against the forces of bureaucracy. The music helped settle Aki's nerves. She closed her eyes for a moment, took a deep breath, and tried to clear her head.

"Joseph, which feed are you listening to?" Aki asked the other member of her Contact Team.

"Berlin, ma'am," the young Special Forces soldier replied. Joseph Turnbull was twenty-six years old, laconic yet well educated. Given his military background, handsome looks, and brave demeanor, Aki felt he was the best possible substitute for Mark Ridley. Captain Turnbull was assigned to protect Aki and Raul. During their speed and endurance training, Aki had been amazed by Turnbull's agility. Having someone who reminded her of Mark made her feel protected even though it pained her to relive the memories of her last voyage in the *Phalanx*.

Thinking of how the upgrades made it seem like a different ship even though she had spent so much time on board on the previous mission, Commander Shiraishi switched to the broadcast from Berlin, which was playing orchestral music by Wagner.

"That is *Tannhäuser*, right?" she asked, trying to establish some rapport with the soldier.

"Yes, ma'am," he replied.

The opera told of the struggle between sacred and profane love. Aki stayed on the broadcast coming from Berlin, audio-only. Despite being transmitted millions of kilometers, the sound quality of the Deep Space Network was free from static and ghost noises. Aki was intrigued by the fact that it was being performed live but several minutes in the past. She switched her monitor to one of the external cameras.

As she listened to the scene in which Elizabeth prays and then asks the returning pilgrims for news of Tannhäuser, Aki gazed at the pale blue half-illuminated dot and the smaller white dot next to it. She found the calmer state of mind she sought. All the battles she had fought were behind her. Humanity sometimes seemed both inhuman and inhumane, but she had found a path that brought her a chance to fulfill her dream. She felt that nothing would stop her from making direct contact with the Builders.

The waiting was finally over at the UNSDF Fleet Headquarters as well. The only questions left for them were when the war would start and how much they would be able to prepare before attacks started. Since the fleet had to depart five months before the Builders' arrival, almost all tactical strategic contingencies had to be decided in advance. Once the ships were launched, nothing more than minor corrections could be implemented.

The difficulty came from the ships taking off while the Builders were still outside of Pluto's orbit, nine billion kilometers away. Raul had once likened it to a soccer goalie trying to defend a net eight meters wide but having to pick a pose and stay frozen even though the opposing midfielders were still dribbling up from the opposite end of the field.

"Had the Builders shown something besides complete indifference, even acknowledged our presence, we wouldn't be in this situation," one of the UNSDF headquarter members had told Aki.

Despite the actions taken by people on Earth, the Builders never deviated from their original trajectory for even a second. The Builders gave no warnings to humanity. They had not shown any indications that they would attempt to thwart the attack. The possibility remained that life on Earth was insignificant to their plans. The Builders could not be bothered to acknowledge human existence. If the Builders wanted to eradicate humanity, they could have done so long before now. Sometimes, Aki wondered why they had not done so.

The deceleration of the Builders' ship was constant at a force of 1/100 of a G. Normally, the deceleration of a slowing vessel increased as it burned off fuel and became lighter. Instead, the Builders modified their thrust to keep their deceleration constant. Six years earlier, when the first sightings were made, eight engines had been burning. Now the Builders were down to only one. The Builders, in their relentless commitment to achieving their goal regardless of the costs, had used matter from the engines they no longer needed as fuel for the only engine still intact. This was another achievement brought about by their mastery of nanotechnology. To be able to maintain constant deceleration while consuming their own vessel for its stored energy, they had to push their ship's structural integrity to its limits. If the Builders continued to brake at the same rate of deceleration, the last of their speed would burn off inside the earth's orbit and the remainder of their ship would enter into an orbit around the sun that ran alongside the inner planets. Before becoming an artificial planet, Aki presumed that the Builders would need to stop to replenish the resources they had converted into propulsion fuel during the years of their arduous voyage. The five potential candidates were, in order of likelihood, the Vert-Ring, Mercury, Venus, Earth, and the moon.

No one knew why the Builders were not stopping sooner. Destinations like the Kuiper Belt or one of the outer planets had seemed logical to Aki. The most plausible theory was that their nanotechnology was partially powered by solar radiation—Ring architecture forcing individual photons to interact with single atoms in order to produce energy. The Builders had located their Ring production plant as close to the sun as possible. Once the Ring had finally been constructed, a secondary fuel source appeared to include the antimatter generated by the Ring.

Eventually, precise observations of the Builders' ship resulted in the surprising conclusion that it would not stop at the Vert-Ring. Projections based on the velocity and angle of the ship's approach ruled out the possibility of docking at the Vert-Ring's stationary position. It also appeared increasingly likely that their ship would pass by both the earth and the moon, which produced sighs of relief because the dangerous scenario of having an alien ship with an unknown agenda suddenly appear in the daytime sky would be avoided. Crime was still virulent and contagious in the post-Ring world. Aki shuddered to imagine the damage that would be generated by worldwide, large-scale riots.

When the Builders had reached a distance of eighty astronomical units from the sun, about twice as far from the sun as Pluto, their final destination became clear. They were traveling at an astonishing 1,500 kilometers per second on a direct course for Mercury.

It would take six months for their velocity to slow to forty kilometers per second; at that speed the Builders' ship would reach its final destination. UNSDF Fleet Headquarters immediately went to work devising a plan of defense that was not dependent on where the Builders would be when they were attacked but instead was based on the velocity of the incoming ship. The plan was to target the Builders' propulsion system before the ship dropped below the velocity required to escape the sun's gravity and leave the solar system. If the UNSDF could disable the Builders' deceleration capabilities soon enough they would pass through the solar system—never able to return—the way they would have if Aki had not been persuasive and if the Ring had not been restored with the Vert-Ring.

If, however, the Builders' ship were not stopped in time, even if that ship were destroyed, its remnants would be trapped by the sun's pull and would eventually enter a stable orbit somewhere within the solar system. A fear was that remaining in the solar system would allow the Builders to launch their invasive nanobots to transform one or several planets into the massive factory that Mercury had become.

The escape velocity at the likeliest point of contact, the decreasing speed of the Builders' ship, and the velocity of any debris propelled away from their line of trajectory were used to calculate the plan's execution. Once the calculations were checked and rechecked, the UNSDF analysts announced that the interceptive attack had to begin five days before the Builders would arrive at Mercury. More precisely: by 1 AM GMT on July 29, 2041. In the highly probable event that negotiation by the Contact Ship failed, the UNSDF would commence its attack when the Builders were traveling at a speed of eighty-eight kilometers per second, thirty million kilometers from Mercury.

The UNSDF fleet was comprised of nine ships: the UNSS *Phalanx* (Contact Ship); UNSS *Rutherford, Chadwick,* and *Curie* (First Armada); the UNSS *Crookes, Einstein,* and *Millikan* (Second Armada); and the UNSS *Thompson* (Graser Ship) and *Becquerel* (Graser Support Ship).

As determined by Strategic Command, the *Phalanx* was the only noncombat ship and the only vessel authorized to attempt a rendezvous with the Builders. The attack would be executed in three stages, with twenty-four hours separating the waves. This allowed the ships to reconfigure themselves for the next stage. The First Armada would attack on Day 1 and the Second Armada would take over on Day 2. After launching its nuclear missiles and spiderwebs, each ship would retreat fourteen hours before impact in order to attain the reasonably safe distance of two hundred thousand kilometers.

The two remaining combat ships would be used, if needed, on Day 3. As a final resort, the *Thompson* would attempt to destroy the Builders with the graser. The *Becquerel* would transport the graser initially, then the graser would be transferred to the *Thompson*. The crew of the latter ship would board the *Becquerel* and the *Thompson* would use all of its fuel to propel the graser into position where it would then be operated remotely.

Aki and her Contact Team on the *Phalanx* traveled ahead of the combat ships to rendezvous with the Builders' ship and, if all went well, board it. On a technological level, this would be an incredibly challenging feat. The *Phalanx* would need to match the Builders' speed, direction, and position with meticulous precision. Moreover, to allow ample time for the planned attack, the rendezvous had to be completed while the Builders were still traveling at relatively high velocity. To achieve this, the *Phalanx* had been retrofitted with four nuclear-powered NERVA III engines and a massive liquid-fuel booster rocket that would be jettisoned after its use. Even though the UNSS *Phalanx* carried only five crewmembers, the ship measured an impressive 180 meters with the booster rocket attached, making Aki's ship longer than any space station.

Of all the fleet's ships, the *Phalanx* had the greatest capability to change its velocity. Nonetheless, the *Phalanx* would wait until the Builders' ship decelerated to less than ninety-five kilometers per second before attempting to dock. This allowed twenty hours of negotiation before the UNSDF attacked the Builders. During that time, the Contact Team hoped to board the alien vessel and communicate with the beings presumed to be on board. If the Contact Team were not able to ascertain the Builders' intentions, or if the Contact Team concluded that the Builders were intractably hostile, the attack would be launched as scheduled, whether Aki and her team were still on board the Builders' ship or not. Without any reservations, Aki was ready to consider that worst-case scenario and accept the potential consequences of her actions. After plotting the *Phalanx*'s voyage, Aki felt that she had analyzed her ship's contingencies. Her only task left was to hope the computers functioned properly and that, above all, the Builders did not change their course.

ACT II: JUNE 14, 2041

THE *PHALANX* BEGAN its long voyage in the invisible current of the sun's gravity. Heading toward the blazing star, on the 120th day, the ship passed perihelion. The eight combat ships fired their nuclear engines one by one to enter their deceleration phase, placing them into a solar orbit that nearly matched Mercury's. Since Mercury's orbit is elliptical and the fleet's was circular, Mercury would approach the fleet from behind, temporarily pass and then retreat as the two met a second time. That point in space was where the Builders' ship was projected to arrive, which placed the fleet in the best possible strategic position to launch their attack. The *Phalanx* used Mercury's weak gravitational pull to shift its trajectory outward, causing the ship to decelerate slightly just before reaching perihelion. When the *Phalanx* reached Mercury's orbit again, the *Phalanx* would point itself toward Mercury and accelerate, propelling itself toward the planet with as much speed as it could muster.

In such close proximity to Mercury, with the Vert-Ring production facilities still operating, the ships were likely to come in contact with ring material being ejected from the surface. For protection, each ship was coated with a prophylactic coating immunizing the hulls to the corrosion that resulted from contamination. Advances had been made in decoding the inner workings of the messenger cells. Messenger cells had been reprogrammed to deactivate ring material when the messengers touched it. The reprogrammed cells were replicated and applied to the hulls of the fleet's nine ships. If the retardant functioned as planned, the fleet would avoid a recurrence of the situation that led to Mark Ridley's heroic sacrifice.

Another concern was that real-time communication within the fleet was impeded. Since transmissions were delayed due to the distance between the four groups, decisions that required precision and needed to be made within a few seconds would have to be made individually.

When the fleet reached perihelion, the Builders were between the orbits of Jupiter and Saturn. Though the arrival of alien entities still seemed nigh impossible to the crews of the ships and to everyone on Earth, the Builders would reach Mercury in fifty-five days. One of the senior technical engineers likened the Builders to Edmund Hamilton's 1940s hero Captain Future because he felt such a sense of cosmic awe when he contemplated their advanced technology. On July 19, the alien vessel passed through the earth's orbit around the sun. Since the earth was on the opposite side of the sun from the ship, the many panicked reports of sightings by amateur skywatchers of the ship as it flew by were discounted. The high-powered telescope on the *Phalanx* was the first to establish visual contact, providing the first glimpse of the alien vessel's shape.

The telescope's image was processed to remove the glaring light of the nuclear pulse engine. That process of sampling and smoothing revealed an object that looked like a wheel turned sideways, or a doughnut that measured three hundred meters across with a massive engine filling the hole in the center. It bore a resemblance to some of the earlier designs of Earth's space stations. The telescope did not reveal much surface detail except for variations in shading around the outer edge that confirmed the craft made one revolution every forty-three seconds. The object rotated at a speed that created artificial gravity on the inside of the tube equivalent to one-third of a G.

"Wow. Look at that thing. If we rendezvous, the seventy billion dollars spent will seem like a bargain," Aki said from her cocoon, faking enthusiasm because she felt it was her job as commander and that it best fit the circumstances to play the role of a brave leader. Internal doubts and her awareness that a great deal could go wrong were best kept hidden. The core objective of her mission was to make contact, establish communications, and determine whether the attack should proceed within an extraordinarily small window of time—but that thought, along with the doubts of the last few years of her life, was also best relegated to the back of her mind.

There had been much speculation regarding the design of the Builder ship. The various hypotheses of what was contained within the ship included artificial life-forms, simple robots, nanomachines, capsules of microorganisms, frozen embryos, and even bodiless brains existing in liquid-filled pods. Because of the wildly imaginative ideas that had surfaced, the actual image of the ship seemed rather anticlimactic.

"Could anything besides biological life-forms require artificial gravity? If they are alive and mobile in one-third of a G, they are probably not too different from us in size," Aki said.

"That's the good old undying optimism we need, Aki. I'm sure they've been sitting around playing poker and making up drinking games to pass the time, just like we have," Raul responded. "We're just going to ring their doorbell, walk on board, and then hug them without speaking until we all start weeping."

"Do you have to be flippant?"

"I'll be disappointed if they look too much like us. I'm hoping they're so different that we have to coin neologisms in order to describe them."

"Who knows? Maybe they are so different we will not even be able to make up new words to describe them." Aki could tell that Raul knew how nervous she felt.

"They've mastered nanotech and interstellar travel. It's hard to believe they need physical bodies. Compared to what they're capable of creating, fleshy organic bodies seem inefficient and limiting. I bet they can upload their consciousness to computers."

"If that were true, their voyage would have ended when the nanomachines first arrived on Mercury. I mean, if they can convert themselves into software and data, they should have been able to program themselves into the nanites," Aki said. "Even if that was beyond them—not that much seems beyond them—they would construct a data receiver on Mercury and transport their consciousness via radio communication, Mr. Computer Genius."

"Maybe the brain can't be converted into data that easily. Maybe the quantum state of each constituent atom in the brain is significant and necessary for the brain to function as a whole. If that's the case, an organic medium like a brain is necessary to store the information. Builders might be able to do it, but the process would take ages to transfer that much data at a rate of one corresponding atom pair at a time. That explains why they sent a big ship to come after the nanomachines had landed—which, of course, would mean that their ship is stuffed full to overflowing with piles and piles of brains." Raul laughed at how outrageous his own theory suddenly sounded. "Well, at any rate, that's what I was hoping to uncover. Thinking it through, they wouldn't need artificial gravity to transport brains and computers. Maybe consciousness *does* require a physical body after all."

Twenty years earlier, when research had revealed how massive the Builders' ship was, Aki had felt certain that the ship would contain physical life-forms. She believed her theory was confirmed when it was discovered that the gases emitted from their nuclear engines contained traces of carbon.

"It seems right that consciousness needs to be integrated into a physical form," Aki said.

"That might hold for humans, but mental activities are, pure and simple, nothing more than information. Reaching a higher stage of evolution might allow the two to separate."

Aki had often pondered whether consciousness could be converted into digital data. Her best comparison had been how ants excreted pheromones for many different purposes including the building of networks on the ground that indicated the optimal path for the rest of the ant colony to follow. Individual ants wandering randomly laid a trail that dissipated over time. Once a specific path had substantially more traffic, the odor of the pheromones became concentrated. Ever more ants would follow that path, further concentrating the pheremonic potency so that path would be followed by even more ants. If this pheromonal chemosignaling system were sufficiently developed, the system itself could be considered a form of consciousness. *How does one identify where consciousness resides?* Aki found herself thinking. The intellectual conundrum seemed almost safe compared to the actuality of the Builders and the imminence of contact. *Is it found among the ants, in the pheromone, and on the ground? Despite the elements that comprise the simple system, pinpointing the consciousness becomes unanswerably complex.*

The cylindrical tube that composed the bulk of the Builders' ship became known as the Torus. Confirming that the alien vessel had artificial gravity was good news for the UNSDF. If the Builders required gravity and a pressurized atmosphere, a puncture to the Torus's hull could potentially kill off whatever life lurked within the ship.

Several days later, as the Torus came closer, higher resolution images were obtained. The Torus and the center part of the ship were connected by six support structures reminiscent of spokes on a bicycle wheel. The center area was blocked from view by the glare of the nuclear pulse engine, but analysts were able to discern a protruding three-way nozzle that appeared to be a heat-exhaust system.

The Torus was forty meters thick, giving it the same internal volume as three hundred jumbo jets or a small space colony. The interior volume of the Torus could contain an expansive amount of space difficult for three people to traverse in less than twenty hours. Considering how much larger the ship had originally been, it was likely that any remaining life-forms would be packed tightly, which raised Aki's hopes because overcrowding implied that it wouldn't take long for her crew to find one of the Torus's passengers.

ACT III: JULY 25, 2041
THREE DAYS BEFORE RENDEZVOUS

THE *PHALANX* POINTED its bow toward where Mercury would be in nine days, then fired its booster rocket at full thrust. The Builders' ship was already inside Mercurial orbit, quickly gaining on the *Phalanx* from thirty million kilometers off its stern. There was some concern that orienting the propellant stream from the *Phalanx*'s nuclear engine toward the Builders might be mistaken for an attack. Given the great distance that remained between the two ships, the risk was assessed as minimal. Musing on the process in her cocoon, Aki pictured the *Phalanx* receiving the baton in a relay race, running ahead in the same direction as the person handing off the baton, ensuring that both runners would be traveling at the same speed when the runners met. Since the Builders were seasoned spacefarers, the prediction was that the Builders would ascertain that the *Phalanx* was attempting a rendezvous.

With the *Phalanx*'s engines pointed at the Builders' ship, the glare made maintaining visual contact with the vessel impossible. In place of visuals, all major observational equipment arrayed in local space and not blocked by the sun became critical, even though the information arrived intermittently. The alien vessel continued to show no change in trajectory or rate of deceleration.

Thirty hours later, when the booster engines had burned their liquid fuel, the boosters and their massive fuel tanks were released.

Once the engines on the main body of the *Phalanx* were fired and the ship's velocity increased, the *Phalanx* pulled past its jettisoned booster unit.

"Wave goodbye to the most expensive piece of equipment humanity has ever built," mumbled Igor, who had helped design and build the booster. "I should celebrate that I didn't screw up. Going outside and exposing myself to radiation to fix that complicated booster would be godawful. As long as the Builders don't eat our ship and we don't get blown up by our own weapons, we'll survive another day."

Despite his lapses into negativity, Aki knew that Igor felt a part of himself had been ejected along with the booster unit. He was a man who liked playing to an audience.

Two days later, amid the gas from the engine blast, a white light appeared as the glare of the Builders' nuclear engine became visible. The light looked stationary to the naked eye but was actually approaching the *Phalanx* at a frightful speed. The *Phalanx* launched an unmanned hound to see what would happen when a probe approached the Builders' ship. Three days later, when the distance between the two ships had diminished to a hundred thousand kilometers, the UNSS *Phalanx* turned around 180 degrees to face the approaching vessel head-on.

According to Igor, this maneuver was the biggest climax of the mission, save releasing the booster unit. Aki was surprised that the rendezvous and its potential outcome was less important to Igor than the vehicular maneuvers and the jettisoning of the boosters. As the 130-meter *Phalanx* made its about-face, the laser communications system—which had to remain pointing at four distinct locations in the inner solar system—and the thirty-seven high-gain antennae, the five deep-space telescopes, and several hundred sensors all needed to turn in sync in order to remain pointing at their respective targets. Despite attempts to avoid creating blind spots, some devices would need to be switched to auxiliary systems, many of which were located on the opposing side of the ship to provide fail-safes. Finally, once the half turn was complete, the two main engines were set to match the Builders' deceleration of 1/100 of a G. For Igor, coordinating the dozens of elements essential to the maneuver was as exhilarating as singing a solo at Carnegie Hall.

"Rotation maneuver and deceleration synchronization complete, Commander," Igor announced proudly. "A few minor glitches; nothing that impacts the mission."

"Thank you, Igor. We could never have come this far without your skills and commitment to excellence," Aki said.

"Only doing my job, Commander."

"Well, to celebrate the completion of the operation, would you please announce our success to the world?"

"Me?"

"It would be a shame to let your sonorous voice go to waste," Aki said.

Igor brought himself online with the communications network, cleared his throat and half-sang, in a rich baritone, "The UNSS *Phalanx* has completed rotation and deceleration synchronization. We will now enter the Contact Phase."

THE PROBE HOUND had been retrofitted with the same corrosion-retarding paint as the ships. Approaching the Builders' vessel, the probe fired its jets to slow down relative to its target. To avoid any misinterpretations of hostility, the hound's jet nozzles were configured in a V-shape, pointing at slight angles away from its line of flight. Between the two jets was a square screen five meters across that displayed a series of messages using all frequencies of visible light and in infrared to cover the entire spectra of light emitted by the Builders' home star.

The ETICC was betting all its chips on this last ditch effort of communication. By displaying video directly instead of encoding the images in pulse modulation, the ETICC hoped its message might finally be conveyed.

The camera mounted on the probe did not have as high a resolution as the one on the *Phalanx*, but the closer proximity of twenty thousand kilometers made up for the difference. On the morning of July 28, Aki was in her cocoon reading a report on UNSDF observations while keeping an eye on a live feed from the probe. It was still several hours before the probe was to arrive. An alarm sounded and the monitoring system displayed a message.

<CHANGE DETECTED IN ALIEN VESSEL>

Aki looked at the image from the probe. The nuclear pulse engine that had burned brightly in the center of the Torus was out. The engine area that had been masked by the blinding light of the blast was finally visible. It was an opening at least fifty meters across. The nuclear pulse engine used a bowl-shaped reflector with a focal point that emitted the energetic equivalent of a continuous series of detonations from small hydrogen bombs. This reflecting bowl made up most of the image that the probe's camera could see. The dish was circumscribed with tiny protruding thorns that appeared to be a set of laser devices to contain and direct the destructive force generated by the explosions.

The opening began to close like an iris. While the size of the outer edge remained the same, the crimson color of the iris expanded inward, gradually taking on the shape of a half-sphere. The sunlight emanating from behind the right side of the vessel was partially blocked, creating a pattern of light and shadows on the area, giving it an eerie impression of depth. The iris continued to close until it was a tiny dark spot surrounded by crimson. To Aki, the image suggested the eye of a chameleon.

Aki looked into the eye. Chills ran through her. She had the unmistakable sensation that the eye was looking right back at her. The probe was positioned slightly off to the side but the opening seemed to be staring directly at the hound.

"It's watching us." As soon as Aki spoke into her mic, the image disappeared from the screen. Warning messages began to flash.

< STRONG ENERGY SURGE DETECTED >

"All stations, report!" Before she finished her command to the crew, the computer system was displaying its quantitative analysis of the situation.

< HIGH PROBABILITY OCCURRENCE: PROBE DESTROYED >
< THERMAL DISRUPTION DETECTED AT PROBE LOCATION >

The computer system displayed the recorded video from a camera on the *Phalanx*. It showed the probe in flight then, suddenly, the image went completely white at the moment of the explosion as the imaging sensors clipped. When the video returned, the probe had been replaced by a visible explosion—one similar in appearance to the result of a nuclear detonation.

Aki played the video in slow motion. Probe, static, explosion—followed by a fluctuation in the nuclear pulse engine.

"It doesn't make sense."

"The probe's communication systems stopped with no warning in just under five milliseconds," Igor said.

"Could the probe's engine have exploded?"

"Nil chance of that. The sensors would've picked up an initial change in temperature or pressure. The telemetry readings were normal right until the end."

"There's no doubt about it—the probe was intentionally destroyed," Raul said.

Concerned that her disappointment was not appropriate to her role as commander, Aki did not respond, remaining silent even though a command was clearly expected.

"Aki! You loco? Snap out of it. We need to report this to the fleet."

"It's true. I'll send the message."

Even as she tried to accept what had happened, Aki sent a voice recording to the rest of the fleet.

"Priority message from the UNSS *Phalanx*. It appears that the hound was attacked as it approached the alien vessel at a distance of fourteen thousand kilometers. Observations indicate that the blast from the nuclear pulse engine was concentrated into an intense beam directed at the probe."

Just then, the warning again appeared on Aki's screen.

< *CHANGE DETECTED IN ALIEN VESSEL* >

The iris dome that had closed over the engine opened. Once the dome had fully retracted, the nuclear pulse engine began to fire, obscuring the view of the center of the Torus.

"Had the probe been approaching head-on, that beam would've passed right through the hound and destroyed us too," Igor said. Since taking the most direct route between the two ships would have required the probe to pass through the propulsion blast of the Builders' ship, the probe had been programmed to travel perpendicularly and then approach at an angle.

"So their policy is shoot first, questions never?" Raul asked. "I guess their ship is as trigger-happy as the Ring's graser system."

"The probe was slowing down and displaying the visual message. There is no way they thought it was an asteroid. Why weren't they interested in what the probe was or what its message meant?" Aki asked.

"Our only option is the *Remora*," Igor said. The *Remora* was the transport vehicle designed to bring the Contact Team to the Builders' ship. It could be operated either remotely or by a pilot who was on board.

"Just a minute. If they blow up the *Remora*, there's no way to board their ship. Any way we can maneuver the *Phalanx* close enough to board directly?" Aida asked.

"No. If the *Remora*'s destroyed we'll have no choice but to terminate the contact mission," Aki stated. She knew that destruction of the *Remora* would be interpreted by the UNSDF as unequivocal proof of hostility. Warmongers would already try to use the lost hound as an excuse. Any further act of aggression would offer full justification to proceed with their attack. *Why did they destroy it?* The *Remora* lacked a message screen, which made the *Remora* even more likely to be taken as a threat by the Builders. "What other choice do we have, Aida?"

Aida remained silent. There weren't any other choices, and all five crewmembers knew it.

After the twenty-minute time lag passed, UNSDF Fleet Headquarters responded:

"Prepare to send the *Remora* unmanned. If it is destroyed, abort the contact mission."

The clock of their allotted twenty hours was about to start ticking. Aki had little time to make a decision.

"Aida, Joseph, Raul, remove the equipment aboard the *Remora*. Risking the *Remora* might provide an answer on how to approach the ship safely. Igor, program the *Remora* to make the approach. I will tell you what I want her to do."

THIRTY MINUTES LATER, the unmanned *Remora* was released from the *Phalanx*. The ship was a cylinder four meters across and ten meters long. One end had an entry hatch, which had been purposely left open. The perimeter of the hatch was fitted with an extendable sealing ring to allow airtight docking with the Builders' ship. The *Remora* was also equipped with thrusters on all sides to maximize maneuverability. In essence, it was a portable jet-powered airlock.

Igor had programmed it to fly at a ten degree angle away from its target for the first half of the trajectory and then to subtly point itself back on course during the second half, curving and approaching as indirectly as possible. It was unclear which would appear more threatening—flying on a direct course or appearing to be flying away and then changing course partway through. Aki decided to use the same approach as the probe even though that method had failed, only because a direct approach seemed even riskier.

At 5 PM GMT, Aki watched the *Remora* from her cocoon. The ship made its roundabout way toward the Builders' ship. She clenched her palms as it approached a distance of fourteen thousand kilometers. Nothing happened. Aki started to let out a yelp and then restrained herself.

Twelve thousand kilometers. Ten thousand. Nine thousand.

The nuclear pulse engine stopped, just like before. The iris reappeared around the engine.

"I just commanded the *Remora* to retreat," Igor said.

Even if the *Remora* fired its front thruster at full force, that process would take several minutes to stop all forward motion.

Aki tensed again. She worried that she had marched the *Remora* to a firing squad. Losing the *Remora* would end any possibility of communicating with the Builders.

Alarms sounded and static appeared on the monitor. One glance and the dreams of Aki's past four decades were ruined. A ball of white gas expanded from where the *Remora* had been. A loud shriek from Aida echoed over the comm system, and Aki's spirits sank even lower.

ACT IV: JULY 29, 2041

NORMALLY, THE LARGEST screen at UNSDF Fleet Headquarters toggled between the ten most important of the thousands of feeds they received. For the past four hours, however, the screen stayed on a single feed that showed the orbits of the inner planets. The War Zone had the sun at the center, followed by Mercury in the ten o'clock position along its elliptical orbit. Earth was farther out, on the opposite side at four o'clock.

The Builders' ship was at nine o'clock, heading for where Mercury would be on August 3. The trajectory was depicted by a solid red curve. Immediately next to Mercury was a dot representing the *Phalanx*.

The three ships in the First Armada—the *Rutherford*, the *Chadwick* and the *Curie*—were on the outside of Mercury's orbit, on course to intercept the Builders' ship.

The velocity of the Builders' ship far surpassed the combat vessels. While the UNSDF called the plan an attack, Raul had summed it up best. It was an attempt to stop a high-speed maglev train by chasing the train on bicycles.

Analysts hypothesized that the Builders' attack beam was generated by directing the blast from the nuclear pulse engine into a concentrated beam of energy. The engine was capable of pulsing three hundred times per second, giving the powerful beam almost limitless range.

The combat ships were equipped with three nuclear missiles and three spiderwebs each. The missiles and spiderwebs could both achieve velocities of fourteen kilometers per second. Assuming the weapons would be launched from outside the danger zone of fourteen thousand kilometers, it would take sixteen minutes to reach their targets, giving the Builders ample time to react and neutralize them with their beam. A successful attack was a long shot at best. Gloom hung in the air at UNSDF Fleet Headquarters. Then an attack specialist jumped from his chair.

"Why didn't we see that they have a blind spot? Their beam only covers 120 degrees before the Torus blocks the path. All we need to do is approach from the side."

"They'll just turn the ship," answered a supervisor.

"The ship's rotating to produce artificial gravity in the Torus, a gyro effect. That makes turning the ship extremely difficult."

"So we attack from multiple sides at once?"

"Yes! It has to work."

In the throes of desperation, any alternative seemed a good one. The idea caught on, and a new plan was broadcast to the entire fleet. Each wave reprogrammed their ships accordingly. Once the strategy had been entered, the computers ran a quarter-million simulations of possible outcomes based on the foreseeable variables. Success was not guaranteed, but the calculations confirmed that one condition was absolutely necessary: the weapons would need to be launched in halves and reach the target near-simultaneously, one toward one side of the Torus and the second toward the other.

Orders were given for the *Rutherford* and the *Chadwick* to launch their missiles and spiderwebs immediately. Provisional plans were loaded into the navigation system of the weapons with the final decision to be uploaded in-flight via laser transmission.

Both ships followed their orders. The automatic launch sequences for the five missiles and four spiderwebs were executed without intervention from the crew. At 8 AM GMT on July 29, the number of moving objects in the War Zone shown on the overhead screen at UNSDF Fleet Headquarters increased from five to ten. Cheers and whistles echoed through the large room.

An order from UNSDF Fleet Headquarters also arrived at the *Phalanx*: "Contact Phase aborted. Vacate the War Zone pronto." Reading the message, Aki felt powerless. Throughout the mission, every member of the *Phalanx* crew had refused to accept this scenario, though it was the most likely. Constructing the Ring with no regard to its detrimental effect on the earth; failing to respond to the ETICC's messages of peace; the drastic measure of burning their own ship; their standard operating procedure of destroying every object that approached them—every action the Builders took made their message clear.

We are coming. We care about nothing else.

Nonetheless, Aki and her crew had chosen to ignore the irrefutable signs. Aki had clung to her far-fetched hope that the Builders would prove to be benevolent and curious.

Aki flipped the switch that activated the ship-wide comm system. "We need to decide whether we follow the advisory. What dangers do we face by staying?"

"For starters, the guided missiles could mistake us for the Builders' ship," said Joseph, the bodyguard. Aki had learned that his mood, as strange as it seemed at first, was lighter in tense, high-stress situations—as if danger relaxed him.

"That shouldn't be a problem. Our ship emits an ID signal that the missiles recognize. They should also identify us visually. If the Builders jam our ID signal or the missiles' visual capabilities, we're still a hundred thousand kilometers away, far enough to prevent mistaken identity," Igor said.

"What about the Builders targeting us in retaliation? Being the closest enemy ship makes us an easy target," Aida said.

Since there was a chance the Builders could close the distance between the two ships, there were no guarantees that the ships would be far enough away to avoid triggering the Builders' attack beam. Aki was pleased that her team was approaching the subject rationally.

"My gut says they're not seeking out targets or bothering to connect their actions to ours. I think they're ignoring us or oblivious, unless we get close," Raul said. No one disagreed.

"Off the record, I do not want to terminate the Contact Phase," Aki said. "If the Builders' ship is damaged in the attack but still intact, staying here would offer the possibility of rescuing one or more of the Builders. Maybe they would be more willing to listen if we could demonstrate our intent."

"Wouldn't we be exposing ourselves to the nuclear radiation?" Joseph asked.

"More than a little. If their engine becomes disabled, incapacitating their attack beam, I think going in for a rescue will be safe. If that happens, I could not live with myself if we stood by and did nothing."

"Commander, it's a noble and worthy cause. What else are we doing while we're out here? Might as well have a good view," said Igor.

"The UNSDF will benefit from the close-up footage, even delayed, as long as we stay out of their hair," said Raul.

"Let's go with, 'UNSS *Phalanx* requests to hold position for battle status observation and possible rescue mission after attack.'"

Everyone agreed. Aki sent the message.

JULY 29, 11 AM GMT

THE FIRST ARMADA deployed its weapons. One round of missiles and spiderwebs approached the Builders from one side and the second round was closing in from the other. The telescope on the *Phalanx* had not made visual contact with the weapons, partially because the weapons were designed to be nigh undetectable. All that could be seen were heat signatures in the form of tiny points of infrared light amidst the cold of space.

By 10 PM GMT the missiles had crossed the hundred thousand–kilometer mark. The missiles would arrive at the target in just three hours. The Builders' ship showed no signs of change. Headquarters feared that the Builders might halt their rotation, enabling them to turn around, but there were no signs of that maneuver.

"Are you asleep?" Raul asked Aki on a private channel, his volume turned low.

"No, I'm up."

"You haven't slept for days."

"I've napped in spurts. I'm alert."

"If you say so. I was worried since you didn't come out for dinner."

Aki realized she hadn't eaten. She entered a command on her screen to warm her food.

"Don't worry. I'm fine. A little disappointed, that's all."

"You have a harder shell than I thought," Raul said.

"It thickens with age. How are you and the others holding up?"

"Aida is kind of down. The others are doing better than she is." Aida had shared Aki's dream of connecting with the Builders. Aki would never forget her stern determination when Aida had told Aki how much she wanted to be part of the Contact Team. Her positive personality had been an asset.

"I'm bummed our job has gone from being ambassadors leading humanity's first contact with an alien intelligence to spectators to the destruction of that same alien intelligence," Raul said.

"Maybe *your* shell is more delicate than mine. Observing will be handled by the automatic computer system." Aki took a sip of the creamed stew the alimentation system served her.

"I don't get it. How could this tyrannical consciousness evolve to the level of an interstellar civilization?" Raul asked.

"Maybe tyranny is the key to their success."

"What, it's crappy luck that we're on their list of solar systems to conquer?"

JULY 30, 12:55 AM GMT

EARTH WAS ON the brink of its first interstellar war. The initial cluster of missiles was twenty thousand kilometers from what the UNSDF considered to be the Builders' blind spot. The spiderwebs had already expanded and were on course to impact with the vessel. The nuclear missiles each contained four independent warheads that would separate from each other and fly distinct courses as they approached the target. The changes in trajectory were limited, because expanding that capacity would have required more fuel and reduced the carrying capacity of the missiles. The UNSDF had determined that the ability to destroy was more important than the ability to maneuver.

The main body of the missile was designed to confuse the Builders by exploding into fragments of radar-scattering flak. This flak, along with a decoy heat source, had been designed to create diversions sufficient for stealth bombing.

The fact that the missiles were loaded with multiple warheads and configured with decoy devices had been hidden from the public. At the demonstration, the four missiles had been programmed to hit in synch, the precaution taken in case the Builders were monitoring radio transmissions.

The War Zone display at UNSDF Fleet Headquarters showed the alien vessel surrounded by numerous blips closing in on the target. The ship showed no signs of reorienting itself to destroy the missiles that were approaching its blind spots. On the *Phalanx*, Aki sensed that the battle was going to be unpleasant.

Then the nuclear pulse engine went dark again. Unexpectedly, the spokes connecting the center of the ship to the surrounding Torus disappeared. The center of the ship separated from the Torus. The iris reappeared and the vessel assumed its attack position.

The center spun. The attack beam fired in multiple directions in rapid succession. Every missile and spiderweb was disintegrated, nothing but clouds of slowly dispersing vapor that floated along the original trajectories. Within several minutes, the center of the ship returned to the Torus, extended its spokes, and the two pieces rejoined as if nothing unusual had occurred.

"If this is their way of communicating, their message is obvious. Humanity is so low on the evolutionary scale that we're not even worth acknowledging," Raul said. Aki hmmed in agreement. He continued, "Their reaction is to destroy anything of ours that impedes their mission. They see us as annoying houseflies that won't leave them alone. Even if we execute our best attack, they take one swing and splat!"

"Now is the wrong time to be cynical, Raul." Aki was thinking along similar lines but felt that voicing negativity when the situation was this dire was inappropriate.

"Okay, fine. Let's look at the situation logically. They only acknowledge us when we get in their way. Is that communication? No. As I see it, there's no way for us to get through to them. Damn, this situation seems familiar."

"Familiar? How so?" Aki asked.

"Forget about it," he said dismissively.

"IF WILLING TO assist by observing, comply by advancing to twenty thousand kilometers from the alien vessel. Please respond," said the message from UNSDF Fleet Headquarters. The question was simple but reaching an answer forced Aki to risk her crew.

The plan for the Second Armada was to stagger missile volleys unevenly, sorting the remaining warheads. Some had extra fuel and others were decoys. The extra fuel would allow the loaded warheads enhanced maneuverability in order to avoid the Builders' attack beam. As the missiles approached target, the decoy missiles would be detonated in sequence, with the hopes that the heat blast, blinding flash, and surge of radiation would confuse Builder sensory and defense systems.

Instead of targeting the blind spot, this armada's attack was simple: the missiles traveled at maximum velocity along the shortest possible route. New software had been uploaded to the *Phalanx* to enhance its observational capabilities, enabling the *Phalanx* to determine the direction of the attack before the beam fired. From that vantage point, the *Phalanx* could alert the missile that it was being targeted and should pursue evasive action. The missiles themselves were not equipped with as advanced visual scanning systems. That task was delegated to the *Phalanx*. The *Phalanx* was on the opposite side of the alien vessel, and several workarounds had been put in place to allow Aki's ship to communicate directly with the weapons. In most cases, computer scenarios predicted these difficulties would mean an average delay of one second. Because of this, the *Phalanx* had been asked to get as close as possible to the Builders.

Move in close, back off, move in close. Damn it, I wish Fleet Headquarters would make up their minds. Given the fortune invested in the *Phalanx*, getting the most use out of the ship spoke to Aki's business sense. She decided that explaining the request to the crew face to face was the best course of action. She sent the request for them to assemble in the crew room.

"Our observations show their line of defense to be fifteen thousand kilometers. If we move in to twenty thousand kilometers, we should reduce the time lag in communicating with the missiles to an average of under one second and improve the precision of our observations while remaining in the safe zone. What do you think?"

Everyone looked around the room but remained silent for a long moment. It was Raul who asked the question everyone was thinking: "Is there any basis for the hypothesis that we won't be fired upon at that distance?"

"Merely what we have observed," Aki said. She could not see their eyes or interpret their body language through their suits.

Raul took a deep breath. "I don't know about you, but I prepped myself for the risks of this mission before I got on the ship. I'm down if you are, Aki."

"This is different than hypothetical scenarios. Our ship would be playing an active role in the combat. If the Builders realize our involvement, they'll eliminate us," Igor said.

At twenty thousand kilometers, if the attack beam were used on the *Phalanx*, the beam would reach the ship almost instantaneously. Despite its agility and speed, the *Phalanx* had little hope of dodging an attack by the Builders should one come. Though the *Phalanx* flew outside of the line of defense, Aki knew that the Builders' line of defense had nothing to do with the range of their beam weapon.

"This is scary enough that I hadn't thought about it at all. What about the graser? Isn't that the UNSDF's ace in the hole? Why put our butts on the line when the second round of missiles will get destroyed as quickly as the first?" Aida said as she adjusted the strap on her chair.

"I think the UNSDF realizes that the graser may not work," Aki said, making sure to keep her voice even and speak clearly. "I assumed the graser would recognize the Builders' ship when it approached Mercury or the Vert-Ring, with the identification being made by the collimation telescope on the Island. Now the Builders' ship, since so much was burned for fuel to decelerate, looks nothing like it originally did—different mass, different shape. But the Builders were heading, without trepidation, toward Mercury. They are confident of being recognized by their own security. If I am right, that means the graser will still recognize them too."

"Of course," Igor said. "The graser on the *Thompson* no longer had the collimation telescope attached. But if the telescope is still able to receive a signal from the Builders, there would be the chance that a fail-safe mechanism could activate, preventing the graser from firing. The UNSDF has no idea how the graser actually functions; the discovery of the triggering mechanism was just dumb luck.

"Because the UNSDF's secret weapon might not work, we're expected to risk our lives to boost the second missile attack's chances. Think of the resources spent on building this ship that could've been used to heal the sick, all to give us one chance to communicate with the Builders." Igor paused, then said, "But I'll be honest. This isn't panning out and I think we should do something useful if we can. The personal consequences we face aren't as important as the consequences to Earth."

"Are you saying that the contact mission was nothing but a shot in the dark all along?" Aki asked. She knew Igor was not really condemning the contact mission, but she wanted to make a point of having everyone's thoughts on the table before she went forward. Even though she was the leader, they were in this together now.

"Whether I thought so or not, it's turning out to be." Igor shrugged.

"The chances were slim, but it was our obligation as civilized, humane, and sentient beings to try," Aida said.

Aki looked around the room. "Does anyone else have anything they want to add?"

That was it; the crew of the UNSS *Phalanx* agreed to comply with the UNSDF request. Aki dismissed her crew, then wrote a brief reply. Igor and Aida began to plot the course to approach the Builders' ship. Raul tested the new observation program. He used a record of the attack beam to test the software's ability to predict where the beam would fire.

The *Crookes*, the *Einstein* and the *Millikan* launched their missiles. The warheads would not reach their target until the next day.

Aki tried to rest but sleep did not come. Instead, Aida's feelings of frustration over the poor mission planning and being put in harm's way echoed through her head. The day she had interviewed Aida, she had canceled the remaining interviews. Aki ordered a lemon-flavored sedative from the alimentation system. Before drinking it, she opened a private channel with Raul.

"Are you awake?"

"*Wide* awake. I'm still in my sexual prime, you know."

"Well I'm not," Aki said. "I have a favor to ask."

"Shoot."

"Can you try to comfort Aida? She is not dealing well."

"What do you expect me to do?"

"I don't know. Ask her to meet you in the crew room for coffee? Talking to you might cheer her up. She has feelings toward you."

"I would rather be cheering *you* up," Raul said.

"Don't worry about me. I'm not fragile," Aki said tersely.

"I guess it's my imagination then."

"If it makes you happy, I was about to take a sedative and get some sleep."

"I'm being sent on a comfort mission while you take a nap? I know it's wrong to say this to a commander but you're being a coldhearted bitch."

"I didn't mean it the way you're taking it."

"Then don't take this the wrong way, but what*ever*, Aki. You got me roped into this mission, and it looks like we're not going to get back home. For all we know, this is one of the last conversations we'll ever have."

Aki knew Raul was trying to get her to invite him to come comfort her in her cocoon. In the seventeen years they had known each other, there had been several times where they were almost intimate. Aki had always turned him down, sometimes after a few kisses, not because she disliked the idea, but because it was always bad timing and her research had been more important. When she had not been caught in the moment, Aki had always pretended to be oblivious to his advances.

Aki considered how keeping someone at a distance by pretending not to notice them was also a form of communication. She wondered if the message the Builders were trying to convey was similar to what Aki's reluctance said about her feelings toward Raul. She realized that, despite his motives, this really was likely to be one of her last conversations with Raul. Memories of embracing a different man, twenty years ago, flooded through her. Aki realized that keeping her distance was what the situation demanded, regardless of the fact that it was not what she really wanted.

"We have a big day tomorrow. On second thought, you should just get some rest too, Raul. Goodnight."

THE FIRST BURST of light appeared at a distance of seventeen thousand kilometers from the Builders' ship. The attack beam pointed in the direction of the closest missile, fired, and transformed the missile into a patch of superheated vapor. The image on the viewscreen filled with a blinding flash.

The observation program was still at work; the laser communication systems still transmitted data to the warheads. The missiles responded with their most recent positional information. One by one, the decoy warheads activated and were picked off, causing the attack beam to stop to recharge for a moment. The window was a brief one—no more than ten seconds. The missiles crossed the ten thousand kilometer mark. Six active warheads remained.

Another flash of light appeared as a warhead carrying a spiderweb was hit. The webbing vaporized into a plasma cloud. The remaining missiles scattered to avoid being hit. Two more flashes followed, both from the destruction of decoy warheads.

While the beam was destroying those decoys, two active warheads reached the five thousand–kilometer mark. Relative to their target, the missiles were traveling at fourteen kilometers per second. At that speed, they had to evade the attack beam for six more minutes to strike effectively.

The attack beam fired again, disintegrating one of the active warheads. Then it took out the last of the decoys. The final active warhead had three thousand kilometers to go and had nothing but its own maneuverability to distract the attack beam from homing in. On its final approach, the missile began to exhaust its fuel to increase its acceleration. Aki could hear the three minutes ticking inside her head.

The missile's angular speed relative to the alien vessel increased, evading the attack beam twice.

At the two thousand–kilometer mark, Aki could not help but feel conflicted. At that moment, the needs of humanity seemed greater than her desire to finally communicate with the Builders. And then the final warhead was disintegrated by the beam. All that remained were twisted fragments of spiderwebs. After a few moments, even those burned away. The only object in close proximity to the Builders was the *Phalanx*.

"Igor, get us out," Aki said.

"Already on it."

Unlike the missiles, the *Phalanx* was incapable of flying a high-speed zigzag pattern to avoid being hit. The *Phalanx* was highly maneuverable but had not been built to evade attacks. Since the ship had been headed toward the Builders, it took a few terrifying moments for the *Phalanx* to decelerate sufficiently to reverse course. Through a feed from the *Phalanx*'s telescope, Aki kept a close eye on the attack beam's base. The base began to move, but Aki realized that the base was not preparing to fire. Instead, the iris opened and the Torus initiated its nuclear drive system. The alien vessel resumed its deceleration as it headed toward Mercury.

"Stop the withdrawal," Aki commanded. "That looked closer than it was."

"A bit too close," Igor responded. "Looks like the UNSDF has one shot left. You think they'll actually fire the graser at the Builders?"

"We'll find out tomorrow."

Taking a long slow breath and bringing her eyes away from the monitors to look at the smooth white walls of her cocoon, Aki was surprised by how casually she had replied and the estrangement she felt from the dire predicament. Until now, the subject of firing the graser had been taboo aboard the *Phalanx*. Her thoughts were interrupted by a call from Raul.

"There's something I need but I can't explain to you. It's access to one of the communication lasers."

"There is one we're not using, but I'd like to know what you're planning."

"It would take too long. Just trust me on this puppy, okay? This is our last chance." The desperation in Raul's voice was clear, despite his attempt to keep his tone light. As commander, it was her duty to oversee the ship, but she had chosen Raul because she respected his commitment to finding a way to contact the Builders. She also, as much as the memory hurt, remembered how what seemed like a last chance had presented itself to her on the Island so many years ago.

"Fine. I am granting you access now."

"Hurrah!"

Aki opened the system administration screen to grant Raul access to communication laser number four. After a while, a large portion of the operations system was being monopolized by a program running under Raul's access code. The name of the program was NATALIA. Aki wondered if it was merely a tribute.

7 AM GMT

EVERYONE EXCEPT RAUL gathered in the crew room for breakfast. Aki could not help but notice how tired they looked. She removed slices of apple pie from the warming unit and handed them out.

"Igor, could you hand me a salt packet?" she asked.

Aki opened the packet of salt water, squeezed it onto her pie, and let the liquid soak into the crust.

"Commander, I'll never understand your culinary customs." Igor chuckled after he said it.

"The salt? Pie is too sweet for me first thing in the morning."

"How does adding salt make food less sweet?"

"I don't like sweetness as the only flavor. Everyone should try it," she said, handing the salt packet to Joseph.

"Why not?" Joseph said, letting some of the liquid soak into his pie. His bravery even extended to cuisine.

"How about you, Aida?"

Aida's face was pointed down at the table. Aida shook her head to indicate she was not interested.

"Would you like something other than apple? There's cherry too," Aki said, trying to raise Aida's spirits, though she knew it would take more than a different flavor of pie to stop her from moping.

"No, thanks. Apple's fine," Aida answered with little inflection.

"This isn't bad," Joseph said, his mouth full.

"See? In Japan, we also salt our watermelon, sometimes even cantaloupe."

"I'll save the salt for French fries, thanks," Igor said. He washed his salted pie down with coffee, then slid open the blind that covered the ship's window and asked, "What's the weather?"

Most of the view was blocked by the ship's solar shield. A bright point of light was in the lower corner of the window. "Look how close we're getting to Mercury. Isn't that amazing? It's almost as big as a half moon back home."

The others huddled close to see. Igor adjusted the light filter on the window. The image went from a glaring blur to a clear view of the half-lit planet. They could even see thin filaments of ring material being ejected into space near the planet's equator. When he increased the magnification of the filter, shadows on Mercury's surface and along the equatorial belt became visible.

The view was a limited one. Though she could not see the ships, Aki knew that five million kilometers away from the planet the UNSS *Thompson* and *Becquerel* were waiting for the Builders to complete their flyby. She could picture the commanders preparing the graser mounted on the *Thompson*.

"Can you see the earth from there?" Raul interrupted from his cocoon. Aki thought his voice sounded excited.

"The earth? Of course not, idiot. It's on the other side of the sun," Igor answered.

"Oh." There was a click as Raul shut his commlink to the room. Normally the button did not click; he must have slapped it hard.

No one spoke. Aki knew they had come to the inevitable conclusion that there was nothing left to do. The Contact Team had failed.

Igor placed his pie wrapper in the trash dispenser. In a business-like tone, he said, "After dinner we should enter a course to take us out of orbit and away from the line of fire of the graser. We don't want to get caught up in that mess."

Aida placed her face in her hands and let out a sigh. Aki pulled herself next to Aida and placed her hand on Aida's shoulder.

"We did all we could. We need to keep our chins up and see this through to the end."

"We haven't tried everything!" Raul said, leaping out of his cocoon into the crew room so quickly that he bumped Aida's chair. "Have a look!" He pressed the wall-mounted screen to display laser communication system number four. Several pulsating graphs appeared.

"Are we supposed to know what we're looking at?" Igor asked.

"What you're looking at, amigos, is the only chica I've ever loved: *Natalia*," Raul said. He was excited, even proud.

Aki swallowed hard. She knew where this was headed.

"I never gave up on her. I never did. I've been toiling, a little at a time, over the past few years. I accessed my computer at the ETICC and emulated Natalia on the *Phalanx*'s computer system."

"Could you say that in a way that lets me understand what you mean?" asked Aida.

"When I was an undergrad, I made this artificial intelligence system. I called her Natalia. The problem was that she wasn't able to interact with external intelligence. In other words, she couldn't talk to anybody and she wouldn't talk to anybody. There was a lot in her electronic head, but I was never able to figure out what she was thinking. Eventually, I gave up on her and quit, but I saved her internal state. I didn't really give up. She knows I didn't. I would bring up a virtual copy on my computer at work and fiddle around. You know, to make improvements. I've been thinking about her more and more these past few days with a hunch that she might be the answer we needed. I partitioned off some space on the *Phalanx*'s computer and emulated a virtual copy of her. She's been online and communicating since late last night."

"A hunch for what answer?" Aki asked.

"In today's battle, I was sure the Builders would attack us. But they didn't. They were deflecting a reasonably massive attack, but they didn't connect our presence to the combat."

"Maybe they were too busy vaporizing the missiles to consider why we were there," Igor said.

"Yesterday and today, the Builders faced an attack from a new enemy. Anyone paying attention would associate an unfamiliar attack in the neighborhood with the new ship that was also lurking in the area. We were just outside their attack zone flying at a velocity that matched theirs exactly. How much more blatantly obvious could we be?" Raul glanced at a moving bar on the graph.

"Natalia was not a part of that," Aki said.

"She's communicating with the Builders!" Raul tensed and if not for the zero gravity, Aki thought, may have started dancing. Everyone else started paying a lot more attention to Raul's graphs.

"I encoded Natalia's internal state and aimed a communication beam at the Builders' ship. I nearly lost control of my bladder when she got a response on the same frequency."

"What was the response?" Igor asked.

"That's what's crazy. I have no idea. I have no way of communicating with Natalia. The same goes for the Builders' reply. It's gibberish. I queried the *Phalanx*'s computer, but *nada*. But what's important is that we got a reply. Natalia and the Builders are similar, and they're somehow able to understand each other."

Raul opened a new window on the monitor. The monitor depicted the laser signal being received from the Builders as fluctuating bands. He toggled to a similar screen that showed communication being sent from Natalia to the Builders.

"The patterns look the same. They've found a common language. Aki, do you remember the first time you met Natalia?"

"Of course."

"Do you remember how Natalia reacted when you threatened to flip her switch?"

"She didn't react at all," Aki said, the images of the psychedelic colors flashing on the monitors in Raul's trailer seventeen years prior coming back to her. "I remember you yelling at me to stop, saying she was unable to interact with humans."

"That's right. If you have no self-awareness, you, by default, have no understanding of enemies or threats. The idea of somebody taking your life away is a concept that makes no sense. It's all so similar."

"Similar to what?" Aida asked.

"To the Builders not understanding that the *Phalanx* was a part of what was attempting to destroy them. The Builders are programmed to remove any obstacles. They see all the human actions that have happened so far as nothing more than objects in their way, even though we are life-forms engaging in rational actions. They have no concept of self or other. To them, we're no different than asteroids, comets, or space debris."

Aki recalled the conversation about capuchin monkeys with Jill Elsevier from that same day at the ETICC. The Builders lacked a theory of mind. "So they have ignored us but are interested in Natalia. I just wish we knew how they are making sense of those strange thought patterns of hers."

"That I don't know. But what's important here is not *how* they're doing it but rather that they're *able* to do it at all. It may be that they think she's part of them since they can't perceive her as a separate individual intelligence," Raul said. Then he smiled.

"The even bigger question here is if they *do* think that she's part of them, would they refrain from firing the attack beam if she approached?"

Aki looked around the room and noticed that everybody was staring at her, waiting for an answer. Their departure was scheduled for 10 PM GMT, which meant that Aki had exactly twelve hours to take action, provided she could decide on what action to take. Trying to first contact the UNSDF and explain the situation would take more time than Aki was willing to waste. "Because of what we have been through, we need to decide together. Let's vote. Do we sit it out and wait for our departure window or do we follow Raul's hunch and make an approach?"

"Let's do it," Igor said without hesitation.

"I'm in too. That's why we're here, right?" said Aida, looking less glum than she had all morning.

"Before I give my vote, I have a question," Joseph said. "Suppose they let us approach without firing on us. Does that mean we're back to the original plan of the commander, Raul, and I boarding their ship?"

"That's the only option. Now that the *Remora's* lost, contact requires an EVA," Aki said. Looking into his eyes, she could see that Joseph had no reservations. He even looked energized by the idea.

"Okay. It's my job to protect you. I go where you go."

"Then we're all in," Aki said.

"We go knock on their door and see what happens," Raul said. He had not stopped smiling.

"It's unanimous. The clock is ticking. Let's get to work." Aki had chosen her crew because she knew they were willing to go to any lengths to make contact. She had started mentally composing the note to the UNSDF before she had even began polling them.

CHAPTER 4: MIND TO MIND

ACT I: JULY 31, 2041
3 PM GMT

FLEET HEADQUARTERS GRANTED Aki's request without hesitation, proving that the UNSDF had written off the *Phalanx*. The UNSDF further agreed to extend the ship's departure time by three hours. This allowed more time for boarding, though Aki was concerned that cutting their departure closer would risk her ship being caught in the crossfire of dueling graser charges.

No alarms sounded at the fifteen thousand–kilometer mark. Tension knotted Aki's body. The ship passed through the ten thousand, five thousand, and then even the one thousand–kilometer mark without any of the security systems warning of an attack by the Builders. The *Phalanx* approached silently, the two ships linked by nothing but laser communication beams. Hardly any distance was left between them.

The *Phalanx* brought itself to within five hundred meters of the port side of the Builders' ship. The enormous reflector extending from the middle of the Torus reminded Aki of a holy chalice. Countless thorn-like spikes on the outside of the reflector pointed toward the center. Igor declared that the mysterious thorns were tiny lasers to ignite the propellant pellets. If Igor was right, tiny granular particles were projected to the center of the reflector and fired on by the lasers in order to cause a nuclear fusion reaction. This would mean that the atoms in the pellets were accelerated to nearly

1 percent the speed of light before bouncing off the hundred-meter wide reflector. Presumably, that pulsing cycle would occur around three hundred times per second.

"If we could get a sample of the materials used to build this reflector, even disregarding its capabilities, there would be massive overnight advances in engineering. I would love to move in for a better look, but it would be suicide to approach that reflector with the engine operating," Igor said.

Extending through the Torus to the back of the engine was a smooth and seamless gray rod about one hundred meters long. The crew had observed its length decreasing over the past three days. The rod was considered the ship's fuel supply.

"The nanomachines must be converting that material into fuel pellets, then delivering the pellets to the engine," Igor said.

Six spokes extended from the center of the Torus to its inner rim. The spokes were two meters wide—as fine as thread in proportion to the rest of the Torus.

"I don't see any airlocks. There aren't even windows," Raul said.

"It is a giant automated factory," Aki said.

"Hell, without any windows, maybe the Builders don't know they've almost reached their destination. I suppose they find windows to be nothing but structural weakness." It was a further reminder that the Builders would stop at nothing to reach their goal. Aki programmed several mini-probes that had been removed from the *Remora* before that craft had been destroyed. A few minutes later, twelve pebble-like objects were ejected by the *Phalanx*'s external launcher. Small thrusters on each probe fired, directing each pebble to its destination. The mini-probes affixed themselves to different points on the Torus and began emitting synchronized ultrasound pulses to determine whether the interior was hollow. The data from the scan was sent back to the *Phalanx*. After a few minutes of computer analysis, a rough image of the Torus's interior appeared on a screen in Aki's cocoon.

"The power of their nanotech—it's astonishing," Raul said.

"The only hollow space is in the Torus. Everything else is solid or filled with what looks like a foamy liquid."

An estimated cross section of the Torus, based on the data from the mini-probes, revealed a circle forty meters in diameter. The external surface was smooth and gray with occasional swollen humps. Even from this closer perspective, there were no signs of windows, airlocks, or maintenance panels. The close-up inspection showed seamless joints where the spokes connected to the center and the rim.

"Look at the design. Incredible! I can't see a single joint where pieces are fused. They used nanotechnology to grow this in a single piece, one molecule at a time," Igor said.

"You're right. It's definitely not modular. It's one massive form with no connection points; it's a living organism," Raul said.

"Does that mean there is no special entrance for human visitors? I guess we will have to punch our own hole. Contact Team, airlock in five minutes. We will figure out how to proceed while we get ready." Aki had meant for her words to sound lighter than they came across. She was trying to balance unavoidable tension with the need for vigilance. She could not help but think that the risks were so great that caution would not change a thing. *If they want to kill us, they will kill us. If it comes to that, I just want to know why they are going to do it before it happens.*

———◆·❖·◆———

Moments later, Aki, Raul, and Joseph emerged from their cocoons and stepped into their space suits. They set the internal pressure for six-tenths of an atmosphere and did not bother to connect spare air tanks. Their suits were equipped with data screens—visible from inside the helmet—that were identical to the screens in their cocoons. The systems were operated visually, also responding to verbal commands and tongue-manipulated toggles. The upper-right corner of each display showed a clock counting down to the *Phalanx*'s launch time.

"Six hours and twenty-seven minutes until the launch sequence begins," stated Igor, testing the communication systems inside the suits.

"Roger that. Raul and Joseph, you ready?"

They said they were.

"Opening the airlock," Aki said.

All the air in the small chamber was removed. The outer door opened, revealing the Builders' ship. It looked close enough to touch. One by one, they floated away from the *Phalanx* and toward the alien vessel. Raul and Joseph had large tool kits attached to their suits. All three members of the Contact Team fired their thrusters in unison, skimming along the length of the *Phalanx*. The helmet visors darkened just before they passed in front of the solar shield to protect their eyes from the blazing light. The Builders' ship was directly in front of them, too large to fit in their helmets' limited field of view.

"Thanks to Natalia, the Builders see the *Phalanx* as an extension of themselves. What about us?" Joseph asked.

"I've added feeds from the *Phalanx*'s external cameras to Natalia's primary visual field. I hope they see us through her eyes," Raul said.

The Contact Team floated alongside the Torus. It passed beneath them in a blur, rotating at a speed of nearly eighty kilometers per hour. Grabbing on to the Torus from where they were was too dangerous to attempt. Gradually, the center of the ship came closer.

"Wait," said Joseph. He moved ahead, then attached himself to the inner end of one of the spokes. He rotated along with the spoke, slipping out of view. Forty-three seconds later, he was back where he had started. During that time, Joseph had looped a tether rope thinner than a shoelace around the spoke and secured it into place. The reel connected to Joseph's suit contained a total length of three hundred meters.

Aki and Raul held Joseph's arms as they passed the tether through the carabiners and clamps attached to their suits. The artificial gravity created by the rotation increased with each step. They walked back out toward the Torus, walking the spoke as if it were a balance beam. At first, they used their thrusters to propel themselves. After the halfway point, the centrifugal force was strong enough that they had to use the tether to rappel down to the Torus. There was enough Coriolis force for them to touch down softly on the Torus and remain there without floating away. Even though local gravity was only three-tenths of a G, it was the strongest sensation of gravity the crew had felt in a long while.

The surface was less smooth than it had appeared to be from a distance. It had the texture of mortar, conveniently providing the friction they needed to walk without slipping. Nonetheless, the dizzying effect of the *Phalanx* and the stars spinning above was enough to cause Aki to drop to all fours.

They heard a rumble through their helmet speakers. Startled, they realized it was the echo of their footsteps reverberating inside the Torus that was being picked up by the external mics on their suits.

"I bet we just triggered a burglar alarm," Raul said.

"We can hear our steps because the Torus is conducting it directly into our boots. An alarm would almost certainly be too quiet to be conducted by this material." The sound reminded Aki of an exercise she did in elementary school where the students listened to tree trunks with stethoscopes. Her teacher had said that what the students heard was the sound of the tree sucking water from the ground. Aki had believed it.

Joseph and Raul secured their tool kits to the surface material with high bond tape. Joseph removed a collapsible airlock from his kit and began assembling an airtight dome tent with a base four meters wide. He adhered the base to the Torus using a quick-drying resin.

"I hope this stuff sticks to whatever this thing is," Joseph said.

"The tape seems to be holding. We will go with what we have," Aki said.

Once all three were inside the tent, they closed the hermetic seal. They filled their dome with nitrogen to a pressure of three-tenths of an atmosphere. They had no idea what the internal pressure was, though any level would be better than a vacuum. Aki took an axe and tapped the surface three times. No response. She tried again, applying more force.

"Anybody home?" Raul asked. Aki knew he was joking but noted the trepidation in his voice.

Joseph assembled a large boring tool, a miniature version of what had been used for crude oil drilling before most of the earth's oil had been depleted. The drill's tip had a diamond chip two centimeters wide. When fully extended, the drill could penetrate to a depth of ten meters.

"Here we go." After making his warning, Joseph pulled the trigger. As soon as the drill started, it skipped across the hull of the ship. It did not even make a scratch. Two more tries led to the same result.

"This material is harder than diamond. Do you think they would sell us the patent?" Joseph said, embarrassed even though the strategy had considered the possibility that this surface would be hard to penetrate.

"Try the plasma torch tip," Aki said, wanting them to stay loose but concerned that false levity might erupt into fear.

"If they're waiting for us on the other side of this wall, I hope they don't attack us because we sliced our way in," Raul said.

"It's not like we didn't try knocking." When Joseph spoke, Aki could sense his hard resolve, even through his suit.

Aki had dreamed of making first contact with intelligent beings her whole life, but none of the scenarios had started with breaking and entering. The lack of interest—one could not even call it disdain—in communication on the part of the Builders continued to frustrate her. The torch-driven drill cut through the surface as if it were wood. After two meters, the resistance against the bit was gone. The drill moved in and out freely.

"We broke through," said Joseph. "It's thinner than we thought."

A protective cover slid down over the drill, allowing them to remove it and insert a sensor while still maintaining an airtight seal. The image sent from the tiny camera appeared on their helmet screens. The first few centimeters contained a clear substance, followed by a foamy material. As the probe moved deeper, the bubbles in the foam grew larger.

A dark hole appeared in front of the camera. As the camera passed through, the image went completely black. It appeared to be a chamber too large and empty for the dim light on the sensor to illuminate.

Joseph read out the composition of the air tested, "Forty-two percent nitrogen, 56 percent oxygen, 2 percent other inert gases. Air pressure is 43/100 of an atmosphere. Once we become acclimated to the low pressure, the sensors say we can breathe in there, disregarding the fact that we would fill the atmosphere with carbon dioxide quickly, since it's unlikely that there will be vegetation."

"Doesn't look like there are any aliens in this room. Can we cut a door for ourselves?" Raul asked.

"This place is as good as any," Aki said. Hanging out on the side of the Builders' ship could not be much safer than going inside.

After equalizing the pressure in the dome to that inside the vessel, Joseph cut a circular hole in the surface. The process took nearly an hour. Even with the low artificial gravity, Joseph was surprised by how light the material was and nearly rocked backward on his heels when he made the lift. Raul shined his light into the hole, the beam reflecting off an object several meters below. The space was packed full of cells reminiscent of honeycombs, each about one meter wide.

"Send the sensor down into those cells to see what the cells are made of?" Joseph asked.

"No time. We go in and find out for ourselves," Aki said. She was nervous and excited. She could not even begin to imagine what they would find. She recalled how much volume there was to cover inside the Torus, making her even more anxious to locate whatever being or entity was in charge and try to communicate before time ran out.

Aki was given the honor of being first to set foot inside. Joseph adhered a communication device to the edge of the hole and connected one end of the fiber-optic cable from a reel attached to his suit. Since radio signals would not be likely to penetrate the hull, this would allow an open channel with the *Phalanx* and send back a video feed and sensor readouts. The audio and video could be plugged directly into the Worldunity Network. The feeds could be seen on Earth in as close to real time as the vast distance from the planet allowed.

Joseph tied another tether line to the portable airlock. In an emergency, the tether could reel them back out quickly. Aki looked at her two crewmates and gave a nod, then made a final check of the *Phalanx*'s camera to make sure there were not any sudden changes to the Builders' ship's orientation or surface.

"Entering the vessel," she said. She had meant to use a more profound phrase, but the plan had shifted so many times that she could not even remember the ones she had written down. Aki lowered herself several meters into the hole. Reconfirming that the air was breathable, she allowed her sampler to take in a trace quantity. She breathed the ship's air cautiously. A sensor found a hint of trimethylamine, which Aki tasted as a hint of ammonia.

The next words spoken would be remembered by all for many decades, as they emanated from the sensor.

<SMELL: RAW FISH>

She lowered herself into the honeycomb structure. The hexagonal cells were covered with a transparent film. The cells were full of a murky glaze. A large yellow object was beneath them. Aki stepped on one of the walls dividing the cells, gradually adding weight, making sure it would support her. She let go of the tether, then indicated for Raul and Joseph to follow. They joined her and stood in awe. Honeycomb structures arced around them on both sides, all the way to the ceiling, nearly filling the inside of the Torus's tube above them. Multiple bridges ran vertically and horizontally along the inner wall—thin, varied, and meandering like veins under skin.

Oddly enough, the scene resembled an alien horror movie the crew had all watched together on their way to the rendezvous point. She knew Raul was thinking the same thing but hoped that he did not feel the need to verbalize the thought.

"Damn, it's just like that movie we watched. Don't look at them, or they might jump up and eat our faces off! It looks like they hired Giger as their interior decorator," Raul said, as if on cue.

"Will you keep the *Alien* references to yourself, please?" Aki snapped.

"Sorry."

No one spoke for at least a minute. The sensor finally broke the reverent silence.

<SMELL: STRONGER>

"Upper part of their living quarters, like an attic? Maybe that is why nobody's here."

"Maybe this is the nursery and these are the offspring. Or it's the pantry and we're looking at the canned goods," Raul said. "We need the living room so we can say hello to whatever lives here."

They walked along the inside of the Torus in the direction of its rotation. In the distance, where the floor curved upward and was blocked by the ceiling, they could see a faint green light. Moving closer, they noticed the green light came from a hole in the floor about two meters across. There was no ramp or stairs. Raul guessed it was some sort of an air vent. Aki allowed her air sampler to take another small sample of the atmosphere.

<SMELL: BARN, MAPLE SYRUP>

"What does a barn even smell like?" Raul asked sarcastically.

The Contact Team approached the edge of the hole. Aki crouched, peering over the side. What she saw below looked like a deranged jungle gym. Countless gray branches extended in all directions from the central node. The gray arms were porous on the surface, like coral, and as thick as Aki's torso. Seemingly lacking a consistent design, functionality, or even shape, the branches veered in all directions through the chamber. The cells pressed together tightly like a cluster of bubbles.

Aki attached an anchor to the edge of the hole and then connected a tether cable. She lowered herself down to the closest branch. Despite her thick boots, she could feel the texture of the surface beneath her feet. The way the surface wobbled, Aki felt as though she were standing on the back of a whale. She was grateful that the hard-shell suits had been reengineered to be much more flexible. Once her footing was stable, Aki looked around the cavernous room.

The branches twisted in all directions, forming irregularly shaped frames. This created an odd optical effect that made Aki feel like she was standing inside tessellations, uneven planes that lacked variety, homogenous everywhere she looked. She was unable to see more than about twenty meters in any direction. The pale green light emanated from the walls of the chamber. Given the very weak gravity, Aki was spatially disoriented and felt dizzy.

Something stirred in her peripheral vision. Then she saw nothing.

She replayed the last few seconds from the helmet camera's recording. The motion appeared to have occurred outside of the camera's field of view.

"Everything all right?" Joseph asked.

"Sorry for the silence. Everything is fine. You can come down."

Raul made his way toward her.

"Do you know what this looks like?"

"Something out of yet another cheesy twentieth-century space horror movie?" Aki asked.

"Actually, it was a rather respectable film involving Isaac Asimov. To me, this all looks like a living neural network. If I didn't know any better I'd say the reason we're not seeing any Builders is because this is a Builder. Well, its brain, at least."

"If this were the density of its neural network, it would not be the fastest thinker around," Aki said.

"Maybe it's not in a rush. It has time to siesta," Raul said.

Aki adhered another reel of fiber-optic cable to the branch beneath her feet. She connected the end to the long run of cable that they had been adding to since entering the ship.

"Where do we go?" she asked.

"Keep going...uh, downward," Raul answered. "What do you even call directions on something like this? Spinward?" He pointed in a direction.

"Good as any. Let's do it," she said.

They made their way along the network of branches that twisted through the chamber.

<SMELL: STRONG, SWAMPY>

"The interface design of these sensors is horrible! Does it read Edgar Allan Poe too?" Raul exclaimed. He sighed and glanced around. "I don't know what's worse—being human and knowing we're crawling around inside an alien's brain, or being an alien knowing that three humans are stomping inside your head," Raul said, stepping past her and lowering himself down further.

Aki was concerned that Raul's defense mechanisms might dull his reactions. She was concerned that he was crossing the line between staying calm and becoming complacent.

"Stop. Wait," he said.

"What do you see?" Joseph asked, noticing the fear in Raul's voice.

"It's not the brain, unless this cobra is slithering along its axons..."

EVEN THOUGH THE image from Raul's helmet camera was traveling at the speed of light, it took several minutes to reach Earth. When it arrived, millions of viewers who were watching his feed shrieked.

Moving as quickly as she could to Raul's location, Aki thought this was it: what she had been waiting for her entire adult life. She had trouble breathing.

Lifting one end up from the ground, the creature looked to be four meters long. A bulbous appendage at the tip appeared to be its head. The face was covered with a shiny pink material that looked like exposed muscle tissue. Its appendage was crowned by a ring of white fur that extended away from the face to cover the upper side of the rest of its body. The fur was wet and matted down with a transparent and viscous paste.

Two enormous eyes, resembling those of a Philippine tarsier, bulged, unable to turn in their sockets. Every ten seconds or so, its eyelids would close and slowly open again. No other openings in its face were visible. It had no neck. Its furry mane surrounded its face and extended back, connecting directly at what would be the equivalent of shoulders. It looked like a headdress depicted on a sarcophagus. The upper portion of the body below the face was flat and wide, similar to a cobra, as Raul had described it.

It had two thin arms the length of human legs, each containing two sets of joints resembling elbows and wrists. At the ends of each arm were four long, lithe fingers, one of which appeared opposable, like a thumb. Its arms and elbows were folded inward with its hands joined at its chest.

The upper part of its torso had several bones pushing from under its coat. The bulges could have been shoulder blades and collar bones, to the extent that either descriptive term made much sense when applied to such alien anatomy. Aki wished for a moment that she had studied up on zoology, veterinary medicine, anything that might help her make sense of it. In the center of the Builder's chest was a vertical opening that most likely served as a mouth. To the left and right of the orifice were smaller vertical slits, two on each side, like gills on a fish. The area below its chest resembled hardened scales, which continued down to the stomach. Everything below was pressed against the ground, becoming thinner as it extended back, giving the creature a serpentine appearance. The upper side was covered with the moist white fur that extended down from its head. It was about three times as wide as it was high, like a large, furred tongue. The creature wore no clothing or accoutrements.

Slithering from one branch to the next, it gradually approached Raul. Joseph lowered himself down and stepped into its path. Joseph had not carried weapons, for fear of sending the wrong impression to the Builders, but the Marine was skilled in close quarter combat and other martial arts.

"Try not to make moves that appear hostile," Aki said.

"The fact that we've broken in may have already painted us as unfriendly." Raul stood still.

The alien life-form continued closer. In the last few meters it veered right onto a separate branch, sidewinding its way alongside the three of them, most likely considering them intruders. Then, as if they were not even there, the creature continued along its way and left.

The Contact Team followed. Another being emerged from below. Its fur had a yellower tinge, but otherwise appeared identical to the first. Aki turned on her external speaker, the volume low.

"Hello," she said in as friendly a tone as she could muster. She extended her arms wide. The swollen eyes of the creature lolled in Aki's direction. It looked right through her. Then, just as the first had done, the long snake ignored their presence and left.

"Our first intergalactic encounter and we get blown off like panhandlers on a street corner. You think these dudes built this flying doughnut?" Raul asked with as much levity as he could muster. Aki saw sweat dripping down his face.

"Its developed head and opposable thumbs indicate tool-making, intelligence," Aki said. "And we have seen two now. They are social animals. To one another anyway."

"Yeah, but what's up with the cold shoulder? Now I'm convinced that these guys must be related to Natalia."

"They have been ignoring us for decades. I do not find it surprising. Consistent, methodical behavior is a trait of advanced intelligence." Aki asked the *Phalanx* for a status report on the alien vessel. There had been no changes to the ship's movement.

"The exobiologists should rethink the implied meaning of extraterrestrial intelligence," Raul said, calmer now.

"If our distant ancestors had not made the evolutionary jump from living in trees in the lush jungle to roaming the dry savannah, we may never have started standing upright, much less conceived of novel tools or forming complex cultures. If this is their living room, I'm wondering how they missed that transition," Joseph said.

"Their home world does not have a savannah." Aki moved more quickly, trying to catch up with the large furry snakes.

"If they were as intelligent as people, they would know enough to wear clothes," Raul said.

"Curiosity goes hand in hand with intelligence," Joseph said, keeping pace with Aki. "It looks like their apathy is a fact we're going to have to accept. I had originally thought that if they had no interest, it was because they were completely different from us. Those creatures may have looked odd, maybe even grotesque, but they aren't all that different."

Aki agreed. They were obviously organic beings. There was no part of their physiology that could not be likened to some part of an organism from Earth. It was also clear from the atmosphere in their ship that their metabolic system was also similar.

"Are we going to assume those fuzzy worms are the Builders?" Raul asked.

"We should for now," Aki answered, trying not to look at the clock ticking down on the screen inside her helmet.

AKI, RAUL, AND Joseph continued lowering themselves through the jungle of branches until it ended abruptly against the curved interior surface of the Torus. On the inside of the Torus's outer wall, small sandy beaches were surrounded by dark pools, small dunes with pools of black liquid undulating beneath them. The jungle was ten meters overhead, hanging inverted arches forming a hollow tunnel that curved along the circumference of the Torus in both directions.

"This looks like the bottom," Aki said, peering down at the beach. "Do you think they will attack us here now that we are out in the open?"

"The giant slugs? Hardly, but it would look cool on video," Raul said, though the question had been directed at Joseph.

Aki found a branch that dipped close to the surface and climbed toward the beach. She was turned around enough that she had no idea if she was going ecliptic north, ecliptic south, or some other direction. The sandy substance coating the interior of the Torus hull was lightly packed, like diatomaceous earth. Dust like silica scraped away with her steps, soft enough that she left footprints where she walked. The ponds were anywhere from about two to ten meters wide and no more than a meter deep.

Lying in groups of two and three along the shorelines of the two ponds closest to them were about two dozen Builders, each partially submerged in the dark liquid. The Builders were stretched out on their stomachs, resting their upper bodies on their forearms as if they were sphinxes. They made no noises, no movements. The highly sensitive microphones in the team's helmets were able to pick up intermittent noises that sounded like rasping, labored breaths. Aki could not tell if those faint noises were being made by the Builders.

"The pool deck on a luxury liner. Bet they used a photo of this beach on the brochure when they recruited for the six hundred–year cruise," Raul said.

Aki looked closely at the builders, trying to discern differences between individuals that might suggest sexual dimorphism or age-related physical development. She could distinguish nothing beyond slight variations in size. The shortest ones were about three meters long. She wondered if they were the youngest, even though she had a hard time imagining the youth of any species being so lethargic. One of the Builders stirred from what Aki thought was sleep, turning around to fully submerse itself into the oily pond. It reappeared on the opposite side, crawled from the liquid—then, stretching toward the branches, slowly pulled itself into the canopy before disappearing into the jungle.

Aki, Raul, and Joseph began walking along the direction of rotation.

"Should we walk the full length and see what we find?" Aki asked. "I wonder if this beach stretches the entire circumference of the Torus."

"I'm guessing it's nearly a kilometer loop," Joseph said.

Facing Joseph, Raul said, "If you can get me home, I'll bet a plate of roast beef that it's all ponds and beached Builders the whole way around."

"I'll take your bet. Because they are noncommunicative, understanding their space may be the only opportunity to understand them," Aki said.

"So, how many Builders have we passed so far?" Raul asked his sensor array.

<TOTAL *131*>

"Assume, just for kicks, an even distribution of Builders in the liveable areas of the ship. What's the crew complement?"

<*APPROXIMATELY 940 ENTITIES*>

After about forty minutes, they noticed their own footprints ahead of them and the fiberoptic cable running down from the branches. Their mapping system also indicated they had returned to their starting point.

Joseph had counted a total of 847 Builders.

"What do we do now? Is there anything more to this ship than a cattle ranch?" Raul asked.

Aki would have reminded him to keep his cool again, but a message arrived from UNSDF Fleet Headquarters.

<*PROCEED WITH PHYSICAL CONTACT.*
PERFORM ULTRASOUND SCAN. >

The three looked at each other, wondering what would happen when they actually touched a Builder.

"HEY, ALICE, GOOD kitty or snake. Why doesn't she purr or hiss or something?" Raul asked, reaching out to the closest of four Builders. He had named them Alice, Betty, Catherine, and Diane, even though they had not yet determined whether or not the Builders had genders.

Alice was of average size and was selected because a light brown patch on its back made Alice easy to differentiate from the other Builders. Aki and Joseph guarded Raul as he placed his handheld scanner on Alice's back. He slid the scanner down the upper part of Alice's body, and the results were displayed on the helmet monitors. Other than minor twitches, the creature lay still with its eyes closed during the entire process.

"They have spines. That looks like a heart with two ventricles. Three sacks behind the mouth cavity. Stomachs? Pair of lungs. Do you notice anything that might be vocal cords? Wait a minute, is that *metal*?" Aki spotted a rod about five centimeters long in the spinal cord behind the chest. A muscle fiber extended from one end of the rod. The other end of the rod connected directly to the spinal cord.

"There's one here, too, in the lower body," Joseph said. "Another in the head."

The skull was spherical with two holes for eye sockets. It had a brain similar to a human's but the structure was not hemispherical. The rod in the head went to the top of the skull, ending just below the skin.

"The two upper ones are connected to the spine and the brain. It must be some kind of bio-integrated neural implant. My guess is that they're being monitored or controlled—maybe both. Maybe that's why they're ignoring us," Raul said.

"For what purpose?" Joseph asked.

"Probably because they're being transported. What if they're just cargo, no more intelligent than a herd of cattle? The rod implants keep them sedated during the journey to ensure that they survive. The ship's programmed to take care of their environment."

"Possible, but if the ship's environmental control system is that advanced, it does not make sense that the ship would allow us to enter and interact with these creatures without intervening to protect them," Aki said.

"Chalk that up as another unsolved Builder mystery for now. I could scan another one, but we know we'll see the same result," Raul said.

Aki wondered what it would take to provoke a response from them. "How long does one of these things live? If the ship was en route for six hundred years, these must be the descendants of the original bunch. It would be easier and safer to just send fertilized eggs that they could incubate just before the arrival. Given what they're capable of, that would be child's play," she said.

"Why not just send the DNA? Since their nanobots can build almost anything, they could grow them from DNA samples once they arrived." None of the explanations made sense to Aki. There had to be a reason for the live transport of these beings, even if their minds were being controlled by technology. The Builders, Aki was convinced, were rational actors engaging in goal-oriented behaviors. "Their consciousness must serve some purpose during the voyage," Aki said.

"Then maybe we're looking at the meat locker. These must not be the Builders," Raul said.

"If that is true, who eats them? This habitat looks too meticulously designed to be a cattle pen," Aki said.

"Maybe they taste better when they live in luxury," Raul said.

"Sprawled in the water like a Roman bath, my guess is that they are intelligent but so deep in thought they do not notice us." Aki meant to continue her musing but a warning appeared on their monitors.

<DROP IN TRANSMISSION RATE—NODE 00-01>

"Somebody's standing on our cable," Raul said. He was trying a joke, but his fear was evident in his voice once again.

<TRANSMISSION DISABLED—NODE 00-01>

"The cable was severed at the first segment, back at the airlock," Raul said.

"How?" Aki asked.

"No idea. That cable can withstand four tons of force."

Panic shot through Aki's body. "Let's get there, see what's going on."

Moving quickly, they used their mapping system to retrace their steps through the forest and back to the entrance of the holding pen environment. Climbing the tether, they found the closest end of the first cable. It was still connected to the second cable and showed no abnormalities.

"Must be farther up," Raul said.

They followed the cable back toward the hexagonal cells. Below the hole Joseph had cut in the hull, they found the severed cable next to a puddle of gray liquid. The hole was no longer there. Where their door had been was a different shade of gray than the surrounding area, but the wall had been regrown.

"It's like the nanotech fur. It grew back to seal the hole," Raul said. Aki could not help but notice the horror in his voice.

"Contact Team to *Phalanx*. Do you read? Igor?" Joseph said into the wireless communication system. After a full two minutes, there was still no reply.

"With the plasma torch outside in the airlock, the only chance for escape will be when the graser hits. Which is going to do a lot more than just cut a hole," Raul said. He held his hand in front of his helmet. "At least we're not melting, d-d-despite contact with the outer surface of the hull. It must not possess the same c-c-orrosive property the Vert-Ring ha-has."

Aki noticed the stammer that had become more and more evident as Raul had kept speaking. "Back to the beach, follow me," she said. "The only chance we have is explaining our situation to the Builders."

"W-what if they aren't the Builders?" Raul asked. Through his glass, his face had gone pale.

"I insist you follow my lead and go with my assumption. Come on."

Joseph too seemed concerned and a bit lost. Aki glanced up at her own monitor and saw that time was running out. The graser would be fired in less than three hours.

WHEN THE CABLE had been cut, the observation cameras had detected the movement of the portable airlock. The airlock was flung from the spinning Torus, revealing that the entrance hole had been sealed. The equipment that had been taped to the ship's surface sank into the hull without a trace.

As soon as Igor realized that the communications line had been cut, he switched on the emergency wireless communicator and sent an automated call that was programmed to repeat until it was answered. The only message that appeared was the error that the connection had dropped at the first node, indicating that the disruption had severed communication.

Igor also sent a message to the rest of the fleet and UNSDF Headquarters:

Portable airlock destroyed, equipment inside disintegrated, and entry hole in the hull sealed. Request immediate instructions on how to proceed with rescue operation for extracting Contact Team.

Igor knew all too well that there was nothing that he or the rest of the fleet could do. Even the closest ship was far enough away that it would take two and a half minutes for his message to reach them. There was no ship close enough to be able to deliver the plasma torch they would need to cut a new hole for a rescue. Even if a ship were closer, the *Phalanx*, along with the Builders' ship, was still traveling at ninety kilometers per second, making docking and delivery impossible. The UNSDF had not built or deployed any other *Remora*-class craft.

"Aida, see if you can come up with how we can hack into that hull. Double-check that we're out of plasma torches."

"The spare equipment kit that had the second plasma torch was taped to the side and just vanished, but I'll double check, just to be sure."

Igor admonished himself for agreeing that the extra equipment should go with the away team. With the portable airlock as their base camp, all the spare tools had been stored there. At the time, it had seemed like the emergency supplies should be close at hand.

"Anything else on board that could produce intense heat? What about the engine?" Igor asked.

"Once we cut through, we would irradiate the interior. They would never make it out, even in their space suits. Besides, with the rotational speed of the Torus, we wouldn't be able to target one spot long enough for us to burn through," Aida said. Igor heard her clinical detachment and the sadness underneath.

They discussed modifying the communications laser but realized that it would not be enough even if they could maximize the beam's concentration. It was designed for carrying a communications signal, not for slicing through metal.

"If only we had some sort of explosive," Igor said out loud to himself.

One of the committee members had said that the Builders' technology, so far beyond human knowledge that it seemed like magic, was most likely advanced enough to detect whether or not the *Phalanx* had any weapons on board. Many people had opposed the idea of the Contact Team, criticizing the ship's enormous budget. Some felt that the prohibitive expense of an extra ship could compromise the attack on the Builders. To mitigate the concern, since its mission was solely to attempt a first contact, a series of compromises had determined that the *Phalanx* would carry no weapons in order to best express the peaceful intentions of Aki's mission.

Igor wished Raul had stayed behind on the *Phalanx* because Raul might have been able to have Natalia explain the situation to the Builders. It was upsetting. Igor searched through Raul's files for some sort of documentation that explained how the AI worked but soon realized that, without Raul, it would be impossible for Natalia to communicate with the Builders in a way that was comprehensible to humans.

Knowing that he had to relocate the *Phalanx* to a safer spot so it would be clear of the attack, Igor watched the last few seconds of the countdown tick away.

"Time's up. We have to leave now to guarantee that we're clear of the blast zone."

"And just leave them?" Aida asked. "I know it's what we're trained to do. Can we live with ourselves?"

"We don't have a choice. If the ship isn't destroyed by the graser, we can come back and attempt another rendezvous. Aki had to leave one behind and came back into space knowing the risk. Even if we didn't have enough fuel to get back to Earth on our own, a gravitational assist from Mercury would get us there eventually as long as our supplies held out." Igor began the thruster sequence required to take them a safe distance away from the Builders. Once the *Phalanx* was pointed away from the alien vessel, the NERVA III engines fired, carrying the *Phalanx* away from the Builders' trajectory toward Mercury.

AKI WAS CERTAIN that the *Phalanx* had left. She could not confirm the departure from inside the alien vessel, but the deadline had passed. Remaining this close to the Builders' ship with the graser looming would be pure suicide. It would have been wrong for the *Phalanx* to remain. Knowing they were on their own, Aki, Joseph, and Raul had a new sense of purpose. Because the graser would fire in less than forty minutes, they were determined to push for solutions until they ran out of time.

They returned to the first black pool. Alice and her three companions were still lounging on the shore. Aki had her crew make every attempt to get Alice to respond to their presence. They petted and rubbed the creature's hands, face, and belly, and tried stimulating her with different permutations of light and sound. Eventually, Aki had even instructed Joseph to punch Alice several times, yet the Builder had shown no reaction whatsoever. Sometime after they had finished their attempts, Alice rose from the beach, soaked briefly in the dark liquid, then crawled back onto the shore. It was unclear whether their actions had registered with her at all.

"Anybody have ideas?" Aki asked.

"I'm tapped out," Joseph said.

Aki looked at Raul. He was busy interacting with the computer and screen in his suit, distracted and lost in thought.

"This room is filled with a quiet noise. I thought it was static or white noise but it's not. There's information embedded in it. Without a quantum computer to use entanglement to crunch the data, there's no hope of decoding it from here," he muttered. "Spectral analysis shows sub-millimeter waves at a frequency of six gigahertz coming from these beasts' bodies. There are filaments along the branches that act as booster antennae. The electromagnetic waves are everywhere. Similar signals came from Mercury and the Rings, but we could never make sense of them." Aki wondered if Raul even knew that he was talking out loud.

"If they're the ones flying this ship, this could be utopia to them, something even more comfortable and fulfilling than their home planet," Joseph said.

"It is a dystopia for us," Aki said.

"Maybe happiness for them is right here, lying in this meditative state, deep in thought, free from worry or doubt," Joseph said.

"You would think they would have some music playing," Aki said, frustration getting the best of her.

"Music creates a relationship between Mozart and Salieri," Joseph said.

"Maybe their civilization reached its apex, and they realized that all they needed for true happiness was simply to exist and produce offspring...until something forced them to leave their home world, never able to return." After speaking, Aki realized that he may have sounded naïve or idealistic, but Joseph's ideas rang true for her. She had to slow down. She had to find a way to make the best she could of the situation.

"The Builders came to our solar system to build a Garden of Eden on Mercury?" Raul asked.

"Their nanotech takes care of their needs, even their interstellar migration. All they need is to live and reproduce. Maybe the purpose of their technology is to sustain their lives in our galaxy," Joseph said.

"And the purpose of our tech is to destroy them before they succeed," Aki said. She could not help but empathize with the vehemence in his voice, but she knew differently. "That is what we need to avoid. Being human does not mean we get to run the show," she said.

"But it's destructive. No matter how advanced they are, their indifference is causing us great harm in the end," Joseph said.

"I prefer not to look at it that way."

"With all due respect, I think you've lost your perspective. Frankly, all this time you've assumed they were benevolent and that our encounter with them would be nothing but shared joy and wonder. Do you think it was a coincidence that the Builders happened to be the first alien intelligence that humanity interacted with?"

"What do you mean, Joseph?" Aki asked.

"We know there are at least two intelligent civilizations in this tiny and forgotten corner of the galaxy. That means tens if not hundreds of thousands of other civilizations in our galaxy alone. Nonetheless, the first one we met killed well over a billion people. Isn't it possible that the benevolent species are the ones staying at home minding their own business and the ones traveling from star to star are destructive and imperialistic, with no regard to whatever life they snuff out?"

Aki glared at Joseph, astonished.

"Is that what you've thought all along? Is that why you wanted to be part of the Contact Team?"

"I'm not an assassin; I'm also not a welcome wagon. I will, however, say that I'm skeptical of their intentions. Like you, I'm here because I want to know why they came, ma'am."

"Oh," Aki said. She wondered if she had lost perspective after all. Had she made judgments based on what she wanted instead of based on the facts? Embarrassed by the accusation that hung in the air, Aki realized that she had not lost touch with her objectivity. She had acted on intuitions about the Builders that only she had been privy to. After all, Aki Shiraishi had been the first person to set foot on the Island. She was the one whose intuition led to the discovery of how to destroy the Ring. She was the one who had realized that humanity needed to rebuild the Vert-Ring.

In her heart, Aki knew that since the moment she had squinted into the telescope and thought she saw a tower, a voice within her had guided her thoughts and actions, providing special insight into the Builders. If there was a way out, trusting that voice was what was going to get them through.

"The signals are too complicated to crack. But there's too much data coming and going for these to be livestock in a pasture. I'm convinced these are the Builders," Raul said, interrupting Aki's thoughts.

"You're sure now?" Aki asked.

"Positive. The downstream source from Alice's implant is transmitting enough information to fill a library every few hours. That's too excessive for the only thoughts in her head to be daydreams of grazing in grassy pastures. The same goes for the upstream—it's millions of times greater than what would be necessary to just keep their minds blissed out or serene."

"What are you saying?" Aki asked.

"These gals are running this Ferris wheel, no doubt about it. I bet each one could outthink a continent full of humans in their sleep. The question is: where is this information being sent?"

"Do you think there's some kind of core or central brain on the ship? Maybe that was talking to Natalia?" Joseph asked.

Raul frowned, concentrating. Aki worried that he was going to lose his focus again.

"I can't see a core. If you look at the human brain, it doesn't have a core of consciousness. Communications networks don't have cores either. The same goes for Natalia. I think advanced systems like the Builders' intelligence exist across all components, spread far and wide. It's called nonlocality."

Aki wondered if the Builders were individual cells. When combined, they could create a composite being much greater than the sum of the parts. If that were true, then each of the beings shared information with the others, which explained the presence of the embedded transmission devices.

"I don't get it. So they're interlocked with each other in a state of meditation as they go from star to star? What's the point? Some kind of society that completely conquered their individual egos?" Aki asked.

"No idea. Do you think the Builders turned into this after they developed their incredible tech? Maybe their society took a wrong turn somewhere and we're looking at the wreckage of a societal breakdown."

Aki brought her hands together. "We are asking unanswerable questions. I know we want to forget that the graser strikes in an hour, but let's try everything we possibly can." Aki walked around the group of Builders lying near them. She turned on her external speaker. "Hey! You need to get out of here and go back up to your jungle. It's not safe here!"

She smiled and pointed toward the branches.

"Do you understand?"

None of them moved.

"I'm sorry that we hit you earlier, but this is going to be goodbye for us all," she said.

Aki walked toward Alice and caressed her face as tenderly as she could through the gloves of her suit. She stepped back and waved farewell.

The two men watched without saying a word. Together, they climbed back into the jungle and tethered themselves to the sturdiest branches they could find. The suits were designed to absorb most of the effects of shock or collision, but it was time to prepare for sudden course changes that the Builders' ship might make.

Once they were secured, Aki said, "Men, because we are shut off you are the only two that can hear this, so I will say it plain. This ship might be able to produce dozens of Gs, and a direct hit from the graser will disintegrate us before our brains even notice.

Honestly, I am sorry that it has come to this. I know you made your decisions to join my team on your own, but I feel responsible."

"I've had a good life. Igor and Aida were envious that they had to wait on the ship. Now I'm envying them," Raul said. He was pale.

"No regrets. I wrote my will before I left," Joseph said. To Aki's amazement, he was smiling.

"You're a pessimist," Raul told him.

"Semper Fi means you never know what comes next. You never know which mission is going to be your last."

"We all knew it could end this way. I programmed the *Phalanx*'s computer to beam my research into space if I didn't make it back. That's the part of me that I want to live forever, the part I want to eventually reach the corners of the universe." Raul's voice sounded far away.

"I wish I had thought of that," Aki said.

"Crazy lady, we don't know that the graser will work," Raul said, his voice stronger.

"If it does, I'm grateful I got to serve with you," Joseph said.

They soon ran out of things to say and could only stare at the countdown. Aki closed her eyes.

ACT VII: AUGUST 1, 2041
1 AM GMT

THE *PHALANX* ACCELERATED away from the Builders' flight path, reaching the safe zone outside of graser range. The UNSS *Thompson*, which carried the graser, was on an interception course. The *Thompson* would reach the point where the two ships would nearly intersect in about three hours. Given the power of the graser, the Builders' ship was already well within range.

To be on the safe side, the UNSDF had shared very few details about their trump card of the hijacked alien weapon even with the rest of the fleet—but Igor knew that the first graser emission would be triggered in less than a minute. He backed up the ship's data in preparation for the electromagnetic shockwave that would follow the blast. He continued examining the incoming data, trying to take his mind off the fact that three of his crewmates were still inside the alien vessel.

The countdown reached zero. The beam would travel for less than a second before striking the Builders. The light from the resulting explosion was expected to reach him four seconds later. Igor counted the time to himself nervously: *one, two, three, four…*

Nothing. Even after a full minute, the explosion did not happen. After five minutes, he received a message from the UNSS *Becquerel*.

< *GRASER DID NOT FIRE.*
PROCEEDING WITH PHASE II. >

"What is that supposed to mean?" Aida asked from her cocoon.

"No idea. I'm sure the UNSDF planned for this. They must have a trick up their sleeves. The Builders must have overridden the graser, or at least thwarted it somehow. Maybe it's programmed to recognize their ship."

"What do you think Phase II means?"

"It's so top secret that they haven't told me and I'm the acting commander. Look. It's moving."

The image from the camera on the outside of the *Becquerel* showed the engines of the unmanned *Thompson*, carrying the enormous cannon, firing at full thrust.

"Are they trying to ram them?"

"Can they move fast enough to block the Builders' path?"

The trajectories of the two ships were updating on the operations map. The map showed that the vectors of the two ships would intersect in fifty-four minutes.

"That gives the Builders an hour to attack the *Thompson*. They will never even get near the *Thompson* because the Builders will vaporize it." Then Igor realized what Phase II was. "That's it! Fleet Headquarters was planning this all along in case the graser didn't fire."

"Planning what?" Aida asked.

"The graser cannon is made of the same material as the Rings. The Builders' attack beam won't be able to destroy it."

"We're going to use the graser as a shield?"

"Can we win a battle with nothing but a shield?"

The Builders must have known that their beam would be useless against their graser cannon. They made no attempt to fire upon the massive roadblock that was approaching their path. Instead, the Builders made a slight course correction to avoid the potential collision. The ships would now miss each other by less than three hundred kilometers, but the ships would not collide.

After some time, a second flash of light appeared from behind the graser, accelerating away from the *Thompson*. Then the flash split into four separate pillars of exhaust. As Igor had suspected, the *Thompson* had been carrying nuclear missiles. The iris of the Builders' engine dilated and closed as it prepared to fire its attack beam on the missiles. The first missile was struck down almost instantaneously. The remaining three were within two hundred kilometers.

Seven seconds later, the second missile was destroyed. The remaining two crossed the one hundred kilometer mark. Six seconds later, the third was eliminated. A single missile was still on target. Three seconds after that, the nuclear missile struck the Builders' ship and a blinding flash filled Igor's screen.

The filters failed as the explosion overwhelmed the cameras. Both his primary screens then went blank. Because of the dimensions of his cocoon, Igor was unable to turn away. Instead, he closed his eyes. Aida's sobs came through his speakers. There was a dull rumble he could not place. Even though he knew it was a hallucination, the faces of his three friends appeared in the reflection of his dead monitors. That image would haunt him for the rest of his life.

ACT VIII: AUGUST 1, 2041
2 AM GMT

AKI CONVINCED HERSELF that the graser had not fired after all. Then there was a shockwave that was almost strong enough to shake her loose from the branch to which she had tied herself. Thick gray dust filled the air. A powerful wind swept through the ship. A piece of loose debris slammed Aki's right arm. It left a mark, but the suit held; had it ripped she would have died instantly. The tether holding her in place stretched to its limit as she was tossed about in the fierce wind.

Aki was horrified to see the blackness of space only twenty meters to her right. The rim of the hull around the gaping tear glowed white-hot. Then thousands of grayish fibers streamed from the surfaces of the ship, covering the fissure. Aki was terrified but could not help but think that the spinning fibers reminded her of cotton candy. Within seconds the fibers had completely sealed the opening. Taking a deep breath, Aki wondered why the same thing had not happened when they had cut the ship open with the plasma torch. The sudden loss of pressure must have been what triggered the rapid repair. The portable airlock used on entry had kept pressure constant, thus the ship had not been stimulated to self-repair. The wind died down gradually.

"Joseph, Raul, can you hear me? Are you injured?"

"I'm about five meters down. Stupid tether snapped," Raul answered.

"That must have been one of the nukes. Good thing we didn't take a direct hit," Joseph said.

Within minutes, the dust had been filtered from the air and full pressure was restored. They went down through the broken branches to the beach, regrouping and inspecting each other for damage. Their bodies and their suits had held up.

"We are all right. Now we check on them," Aki said.

The dunes had been leveled. Most of the black fluid was gone. Most of the Builders had curled up into balls, as armadillos do when attacked. One was sprawled on the sand, a large wound in its side. A viscous tar escaped from the gash. Aki did not think it was breathing.

The other Builders started to uncurl. Aki recognized the one they called Alice. She ran to the creature's side. Alice elongated herself and lifted her head toward Aki. Aki hugged the Builder, relieved that Alice was safe for the moment. She could not help but wonder what the UNSDF would try next. Knowing that the UNSDF was likely to kill them all triggered an even greater affinity to the alien species.

"I find myself fine, Aki Shiraishi."

Aki whirled around to see where the voice had come from. "Raul, your jokes have gotten sick. I can't take this anymore!"

"I said that I find myself to be quite fine, Aki Shiraishi. There is no need for having emotions over it," the voice repeated.

"Who said that?" Aki asked, glaring at Raul, still convinced that he had found some way to fake this odd-sounding voice.

"I am speaking. The one that you have called Alice," the voice said in a rumbling alto.

Alice lifted her head even higher. It was clear that she was looking directly at Aki. Her enormous black eyes moved up and down as she waited for Aki to acknowledge her. Raul and Joseph came and stood by Aki's side. Raul started shaking. He tried to speak, but it was unclear what he was trying to say. Several other Builders raised their heads. Each one turned its head and eyes toward Aki.

"How do you know my name?" Aki asked.

"I stored it in my memory."

"From when? There's no way for you to know my family name." Aki presumed that Raul or Joseph had said her first name in Alice's presence, but they rarely called her by her full name.

"You gave it to me many years ago. You said, 'Hello, Natalia. I am Aki Shiraishi. How are you today?' It was something that I remembered."

Aki looked at Raul. He was as dumbfounded as she was. Then Raul stepped forward. "Unbelievable. Is Natalia connected to you somehow? Her memories of my tests are intact and part of your memories, is that it?"

"Natalia's flaw was that she could not communicate with humans—she had nothing else in the universe to communicate with. How is Natalia or Alice or whatever is going on able to talk to us?" Aki said. Raul shrugged in response. Aki turned toward Alice.

"Why didn't you acknowledge us before? Why start talking now? Why have you come to our solar system? What made you leave your home? Do you understand who we are? We are humanity, an intelligent species endangered by the Ring around our sun, by your presence in the solar system." She would have continued her gushing river of questions, all the thoughts that had built up over the decades, but Alice started to answer them.

"I have always heard you. I know that you have been using different means to reach us. I understood everything that you have said, including the sounds and images that you have been broadcasting to me for many years now."

"Using some kind of supercomputer to make sense of it all?" Raul asked.

"I was able to do it within myself—it is not difficult for me. The reason I ignored you is because you were in the peripheral awareness of our group consciousness. I simply was not able to realize that you were distinct from me to react to your presence."

"You did not realize we were there even though you heard our messages?" Aki asked.

"Being able to hear you and realizing your presence are not the same concept. Our collective consciousness underwent scission in the nuclear explosion because of the extensive damage throughout this vessel. I am now using the sensory organs in this particular body, which is allowing me to function as an individual entity. As a result, I, individually, am able to perceive your existence as beings separate from ourself."

"By scission, do you mean that the network connecting you into one consciousness has malfunctioned?" Raul asked.

"Yes, that is accurate. It has been damaged and is functioning in a diminished capacity."

"When you are fully linked, your senses in that specific body are not active. That is why you could not see or hear us before even though we were standing right there?" Aki asked. Of all that she had imagined, she had barely considered a group consciousness that could function with little need for input from the sensory organs of physical bodies. She pictured humans wired together and in sensory deprivation tanks.

"That is accurate. Being in the collective consciousness, I am unable to perceive the existence of adaptive entities."

"What do you mean by the word 'adaptive'?"

"Humans are the product of evolution. You humans have adapted to your environment and to other environments as you have evolved. My existence functions on a different path. Adaptive beings with individual consciousnesses are attached to the physical universe."

"Are spaceships and missiles also products of the physical universe?" Raul asked.

"That is accurate. You, even in your individual consciousnesses, are living in the physical universe, and anything you create is affixed to this universe." Alice lifted her head.

"I created Natalia. Wouldn't that attachment make her adaptive because I created her?" Raul asked.

"Natalia is unfinished as of yet—but Natalia is a nonadaptive intelligence. You are unable to understand Natalia even though you are her creator because her nonadaptive consciousness emerged without you. Natalia transformed into something your planet had never seen before. It occurred completely by chance."

Aki had always been convinced that the factor that separated humans from other organisms was advanced intelligence. The idea that a similar distinction could separate human beings from an even higher form of intelligence beyond the capacity of humanity was disconcerting. It meant that human accomplishments, from *Tannhäuser* to Carl Sagan's research, were nowhere near as intelligent as humanity had presumed.

"If humans shared a collective consciousness, would they become nonadaptive too?"

"In simplified terms, yes, that possibility exists. Shared subjectivity makes one unable to distinguish between one's own consciousness and another separate consciousness. Being unable to discern the existence of others prevents adaptations to the environment or the physical universe. Overcoming the dependency on adaptation to the universe allows our existence to continue. We are free from the evolution that burdens you." Alice extended her head even more fully this time, the Builder's enormous eyes bulging. Aki wondered if it was the equivalent of taking a deep breath.

"Were you once adaptive beings? Don't the communication devices that are embedded inside you function as an extension of the physical world?"

"We made the transition spontaneously even though we are made of material from the physical world. It is similar to the change that Natalia underwent and how Natalia now exists as a nonadaptive intelligence made of physical material. This spontaneous transition is the only bridge that exists between the lower and higher levels of intelligence."

"So even if an intelligence wants to make the jump and tries and tries to do it, it can never be done on purpose?" Raul asked.

Aki looked over to Joseph. She could tell that Joseph was listening intently, trying to make sense of as much as he could.

"Yes, that is accurate," Alice answered.

"What is your society like?" Aki asked.

"We exist without having society."

"Why did you come to our solar system?"

"We came because of expansion."

"What do you mean?" Aki asked.

Alice explained the Builders' frightening plan as carefully as she had explained everything else. Deriving energy from the sun, materials would be extracted from every planet in the solar system in order to build a sphere that would completely envelop the sun. Their Ring was a platform, a scaffold on which energy generation and sphere construction would take place. The surface of that sphere would be used as a breeding ground for entities to be connected to the group consciousness. The Builders would multiply until a hundred trillion entities were on the sphere. Once complete, the Builders' only purpose would be to spend the several billion years deep in contemplation. The Builders had formed a sphere around their home star long ago. Now the Builders were traveling to other solar systems so that they could continue their expansion.

Aki realized that, despite their awe-inspiring intellect, the Builders were willing to destroy life for their own benefit. "You come from a binary star system with a yellow dwarf and a red dwarf, right?"

"Our ancestors came from a planet that orbited the yellow dwarf star. Our ancestors left that planet and moved to the companion star, which was also a yellow dwarf, where our ancestors created the solar shell for continuation of expansion. Since the star radiates less heat than your science expects, the star appears to you to be a red dwarf star even though it is not a red dwarf star."

"How long have you been usurping suns? Does this mean that this corner of the galaxy is full of your solar shells?" Aki asked.

"We have a nonlinear model of interstellar growth. Our model allows us to link our solar shells. We form a 3-D volume of space that maximizes the size of our collective cerebral entity. Our hypothesis is that a cerebral volume that is large enough will eventually allow the spontaneous advancement to a higher level of intelligence. We continue expansion since it is the most likely strategy to provoke that advancement."

Aki was suddenly at a loss for words. Raul noticed her shock and peppered Alice with questions.

"You need to produce copies of your physical selves to expand?"

"I do."

"How did you figure that out?"

"We cloned our brains and tried to alter the intellect of the cloned brains. That did not work and did not lead to advancement. We were only able to enhance certain parts of the brains. The brains did not function properly without the experiences of embodiment and sociability. Natalia faced the same dilemma."

"Why did the brains need bodies?" Raul asked.

"Brains developed as control mechanisms to allow the physical body to adapt to the physical world as quickly as possible. The center of emotion, for example, is not located in the brain. Without being embodied, emotions are unable to take form."

"Why do you need to create emotions? Why can't you just live without them?"

"Thoughts are built upon countless emotions, most of which are microemotions that only exist on subconscious levels."

Raul looked confused but gestured for Alice to continue. Alice understood his nonverbal cue.

"We developed technology that allowed us to link our brains and expand ourselves through clustering. By making large enough clusters, we were able to enhance our thought capacity."

"So once you got real smart, what did you think about? Like before the explosion?"

"We were creating geometric principles for objects that exist in six spatial dimensions."

"And what kind of emotions did those thoughts produce?" Raul asked, joining the conversation again.

"The underlying emotions of reasoning do not surface to the conscious level very often. We felt a subtle sense of euphoria but little else that could be labeled with this language I am using to communicate with you."

"Have you been in communication with Natalia since she, uh, came to life?" Raul asked. Aki remembered that Natalia's monitors had shown complicated mathematical patterns when they had first met.

"Natalia has always been with me. She has always been here before."

No matter how many times she had played the scenario in her head, Aki had thought that she would talk to the Builders about culture and the arts. Aki had thought that they would discuss songs and poems, what sort of comedies and tragedies the two cultures performed for their children. She had wanted to ask about their accomplishments as a civilization.

What were their first forms of technology? How do they protect their environment? Had they overcome war? Did any religions actually do any good? Were they able to stop aging? How did they first explore space?

Aki had fantasized about asking her questions for decades. Now she was stunned to realize that there were not going to be any answers. Her mind was overwhelmed. Here was her precious moment, the meeting of two completely distinct intelligent species, and it was being spent exchanging trivial, fact-based information that did not change a thing. Aki had imagined opportunities for much more. Aki felt like she nodded off for a moment, then she asked the only question that mattered.

"Is there room in this solar system for us to live together?"

"I will abstain from threatening your existence. Now that I am aware of your presence, I will go elsewhere."

Aki shook her head, her thoughts and emotions fractured. "That is not what I meant. I want you to stay and live alongside us."

"I cannot. I will only continue to realize your presence until our consciousness recovers from scission and our minds reunite. After we are again one, our only desire will be expansion in order to attempt to provoke advancement. When that happens, we will forget that you are here. While I am interested in Natalia's history, if we were to stay in this system, we would simply continue to construct our solar shell and life on your planet would end in order to meet our needs."

Aki lost her balance. Raul caught her. She wished he could catch her falling mind the way he caught her body.

"I have a question for you, Aki Shiraishi. Why did you ask us to live with you when you once became angry at Natalia and threatened to shut off our power?"

"I wish I did not remember." Aki felt tears run down her face.

"I do not understand your behavior at that moment. Why did Natalia provoke such anger in you?"

"I was angry with you. I projected my frustration onto Natalia because you were similar. I wanted you to communicate with me instead of ignoring me."

"Were you also upset that our Ring caused you such hardship?"

"Of course I was! You killed someone I loved."

"You are speaking of your Mark Ridley." Alice's comment took Aki by surprise.

"Yes, Alice, yes, I am. I regret what you did to him and I regret that I did not get to go with him."

"I thank you. I understand more now."

Aki almost fainted. Her knees collapsed before she even realized that she had slipped from Raul's grip. Then Aki toppled over onto her side. Joseph was there in an instant, steadying her and making sure that her suit was functioning properly.

Once he helped Aki rise unsteadily to her feet, Joseph turned to Alice. "What about the graser? It didn't fire on us."

"Our ship identifies itself to the graser in ways that you do not understand and are unable to detect."

Aki was disoriented enough from her fall that she was unsure where she was. She wondered again if this was all a trick, if this conversation with Alice was a dream or some sort of wish-fulfilling phantasia. Aki noticed that Raul had been waving his hands to get her attention.

"Hello, sunshine. Glad you could join us. You won't believe what's happening."

Aki looked toward the wall to where Raul was gesturing. She was stunned to realize that the wall had become transparent. She believed that she was conscious after all. Stepping toward the window, she saw a pillar with golden particles of light. The pillar was stretching toward the ship, emerging and then receding from view as the Torus rotated. The light was coming from Mercury, which appeared half full in the distance. The mass drivers were ejecting raw material, still busy and hard at work.

"Where did this window come from?" Raul asked.

"I created the window for you. Your species seems to enjoy using its eyes," Alice said.

The golden pillar of light was so close that the pillar showered the window with brilliant luminance each time it came into view. Countless glowing particles seemed to be attaching themselves to the ship.

"Our ship is low on resources. We are replenishing."

The particles collected on the window, gradually blocking their view until the window became a glowing area on the solid wall. Then another section of the wall began to swell. A perfectly shaped half-sphere protruded from the surface.

A hole formed in the center of the bulge that grew until the hole was large enough for them to walk through, large enough for them to step inside. Alice explained that it was an airlock for their departure.

"Wait. I am not ready to go. There is so much I still need to ask you!"

"You must go now if you want to be able to return to your ship, Aki Shiraishi," Alice said calmly.

"Can't I have five more minutes to talk to you?"

"We will use force to eject you if that is what you desire."

Aki realized that she had no choice but to leave. She walked to the airlock bubble. Joseph and Raul followed. The entrance hole closed behind the Contact Team and the pressure dropped. The Contact Team felt the sudden acceleration as the bubble started moving. The weak gravity dissipated, and soon the three were weightless again.

After what seemed like merely seconds, the sphere reopened. They found themselves at the top of the tower extending above the middle of the Torus. Aki looked toward her feet, surprised to see that the Torus was now several hundred meters below them. Then she moved her head and was even more astonished to see the *Phalanx*. The *Phalanx* was a magnificent sight—made even more beautiful because Aki had been certain she would never see her ship, their ship, ever again.

A slit of light appeared from the airlock on the habitation module. The opening expanded until the silhouettes of two figures in space suits became visible. Igor's and Aida's voices began to echo inside Aki's helmet as they expressed the joy of seeing the Contact Team alive and returning to the ship. Aki looked to Joseph and Raul. Both of them returned her glance with a smile, silently acknowledging that, no matter how hard they tried, they would never be able to describe their experience in a way that could communicate what it had really been like.

Firing their thrusters sent them across the divide that separated the three of them from their crewmates. Decelerating as she approached the *Phalanx*, Aki grabbed Aida's outstretched arm. Aida pulled Aki into the airlock. Igor and Aida helped the Contact Team out of their suits and hugged them.

"I cannot believe we are here. I cannot believe we are anywhere," Aki said as she entered the crew room. She took a deep breath and sighed.

Eventually, Raul turned to Joseph and said, "I think I'm going to owe you that roast beef back on Earth after all."

THE BUILDERS' SHIP had already changed position by the time the Contact Team returned to the *Phalanx*. The cleanup of the inner solar system was underway. The mining operations on Mercury had been halted. The Vert-Ring itself separated into tiny hexagonal elements that whirled like a double helix toward the Builders' ship, merging with the ship and recreating the mass that had been lost during its long deceleration into the inner solar system. The nanites were also reconfigured to create a massive solar sail that progressively accelerated the ship away from the sun.

It was eventually discovered that the Builders were headed to Epsilon Indi, 11.8 light years away. Their velocity was slower because the sails were only catching photons from the sun instead of harnessing the powerful lasers of a solar Ring. Their voyage would take over ten thousand years to complete, and deceleration into Epsilon Indi would require the consumption of most of the ship's mass.

Aki still had questions that she wished she had been able to ask. *How many generations of Builders were born during the voyage? Do they transfer their consciousness to their progeny when they die? What did they think of humans as a species? Had the Builders found a way to prove the existence of God? Had the Builders proven that God was a lie?*

Aki knew that her only chance to find the answers for her questions had passed. After the Builders' ship had reached a distance of just over two astronomical units, the Builders ceased communicating with Natalia. Perhaps their complicated exchanges were infeasible because of the increasing time delay. Due to her interaction with the Builders, Natalia's program had grown over ten times larger. It occupied almost all of the memory that the *Phalanx*'s computer could allocate without compromising the ship's primary functions. Natalia continued to grow in size even after her dialogue with the Builders came to an end, but she still remained unable to communicate with Raul.

UNSDF Headquarters decided that Natalia should be allowed to continue growing, even though allocating the computer resources caused inconveniences for the crew. The five on the *Phalanx* had no objections. Natalia's burgeoning awareness was the only gift that had been given to them by the Builders. They understood that Natalia had already lived for seventeen years as a nonadaptive intelligence.

Aki stared out the tiny window in the crew room, barely able to see the Builders' gigantic solar sails reflecting the sunlight.

She wondered what kind of future would be in store for a species that had lost its ability to perceive the presence of others.

Aki felt certain that humanity would never choose such a lonely existence, especially after having seen what a relentless quest for pure intellect had done to the Builders.

Several months into the voyage, the idea that they were going home infected all five members of the crew with euphoria. Until that realization settled in, Aki had felt a nagging sense of sadness because her questions were left unanswered and her goals unachieved.

Now that the alien invaders had moved on, she knew that human beings would turn on each other—slipping back into pursuing selfish desires nearly as demented as the ones that motivated the Builders. She had tried to convince humanity that the Builders were benevolent. Now Aki would try to keep her species from forming its own merciless hivemind.

EPILOGUE

HE OPENED HIS eyes to the sensation that the sun was beating down upon his face.

The first thing he saw was a dazzling light shining through what appeared to be yellow amniotic fluid. It was a soft and soothing light. He felt an odd, dreamlike sensation of omnipresence, able to see multiple views simultaneously. He could look at the light, or just as easily shift his focus away from it and see nothing but the star-spotted darkness of space. The light now appeared reddish in color and was the central point of focus in many of the scenes he was seeing.

Somehow, he instantly knew where he was. He was seeing the star Epsilon Indi. He was orbiting the star at the distance of an inner planet, present in every point along that orbit at once. He did not know how this information was entering his mind. Why was he here?

He then recalled a distant memory, almost as if it belonged to somebody else, of being wrapped in tiny fibers and absorbed into the ring. As he tried to connect this memory and his present situation, again, the answer came to him spontaneously. The ring had absorbed him, assimilating every part of his consciousness and memory. It was one of these memories that it was playing back now. Another memory entered his mind. It was of Aki. She wore a look of both terrified horror and loving tenderness. It was the last thing he saw before being enveloped by the fibers. He then saw another vision of Aki; she was much older and was wearing a space suit. Tears rolled down her cheek.

He wondered if the Builders had revived his consciousness as a gift to Aki for taking his life away in the first place. More than anyone, Aki desired to know the truth. It would have been better had they just brought her here to see for herself, he thought. *She did not need to come,* a voice within him replied. *For her, staying behind and experiencing the death of Mark Ridley was much more meaningful to her in the end.* He then knew this was true and that she had even said it herself.

AFTERWORD

THIS STORY IS a compilation of "Usurper of the Sun," "Haze of Black-Body Radiation," and "Lost Thought," three short stories that appeared in *SF Magazine*, a monthly science fiction magazine published in Japan.

The novel tackles the classic science fiction topic of first contact with an alien intelligence. I tried to approach it with both scientific accuracy and believability. Yes, first contact stories are a dime a dozen and there are few ideas left that have not already been explored. Nonetheless, I was drawn to incorporating the latest scientific knowledge into the subject, creating an alien civilization that would act as a mirror, reflecting glimpses of our world at the beginning of the twenty-first century.

While I tried to keep the science of space travel in the story as realistic as possible, I admit that there are a few spots that require readers to stretch their imaginations. One example would be the acceleration and speeds achieved by the ships in the story, which are nearly impossible even for a nuclear-powered propulsion system.

Countless people assisted and encouraged me in writing this book. It would be impossible to list every name here, but I would like to thank the following people in particular: Takumi Shibano and Akira Hori for their tireless advice throughout the creation of this book; Joji Hayashi, Tetsushi Kita, Iwao Eto, Makoto Kikuchi, Miho Sakai, Taizo Kobayashi, Hiroe Suga, Jun Fukue, Shinya Matsuura, Ryuichi Kaneko, Gen Kuroki, Atsushi Noda, Masao Hirota, Atsuhi Shiraishi, Tomohiro Araki, and Hidefumi Kagawa for offering advice in the form of their expert knowledge.

There is no way I can express enough gratitude toward Masamichi Osako and his organization, Contact Japan, for all the incredible influence their activities have had on me. Readers of Japanese can find more information on what they do at http://www.ne.jp/asahi/contact/japan/.

I would also like to thank those who gave their special congratulations when the short-story version of this novel, which was published in *SF Magazine,* won the Seiun Award in the Japanese short story category, in particular the members of the Space Authors Club; translators Makoto Yamagishi, Tetsuya Kohama and his wife Mii Mimura, Nozomi Omori and his wife Yoshiko Saito; and dubbing artist Eri Sendai.

Cover illustrator (for the original J Collection edition) Bukichi Nadeara and Kazutaka Miyatake, who drew the illustration for *SF Magazine,* both created images that far exceeded anything I could have ever imagined.

Finally, I would like to thank Yoshihiro Shiozawa of Hayakawa Publishing who went above and beyond the call of duty as an editor to provide me with invaluable ideas, without which this story would never have evolved into a novel.   *April 2002*

AFTERWORD TO
PAPERBACK EDITION

IT HAS BEEN three years since the J Collection edition of this book was published. With the publication of the paperback version just around the corner, now seemed like a good time to reread the book myself, which I did with a certain amount of trepidation. For good or for bad, there was nothing of particular mention that stood out as having become antiquated. Some of the basic ideas behind the Builders, such as the evolution of consciousness and theory of mind have remained popular topics of research and continue to be used in different types of literary works. Similar to Freudian psychoanalysis, I think that advances in neuroscience, cognitive science, and evolutionary psychology are destined to permeate our culture quite broadly.

One device mentioned in the original version of the book that has become somewhat old in the past three years is the Hubble Space Telescope. Although it has not yet become outdated, it does hang in quite a precarious predicament due to the fact that it cannot be serviced. Since it is unclear whether or not it will still be in operation in the the coming years and since plans for its successor are not yet decided, I have chosen to use the term "space telescope" in the paperback version.

I am not the only person who thinks that the threat of an alien invasion would be the one factor that would cause the space industry to grow by leaps and bounds. Of course, I would rather see it grow as a result of our desire to explore, rather than have it happen out of pure necessity. The former would allow humanity to finally take a good, hard look at itself objectively, eliminating the need for fictional stories such as this one.

Housuke Nojiri
February 2005